TASTE
test

TASTE *test*

KELLY FIORE

WALKER BOOKS
AN IMPRINT OF BLOOMSBURY
NEW YORK   LONDON   NEW DELHI   SYDNEY

First published in the United States of America in August 2013
by Walker Books for Young Readers, an imprint of Bloomsbury Publishing, Inc.
www.bloomsbury.com

For information about permission to reproduce selections from this book, write to
Permissions, Walker BFYR, 1385 Broadway, New York, New York 10018
Bloomsbury books may be purchased for business or promotional use. For information
on bulk purchases please contact Macmillan Corporate and Premium Sales Department at
specialmarkets@macmillan.com

Library of Congress Cataloging-in-Publication Data
Fiore, Kelly.
Taste test / Kelly Fiore.
pages   cm
Summary: While attending a Connecticut culinary academy, North Carolina high schooler
Nora suspects someone of sabotaging the academy's televised cooking competition.
ISBN 978-0-8027-2838-8 (hardcover) • ISBN 978-0-8027-3475-4 (e-book)
[1. Cooking—Fiction. 2. Contests—Fiction. 3. Reality television programs—Fiction.] I. Title.
PZ7.F49869Tas 2013   [Fic]—dc23   2012027331

Book design by Regina Flath
Typeset by Westchester Book Composition
Printed and bound in the U.S.A. by Thomson-Shore Inc., Dexter, Michigan
2 4 6 8 10 9 7 5 3 1

All papers used by Bloomsbury Publishing, Inc., are natural, recyclable products
made from wood grown in well-managed forests. The manufacturing processes
conform to the environmental regulations of the country of origin.

For Mom,
who taught me to do
all the things I love most

For Matt,
who is so much more
than a better half

For Max,
who changed everything
for the better

Cooking is like love.

It should be entered into with abandon or not at all.

Harriet Van Horne

TASTE
test

NACA

North American Culinary Academy
2929 Lakehurst Mountain Road
North Sullivan, CT 21842

Miss Nora Henderson

c/o Smoke Signals BBQ

1745 Deerfield Pike

Weston, NC 11112

Dear Miss Henderson,

Thank you for your application to the North American Culinary Academy's *Taste Test* Competition. After careful consideration of the applications received, we are pleased to offer you a spot for the upcoming academic semester.

As you know, *Taste Test* is a televised competition where teenage contestants vie for a scholarship to the International School of Cuisine in Paris, France, as well as $50,000 to be used toward a career in the culinary field. The competition requires parental consent. Please be sure to have your parent/guardian sign and return the enclosed forms.

Throughout the semester, you will attend culinary classes with an academic focus. All filming will occur based on a schedule to be determined at the start of the program semester. You will receive an itinerary upon arrival; acceptance to the program commits you to attending the school and participating in all scheduled filming.

The competition requires parental consent. Please read through the enclosed documents and be sure to have a parent/guardian sign the disclosure and release forms.

Congratulations on your acceptance. We look forward to meeting you.

Best wishes,

Kathryn Svincek

Kathryn Svincek
President
North American Culinary Academy

CHAPTER one

You, Me, and a Pig Butt

Dad shoves the pointed end of the thermometer into the thickest part of the meat. It reminds me of movies I've seen in history class. The word "impale" comes to mind.

"I could list my reasons for going, Dad. Again."

Silence. I flop down on the back steps and brush away the loose strands of dark hair gathering around my face.

"You know that this is an amazing opportunity, right? I'll be able to get into any culinary program I want in the fall."

Dad grimaces. "I figured I'd have you here for the off-season, Nora. We don't shut down just because things get slow."

I kick at some rocks with the toe of my boot.

"It's just for the semester, you know. I'll be back by Memorial Day."

"If you don't win."

"Right. If I don't win."

The faded red flannel of Dad's shirt strains across his shoulders as he heaves the massive hindquarter out of the smoker and onto a tray. Like a reflex, I'm off the steps and at his side, steadying the wobbly legs of the metal folding table. Once the meat's settled, we both take a step back to marvel at it.

Pork isn't exactly pretty when it's cooked, but when you're talking about meat, it isn't about looks. It's the way the chunks crumble and shred like good mulch, the way the fat becomes a river that slides, then soaks right in.

"Well, that's a beaut."

Dad yanks a sheet of foil off the tube and covers the tray with the same care a father would show a newborn. Makes me kind of sad, seeing him be that gentle. It reminds me of when, years ago, he carried me, fast asleep, from the cab of the truck to my bedroom after a barbecue contest in Raleigh or a festival in Charlotte.

"I'm not trying to make your life harder, Dad..." The words are heavy and thick in my mouth.

"Nora."

He looks at me, tossing a bath towel over the wrapped tray. His eyes are the same deep blue as mine, but today they look like shadows of their former selves.

"It isn't like I don't want you to go."

He falls silent for a minute, one hand resting on the foil mountain.

"It's just that I want you to stay."

Dad's never been one to stop me from doing what I want to do. I guess that doesn't mean he always liked it.

"Anyway," he says as he turns away and yanks off his gloves. "It's a little late now, right? You got about half a day left in Weston, and I got near double the amount of work than usual since Al took off for Barbara's wedding."

I wipe my hands on my jeans and squint up at him. The brim of his Panthers hat is shading his face, but I can see his eyes are damp. I gulp down a lump, the one that's been threatening to turn to tears for the last few days.

"I'll go get started on the sauce."

I pat his shoulder before gripping both sides of the metal tray and yanking it up into my arms. The truth is that, as guilty as I feel about Dad's sadness, it can't erase what's really coursing through me.

Pure, sweet anticipation.

Finally, an opportunity to get out of this ass-backward town. A chance to be more than just the girl behind the counter of a roadside barbecue joint.

My family has owned Smoke Signals BBQ for almost twenty-five years. It was called Willy Woodchuck's when Dad bought it, and there are still a couple of the old signs in the back boasting a bucktoothed beaver. I can't say that I'm sorry Dad changed the name.

Owning a barbecue business in the South—it's kind of like being a pastor in a town full of churches. You're always looking to recruit. See, barbecue is its own language; there's a dialect to it. Different regions do things their own way, like how they say "pop" instead of soda in the Midwest, or "skeeters" down here for mosquitoes. In Texas, it's all about the beef. Kansas City—they focus on the sauce. But here, in North

Carolina, it's something else entirely—and that something else is pork.

The screen door slams behind me as I struggle into the kitchen. I manage to unload the pan onto the counter and push it back against the wall, rubbing my arms where a bright-pink indentation is surfacing.

I start dumping the barbecue sauce ingredients into a metal mixing bowl. It's Saturday, so I'll need to chop twenty-five pounds of pork butt and scrape the pan drippings into a pot for gravy, and all that before most of my friends are even awake. But for once, I don't mind. It sort of feels like . . . I don't know, a rite of passage or something.

It's what gave me my ticket out of here, if you think about it.

I pour the sauce into a pot and fire up the stove. Leaning against the refrigerator door, I pull the letter out of my pocket for the hundredth time. The feel of the paper is thick and silky, almost like fabric.

When I reread the words, I can hear Kathryn Svincek's clipped Connecticut accent enunciate each and every sylla-ble. I still can't believe that I actually made it into the program. Even when I applied, I knew it was a long shot.

The first time I watched *Taste Test*, I couldn't tear my eyes away from the screen. Twenty contestants competing against each other in an enormous arena—it probably sounds like any other reality show. But the differences made this one addic-tive to me.

The arena was a kitchen unlike any I'd ever seen.

And the contestants were in high school.

The show's been on for four seasons. The first cast was a bunch of privileged kids—sons and daughters of important chefs and famous restaurateurs. "Legacy contestants," my best friend, Billy, called them.

But the producers must have gotten as bored as the viewers did with the fancy-shmancy ingredients and TV-star judges. The last few seasons have had a crazy mix of people. There were still the privileged kids from New York City, but there were also pizza flippers from Chicago and cheesesteak line cooks from Philly.

The mix of personalities, the drama, the hookups—that's what makes the show popular. But that's not why I like it. For me, it's all about the cooking. During every episode, I think about how I'd approach that day's challenge if I were there, too. And, between you and me, I think I've had some pretty sweet ideas.

It was Billy who actually convinced me to send in my application in the first place. During an ordinary lunch period in the Weston High cafeteria, Billy watched me carve a lacy pattern in my reconstituted mashed potatoes and grimaced.

"I don't know why you bother buying lunch." He took a bite of his sandwich. "You always end up wasting half of it."

"That's because it's gross."

"Of course it's gross. It's *school* food. What do you expect?"

I just shrugged and took a sip of milk. Billy shook his head, his auburn, too-long-for-varsity-sports hair sort of shifting over his eyes.

"I can't believe you're wasting money on this crap when

your family owns one of the best 'cue joints in town. There must be leftovers you could bring—"

"Um, excuse me? *One* of the best?"

"Okay, fine—*the* best."

"That's what I thought. Still, I'm not eating that stuff for lunch."

"Are you crazy? Why the hell not?"

Billy swiped away my fork, the tines still coated in potato puree. I lunged forward to take it back, but he held it high above his head and kept me back with his other hand. I fell back into my seat, pouting.

"Because."

Billy rolled his eyes. "Because why?"

"Because it's what I cook *every day*. It's what I smell like; it's all I see. It's everywhere. Half the time I think I might end up being a vegetarian in protest."

Billy looked unsympathetic. "Then if I were you, I'd be slurping down slaw at lunch every day."

"I can start bringing you some."

"I might take you up on that." He cocked his head at me. "Speaking of cooking, did you watch *Taste Test* last night?"

I perked up. "Of course—you know I never miss an episode. Did you see Brian's glazed pork loin?"

He grinned. "Looked familiar, huh?"

"Duh—I've done that dish a dozen times. The only difference is that I don't use froufrou Meyer lemon preserves. Orange marmalade works just fine."

"You know," Billy said, toying with a Ho Hos wrapper, "they're accepting applications."

"Who is?"

He looked irritated. "The *show*, Nora. *Taste Test*. There was an ad at the end of the show."

"So?"

"So, what if you applied?"

"Are you kidding?" I scoffed, crumpling a napkin in one hand and tossing it across the table at him. It landed in his lap. "I am the least likely, least interesting potential contestant ever."

"I'm serious! You should do it. Remember Felicia, from season two? Her family owned that diner in Georgia, the one that was in an old bus? It wasn't like she grew up sautéing lobster in Paris or whatever—she was raised in a local dive just like you were. And she almost won!"

"Yeah, until Roman came out swingin' with that lamb shank flambé."

I fingered the edge of my disposable tray before scooting it off the side of the table and into the trash can.

"Look, Billy, I get what you're saying. I need to be proud of where I come from and all—"

"No—well, I mean, yeah, you do—but, no, I'm serious about the audition thing!"

His green eyes were sort of sparkling. It's what I remember most about that day—how intent Billy was. How sure.

"Think about it, Nora. Think about the people who win *Taste Test*. Okay, season two it was that douche bag Roman, but since then? Tressa, the surfer chick from Baja? And Jacob— what was he? A line cook at an *Applebee's*? These are *regular kids*. They work hard, they cook good food, and they win crazy money. Tressa's even got that show now on Eat TV."

I shrugged again, but I'd started to feel a tug of interest, as if a fishing line were reeling me upward in my chair.

It was true. They *were* just everyday, average teenagers. And, hell, half of what Jacob made was amateur stuff. Shock-value crap like caviar ice cream or avocado cheesecake. When it came down to it, the food was always creative, and that's how he won. I'm just not sure if how the dishes *tasted* was ever really measured against his fun ideas and witty banter.

I didn't hear the bell ring until Billy was standing up, slinging his backpack over one shoulder. Hastily, I scooped up my books.

"So, let's just say, hypothetically"—I was practically running to keep up with his freakishly long legs—"that I *might* want to send in a tape. Just for fun or whatever."

He smirked but kept looking forward, weaving through a crowd of giggly freshmen. I stifled the urge to groan. Those kinds of girls always reminded me of rock-star groupies with unlimited access to Lip Smackers. I bypassed the ones batting their sparkly lashes at him, ignoring my desire to warn them of retinal scarring caused by glitter. Billy and I have been friends since middle school, but it's only been in the last year or so that girls started noticing him in *that* way. I blame his hair—it's deceivingly cool.

"Okay, sure. Hypothetically."

He was watching a platinum blonde adjust her miniskirt. I snapped my fingers in front of his face.

"Hello?! Are you paying attention?"

"Jesus, Nora, yes. I heard you. You're hypothetically applying to *Taste Test*."

"Right—I mean, what would I even *say*?"

I thought about my stats. Born and raised in North Carolina by a single dad. Mom died when I was a little more than a year old, so it's not like I remember her. And then there's Smoke Signals. I blew out air between my lips.

Forget it. No big-city judge is going to be interested in how I learned to use grape jelly and chili sauce to shellac chicken skin until it's crispy or how I figured out that you need to let the onion sweat out its juice before adding it to slaw. There's nothing fancy about barbecue.

Billy frowned down at me as we reached his locker. "Stop it."

"Stop what?"

"Stop talking yourself out of even trying. What's the worst possible outcome? They reject you? You continue living the same life here? You'd be doing that anyway, you know."

It took a day and a half for him to finally persuade me to sit down in front of his mom's computer while he fiddled with the camera perched at the top of the monitor.

"Can't we just use a normal video camera?" I grumbled, fixing my hair in the dark reflection of the screen.

"No."

The monitor flashed briefly and my face, a little blueish, popped up.

"Besides," Billy said, readjusting the angle, "this way we can send it in to the website as a digital file. No getting lost in the mail."

I knew what he was getting at—he thought I wouldn't send it if I had the option. That I'd convince myself that the whole idea was a moronic waste of time. Too bad he's such a techie-geek. Wonder what the girls at school would think of the half dozen computer programming books next to his bed and his nights playing weirdo online warfare games until 3 a.m.

I can't help but smile now as I run my fingers over the slightly raised, crimson emblem at the top of my acceptance letter. Everyone's heard of NACA—the North American Culinary Academy is where the best of the best go. It's like Juilliard for chefs. I went to a college fair last fall at Weston Community and spent the whole time thumbing through a NACA brochure I'd swiped at the transfer office. It's not like I thought I'd ever get to go there or anything. It was just a dream.

Kind of like the dream I'm living now . . .

"Y'all packed?"

I jump, dropping the letter.

Joanie, my dad's girlfriend, is standing in the doorway smiling at me. Her bright-red hair is piled on top of her head like a mound of coiled spaghetti and she's wearing her cat-eye glasses, the ones with the zebra-striped frames.

Joanie's been in my life as long as the restaurant has. She was head server before she and Dad started dating and her gruff exterior and high-pitched laugh remind me a lot of Smoke Signals itself—a little rough around the edges, but comfy and warm.

I reach down and snatch the letter off the floor, my cheeks

pink. This isn't the first time Joanie's caught me rereading it. She walks over and gives my shoulder a reassuring squeeze.

"Don't worry, honey. If I'd gotten an opportunity like that at your age, I'd frame that damn thing and wear it around my neck like a medal."

"I just don't want my dad walking in and seeing me reading it, you know? I don't want him to think I'm . . . ," I trail off.

"Counting the seconds?"

"Right."

Joanie sticks a long-handled spoon in the simmering pot and gives it a good stir.

"You know, Nora, your daddy wants nothing but the best for you."

"Yeah, I know."

"Do you?" Her eyes are uncharacteristically serious behind her funky frames. "I know he's been giving you a hard time about leaving."

I give her a half smile.

"That's just Dad. He likes to make things as difficult as possible."

Joanie shakes her head.

"He's just bustin' your chops, honey. He practically bursts with pride every time someone comes in here asking about you and your trip up North."

My upcoming TV appearance is a big deal in Weston. Anytime *anyone* gets out of here, it's news. Even when they're being shipped up to the State Pen, it's like they've made it big.

"So, anyway, you didn't answer my question." Joanie opens

the fridge and starts pulling out ingredients for the macaroni salad.

"What question?"

"Are you all packed?"

I shrug, wiping my hands on a nearby rag.

"Sort of. I guess so. I mean, I'm not exactly one of those girls who needs to bring six different purses and shoes to match."

I glance down at my dirty jeans and scuffed boots. My thick chestnut hair is knotted on top of my head, and it hasn't been washed since yesterday morning. I'm what you'd call low maintenance.

"You said they gave you a list or something?"

"Yeah." I grimace. "Don't remind me."

A few days after I sent in my acceptance, FedEx delivered a thick envelope of rules and requirements. There was a moment there when I was paging through the dress code and behavioral contract that I felt a stab of panic and the urge to run. I'd read some of the rules out loud to a couple of the servers.

"Think about it." Mary, a junior at my school, pointed to the photo of two NACA students on the cover of a brochure. "Everyone wears aprons over their clothes during class. You won't have to think about what to wear, Nora. It's like the mother ship's calling you home!"

"Yeah, but what about all this?" I showed her the list of commitments I had to sign. "No gum chewing? No fast food? No *phones*? I mean, if I grab a cheeseburger and a pack of Trident, does that mean I'm out on my butt? Am I cut off completely from the outside world? It's like communist Russia!"

Dad had walked in just as I chucked the folded papers on the counter. He picked them up, frowning at me, but I couldn't meet his gaze. When he realized what they were, he tossed them back down. A stab of guilt sliced through me then—the same guilt that's set up shop in the center of my chest for the last few days.

But this afternoon, when I head back out to the smoker and watch Dad adjust the thermostat, I can't help but smile. I guess I've been pretty lucky to be raised here. Of course, it's not like barbecue is all that sophisticated or whatever. But it's what I know—a legacy of my own, I guess you could say. I just wish my dad understood—wanting to go away doesn't have to change where I came from.

"You about ready?"

Dad's body tenses a little when he hears my voice. He turns around slowly and I wait for the inevitable last-ditch effort to get me to stay.

Maybe he'll offer me a raise.

Or a car.

Hey, that one's actually tempting . . .

But the expression on his face is one I haven't seen before. It's hard to put into words, but if I had to, I think I'd call it resignation.

"You get Billy to load your bags in the truck?"

His tone is gruff. He doesn't look me in the eye.

"He's helping Dottie clean the fryer, and then he's going to do it."

"I can grab 'em for you."

"It's okay, Dad. Billy'll do it."

We slip into an uncomfortable silence. The only sound is

the crunch of driveway gravel beneath our shoes. I try to think of what to say.

I'm sorry?

I'll miss you?

In the end, I just listen to the *whoosh* of cars passing on Route 19, a sound as familiar to me as breathing.

Dad fishes his keys out of his pocket and tosses them through the window of the truck and onto the front seat. He shoves both hands in his jeans pockets and looks at me.

"You better get the rest of your good-byes said, kiddo. No plane's gonna wait for you."

Joanie and Billy, along with a handful of other people from the restaurant, have gathered out in the dusty parking lot. I give a few hugs and shake a few hands, slap a high five here and there and say a lot of "thank yous" and "yessirs."

When I get to Joanie, she puts both hands on my shoulders and looks me in the eye.

"Remember what I said," she urges. "Your daddy sure does love you. And I couldn't be prouder of you if you were my own daughter."

I gulp down that lump again as Billy walks me to the passenger side of the truck. I squint through the sun at his face. He's looking out at the road, away from me.

"So I'll see you in a few months, right?"

"Yup."

"Okay." I give his shoulder a halfhearted punch.

It's only when I'm reaching for the door that he grabs my hand and pulls me into him. My stomach tenses up, like it's bracing for impact. He smells like soap and wood chips.

"I'll miss you, Nora," he whispers against my hair.

"I'll write," I promise, pulling back to look at him. He's staring at me with this unsettling intensity, like there's something else he wants to say. Like there's something else he needs to do. I swallow hard. His lips part slightly and I feel a pull, gravitational or otherwise, drawing me in. It's not just that he's going to kiss me. It's that I might actually want him to.

"You 'bout done?"

We both jump backward. Dad's looking at us through the driver's side window, his face screwed up into a scowl. Before I can catch my breath, before I can even think, Billy leans down and swiftly brushes his lips against my cheek.

"Bye, kid."

He's walking away before I can say anything back. Numbly, I climb into the cab of the truck.

"Buckle up," Dad reminds me. They're words I've been hearing from him for as long as I can remember, the same ones he used the day we brought the truck home from Jones Motors. His voice is the same as it's always been. It's me who's different. The butterflies in my stomach, the dull ache in my chest—my body hasn't quite decided where it wants to be or how quickly it wants to go there. It isn't until we're at the end of the driveway that I finally let myself look in the side-view mirror. By that time, all I can see behind me is dust.

The planes at Weston Municipal Airport are what people call "puddle jumpers"—commuter planes that take you to international airports in the bigger cities. I watch through the windshield as one taxis the short runway and glides up into the air. It looks easy enough—but, then again, it's my first time flying. I can't help but wish the plane looked a little more like a jet and a little less like a Volkswagen bus.

Watching the planes take off is a good distraction. For a while, Dad and I sit in silence, our necks craned upward and our eyes trained ahead. Even when we get out of the truck, we look everywhere but at each other.

I can count on one hand the number of times I've said good-bye to my father. Twice for summer camp. Once when I stayed for a few weeks on my aunt and uncle's horse farm. An overnight field trip to the state capital.

And today.

"All right, North Star."

Dad sets my bags at our feet. I smile at the old nickname.

"Remember to send time sheets to payroll on Thursdays," I say, lifting my duffel up with one hand. "And don't forget that Dottie is off next week to see her sister's baby."

"I can manage the restaurant. Don't worry about me."

Dad's face is suddenly serious. He grabs me by both hands and I can see that his brow is stippled with sweat.

"Listen," he begins. "You got as much talent as any of those yahoos from fancy restaurants or boarding schools. You know food like you know yourself, like you know me. It's a part of your family as much as I am."

He swallows hard.

"I love you, Nora. Knock 'em dead up there."

"Thanks, Daddy."

It's barely a whisper as I lean into his chest. He gives me a tight squeeze, then abruptly lets go.

"All right now. You get up on that thing and claim yourself a window seat. Otherwise you're gonna be hurlin' halfway through West Virginia!"

I can't help but laugh as I hoist my bags up onto a flatbed cart.

"I'll call you, Dad. At least while I still have my phone."

"I know you will."

"Don't forget to order the to-go containers tomorrow. Oh, and the paper cups are low—"

"Have a good time, Nora!" Dad yells, waving me toward the tarmac with one hand.

Only moments after I settle into my seat, the plane's subtle humming revs up to a roar and we begin to speed down the runway. I feel a sudden reverberation, a strong thumping in the core of my body. It takes me a few seconds to realize it's the strength of my heartbeat, adding its momentum to the thundering motor as the plane takes off.

North American Culinary Academy
2929 Lakehurst Mountain Road
North Sullivan, CT 21842

Intake Survey

Please fill out the following and return it to the nearest production assistant upon arrival.

1. Name: Nora Henderson

2. Hometown: Weston, North Carolina

3. Describe what you are most looking forward to during your semester here. Winning. No, seriously, I'm excited about cooking in the arena and learning from professional chefs.

4. Describe what you are least looking forward to during your semester here. Missing my father and my best friend, Billy

5. Do you have any concerns you need to share with the filming crew or production staff? I have a very strict policy against glittery eye makeup.

I have read and understand the following:

Initial here

NH All outside correspondence will be monitored 24 hours a day.

NH Upon arriving at the airport, you will turn in all communication or data-processing devices, including but not limited to: cell phones, smartphones, handheld translators, and electronic book devices.

NH All non-written communication outside the academy will be limited to emergency situations. Contact off campus will require authorization from the production team.

Please fill in the enclosed forms. Be sure to include updated contact information for both your Emergency Contact designee and your health insurance provider.

CHAPTER two

Sleeping with the Enemy

I really, really wish I'd brought a coat.

It's eight thirty at night, it's winter, and I'm in Connecticut. Standing outside the academy dorms, it is colder than cold. I'm starting to regret that I didn't take that packing list more seriously.

I glance around at my competition. Two girls, both blond, are hopping from foot to foot, giggling and whispering to each other. A guy with shaggy hair chews his nails, while a beautiful girl with caramel skin leans up against a nearby pillar. A tall boy with a couple of facial piercings is talking to a petite brunette, who whips her dark hair over one shoulder and giggles.

An hour ago, at the airport, we had to fill out some paperwork and turn in our cell phones. Honestly, it went over better than you'd think—of the twenty contestants, there were only one or two criers, a couple of phone-kissers. One guy almost smuggled his through by disguising it as a calculator. But by the time we made it onto the charter bus, a bubble of nervous anticipation started to inflate in my chest. I'd plopped down in a seat toward the front and glanced at a girl sitting behind me. She was staring out the window with a bored expression, twirling a lock of shiny black hair around one perfectly manicured finger. When she noticed me, her chocolate-brown eyes narrowed.

"Um, can I help you?"

"Sorry." I smiled. "I'm Nora. Nora Henderson."

I reached my hand over the back of the seat. She stared at it as if it were a weapon.

"*Enchanté*," she replied, raising one professionally arched eyebrow.

On—shan—what?

Just then, a tall, impressively built guy with wavy blond hair slid easily into the seat next to her. He looked from me to her, eyebrows raised.

"Hey, Joy," he said, his voice deep and velvety smooth, "long time, no see. Making friends already?"

"Yeah, right."

Joy gave me a disgusted once-over and I blinked hard. Mr. Universe flashed a dazzling smile and stretched a deeply tanned arm around Joy's shoulders.

"Come on. You know that NACA's famous for slumming—they have to take on *some* amateurs to make things interesting. She'll go back home in a few weeks once she realizes she's up against people like us. If she manages to last that long."

"Christian, please. Don't give her that much credit. She'll be gone by *tomorrow*."

The fury rushed up my neck and into my cheeks, but before I could muster a snarky retort, a gigantic man, half Santa Claus, half Shrek, stood up from his seat in the front of the bus and clapped his enormous hands.

"Welcome, chefs!" he boomed. "I'm Benny Friedman, one of the executive producers. On behalf of the show, I just want to say how excited we are that you're here. There's an amazing amount of talent on this bus and we're sure this will be the best season of *Taste Test* yet!"

As the bus pulled out into the New England night, Benny began to lumber down the aisle, handing each contestant a black folder with the *Taste Test* logo emblazoned across the cover.

"In these folders you'll find your orientation packet—campus maps, contestant dossiers, a daily agenda. Every morning, you'll get a schedule detailing where to be and when. There's a list of the amenities you'll find in your dorm—we've just renovated the fitness center, and the academic center was recently stocked with over two thousand cookbooks and chemistry texts."

Behind me, Golden Boy called out, "What about the on-site spa? I'm just not myself without a daily massage."

People chuckled and Benny looked amused.

"Well, Christian, you'll just have to be someone else for a few months. Unless, of course, you'd like to hire your own personal massage therapist."

"That could be arranged," Christian retorted. Joy gave a little giggle and I rolled my eyes.

When Benny reached my seat, he smiled before handing me my folder.

"Nora, right?"

"Yes, sir."

"Please—none of that 'sir' stuff. It's Benny." He leaned against the seat in front of me. "My assistant grew up just outside of Charlotte. That's not far from your hometown, is it?"

"Not too far—about fifty miles or so."

Benny nodded. "Well, she tells me your dad's restaurant is famous down there. That his pork butt is the best she's ever had."

Behind me, there was snuffle of laughter. I swallowed hard.

"Thank you, sir. I mean, Benny . . ."

He patted my shoulder and moved on. I forced myself to sit up straight.

That was good. He singled me out. Everyone saw him talk to me. It doesn't matter that he said—

"Pork butt?"

The voice was an equal mix of revulsion and superiority. I turned to glare at Christian.

"It's barbecue," I snap.

He nods knowingly. "Oh, right. Hillbilly food."

I narrow my eyes and bite down hard on my tongue before turning toward the window and staring out at the cold northern night.

It only took fifteen minutes to make it to the NACA campus, but the bus had to park several blocks away from the dorm. By the time we make it to our home away from home, I've just about lost the feeling in my fingers. Benny holds up his hand and gestures for the group of us to come closer.

"I'm going to take you on a quick tour through the facility

before we get to your rooms. Now, keep in mind that this dorm was renovated specifically for *Taste Test*. This building, your classes, your labs—*everything* is separate from the rest of the school. And what you see in here? Well, it's not exactly what you might expect from a college dorm."

So, you know Buckingham Palace?

Yeah, apparently I live there now.

Even *my* overactive imagination couldn't have conjured how luxurious our building would be. The first floor has three common areas—a big state-of-the-art kitchen, a wood-paneled library, and a swanky lounge. There are elevators with shiny gold doors, and the furnishings are the kind you'd see in a museum or fancy restaurant. Every stationary object is draped in velvet or silk.

As we head for the second floor, Benny points down a long hallway.

"Down there is the entrance to the arena."

At the end is a heavy-looking set of metal double doors. Two security guards stand on either side of them.

"What are *they* for?" a girl asks, nodding toward the uniformed men.

"Just a precaution. One season we had a little scuffle with some press disguised as guests of a contestant. We don't let anyone down there except the competitors, the judges, and the film crew."

You wouldn't think that a TV show would need that much security, but as we head upstairs, it becomes more and more obvious that armed guards are only one strategy used to keep tabs on the building—and on the contestants. There are cameras monitoring us in the stairwells, in the hallways, in the elevators until 10 p.m. every night. I don't know if they're really for safety purposes, or for catching juicy footage for the show.

When we arrive on the second floor, Benny glances down at his clipboard and starts pointing to the doors on either side of us, showing people their assigned rooms. We reach room 212 and he gestures to Joy. She skids to a stop and teeters a bit in her knee-high black patent boots. Compared to everyone else in their jeans and T-shirts, she looks like the Abominable Fashionista.

"Joy Kennedy-Swanson, we have arrived at your destination."

Joy shifts her Louis Vuitton train case from one hand to the other. "It's about time. I can't carry this heavy thing for one more second."

Benny is looking back at his paperwork.

"And your roommate is . . ."

He runs a finger down the page, then looks up . . . at me.

"Nora Henderson."

Aw, crap.

"Try not to have too much fun, girls," he says, grinning.

I'm tempted to say something snarky back to him, but instead, I shove my key in the lock and push the wood-paneled door open. The room is dark and I grope for the light switch.

I've seen dorm rooms before. Cinder blocks, eggshell paint, pressboard furniture.

This is *not* that kind of dorm room.

I guess I should have realized our rooms wouldn't be the dorms I was expecting. Instead, there's a big bay window in the center of the far wall and a large sitting area right in the middle of the room. On each side, there is a bedroom-like setup that is identical to the one across from it. Each of us has a laptop computer sitting on a dark wood desk. The queen-sized beds are covered in pale-green duvets filled with thick feather blankets. It's like staying at a hotel—except better, because I get to actually *live* here, in the lap of Egyptian cotton luxury, for five months!

I turn to Joy, expecting her to be equally impressed, but she walks right into the shared bathroom and shuts the door. She's tossed her purse on one of the beds, and her shoes are kicked off in front of the nearest closet.

Okay, then. I guess she's chosen which side *she* wants . . .

She reemerges, a disgusted look on her face.

"I cannot *believe* we have to share a bathroom. I mean, HELLO? They can't actually expect us to cohabitate in *here*."

She says it like this room is some dirty shack instead of a presidential-style suite. I gawk at her.

"You're kidding, right? I mean, this place is gorgeous."

She gives me a slow once-over.

"It would be a lot more gorgeous with separate bathrooms."

She picks up her purse and begins rummaging through it. Finding a tube of lipstick, she applies the cotton-candy color with a practiced hand. I imagine shoving it up her surgically altered nose.

"Well"—I toss my duffel up on the table next to me—"I guess you can try to switch rooms." I'm half-hopeful she might consider it. The less time I have to spend with this chick, the better.

"What, and risk looking like the spoiled rich girl on the show? Not a chance."

A little too late for that.

She turns her back to me, which I take as a signal that our conversation is over. A little relieved, I start pulling my far-too-lightweight clothing out of my bag and cram it into the dresser drawers. Out of the corner of my eye, I see Joy hanging a shiny sequined dress in her closet. I look down again at my balled-up T-shirts. Maybe I should at least lay them flat and try to get some of the wrinkles out.

I pull out two framed pictures from the bottom of my bag—the only mementos I bothered bringing from home. One is of Dad and me at a barbecue competition last summer. We're wearing our matching Smoke Signals aprons and holding spatulas. I remember it like it was yesterday—how we'd woken up before dawn to make sure the meat would be perfect, how excited we were when we won first place.

The other one, a smaller gold frame, is of Billy and me at last year's junior formal. We're in one of those contrived, ridiculous poses that school dance photographers force you into. Billy's standing behind me and he's got his arms around my waist. Both of us are laughing.

"Who's the hottie?" Joy is peering over my shoulder. I set both pictures down and give her a sweet smile.

"That's my dad, Joy. He's taken, though. Sorry."

"You're hilarious—I was talking about your Rent-a-Date. I can't imagine a guy like *that* would actually go to a dance with you for free."

"His name's Billy and, I promise you, his attendance was completely voluntary."

"Is he your boyfriend?"

"No," I say slowly, narrowing my eyes. "Just a friend."

"Hmmm."

Joy is twirling her hair again and I feel the not-so-sudden desire to yank it out of her head.

"Well, I hope *he'll* be coming to visit. He'd be a much-needed distraction from this place."

"Um, don't you think your *boyfriend* might mind?"

"What boyfriend?" She looks genuinely confused. I roll my eyes.

"The jerk-off on the bus? Big muscles, blue eyes, huge ego? The one who was kind enough to come to your rescue when I committed the colossal mistake of speaking to you?"

"Oh, him."

She waves a hand dismissively.

"He's not my boyfriend. Not that I would mind some quality time with Christian Van Lorton, believe me."

Christian Van Lorton . . . why does that name sound so familiar?

"Anyway," Joy says, glancing at her diamond-encrusted wristwatch, "I'm going to find some fun in this building if it kills me. And until your friend Billy joins our happy home, I need to find someone to occupy my—"

"Bed?" I ask innocently.

"Time," she corrects me, tossing her hair over one tan shoulder.

She flounces out, letting the door slam behind her. The room reverberates in her wake. Joy knows how to make an exit. Sort of reminds me of those old Godzilla movies—you know, the whole city is demolished, but they're relieved the worst is over. At least until the sequel.

An hour later, I'm freshly showered and in an old T-shirt and pajama pants, curled up in one of the overstuffed silk armchairs. I've decided that the best possible use of my time will be to read through the paperwork I've been given. If I can memorize the schedule and learn the campus map, hopefully I'll have a leg up on my roommate and her beefcake boy toy.

There are three floors in the *Taste Test* dorm, as far as I can tell. I've seen what the first and second have to offer; apparently the third is where the magic happens and the show gets made. All our classes are in two lecture halls—both across campus—and all our meals, meetings, and production interviews are in the dorm itself. Along with the competition, of course.

When my stomach growls, I remember that I haven't eaten anything since my farewell BLT at Smoke Signals. According to my "Dorm Life" handout, the kitchen is open twenty-four hours and is fully stocked with "various snack foods." Visions of fruit snacks, kettle chips, and grilled cheese dance in my head. I yank my hair up into a ponytail and tuck my room key in my pocket before heading out the door. A successful fridge raid will do me a world of good right now.

Wow.

They weren't kidding when they said "stocked."

I'm peering up into a kitchen cabinet like it's a Nabisco Narnia: there are a dozen kinds of sugary cereal; twenty-five types of candy are lined up in colorful rows; and countless bags of chips threaten to tumble off the top shelf. I'm kind of surprised the producers are encouraging binge eating, but I guess it'll make for good footage. Eventually, they'll catch some depressed, homesick sap gulping down chocolate bars and sobbing into a napkin. But hell if it's gonna be me. I pull down a box of cornflakes and start searching for a bowl.

"Last cabinet on the right."

I turn to see two girls perched at one of the nearby bar tables. One is a chubby redhead with short hair and a face full of freckles. She's wearing a blindingly pink pajama set—think Pepto Bismol on steroids—and is smiling.

The other girl has pale eyes and very long, very blond hair. She gets up from her seat and walks over, holding an empty ceramic bowl in one hand. She can't be more than five feet tall and she reminds me of a girl I babysit for at home, which means she looks about nine years old, give or take.

"I already opened the Sugar O's, if you're interested," she says, setting her bowl in the sink. She wipes one hand on her blue cotton robe before reaching to shake mine. Her fingers feel ice-cold and tiny in my palm.

"I'm Giada," she says. "Giada Orsoni. But everyone calls me Gigi." She gestures to the other girl. "And this is Angela Moore."

Angela gives me a wave as she polishes off her cereal.

"Nora Henderson."

"Ah, yes. *Joy's* roommate."

Angela and Gigi exchange a look.

"I can't blame you for escaping down here and drowning your sorrows in carbohydrates," Gigi says sympathetically.

"Actually, she took off an hour ago to find someone more interesting." I shake some cereal into my bowl. "I obviously do *not* meet her standards."

"No one does," Angela says, getting up to join us. "I wouldn't worry about it."

"You make it sound like you know her."

She shrugs.

"When you live in New York City and you run in the culinary circle, there are certain people you just know by reputation."

"So, you're from New York?"

Angela shakes her head. "New Jersey, but I go in to the city all the time. I practically live there."

"How about you?" I ask Gigi.

"Here, actually. Connecticut, I mean."

I nod and chew my cornflakes. I guess these girls won't be too impressed with stories of Weston—the Little League parades, the basket bingo, the tractor pulls.

"You're from Georgia, right?" Angela asks.

I take a sip of orange juice and shake my head.

"North Carolina."

Gigi cocks her head. "You don't really have an accent."

"Should I?"

She shrugs.

"Everyone I've met from the South had that twang when they talked, you know?"

"Some do. My dad, his girlfriend—they both say things like 'warsh' and 'y'all.' But I think most people our age have tried to avoid the stereotype."

Angela grimaces. "I know what you mean. When you're from Jersey, people assume that you're either related to Tony Soprano or the cast of *Jersey Shore*."

"So, here's an important question," Gigi says as she leans in conspiratorially, chewing on a Twizzler. "What do you think of the *guy* contestants so far?"

"I've only met one of them, really." I shrug. "Well, I don't even know if 'met' is the word for it. He decided that the best way to mark his territory was by insulting me in every way he could."

Angela nods. "The blond guy on the bus, right?"

"Yeah, Christian Vonder-Shmookin, or something like that."

"It's Christian Van Lorton," she corrects me.

"You know him?"

"Sort of. More like know *of* him."

"Whatever, he's obviously one of those people who thinks he's the greatest thing to happen to the kitchen since the blender. Maybe even since the fork."

"Yeah, well," Gigi pipes up, raising her eyebrows, "I don't know about that, but I do know that he's freakin' fine. Seriously hot."

I roll my eyes. "Ugh. How can you tell? His massive ego blocks his face."

"And there are a few others worth a second look," Gigi muses. "Pierce something-or-other—did you see him? He's got that eyebrow ring—super sexy."

"Um, super *cliché*," Angela points out. "That is *so* five years ago."

"Well, the less competition for his attention, the better—and, since *I* don't have a roommate to contend with, I'm thinking my odds are looking pretty good."

"You snagged a single room? How in the world did you manage that?" I ask, my mouth full.

Gigi grins. "I'm not sure. But I'm definitely not complaining!"

On the other hand, Angela's roommate, Sky, is giving Joyzilla some competition for the World's Least Likable Person award. She's some kind of vegan tai chi instructor who developed her own biodynamic veggie burgers and apparently spent her first two hours here meditating with gongs, then filled the bathroom cabinets with all kinds of elixirs and supplements.

When we make it back to the second floor, Angela gives us a wink before heading toward her room. "Be sure to look for me in the morning. If I'm not at breakfast, it's because I strangled her with her Kabbalah bracelet."

Gigi and I both laugh as she disappears around the corner. I head in the opposite direction toward Casa Nora y Joy(less).

So, I don't quite feel at home and I'm not *completely* comfortable, but going downstairs helped me loosen up a little bit. It's nice to actually laugh with some people here—I was a little afraid I was stuck in the land of the snobby and the snobbier.

Before bed, I decide to e-mail Billy. I feel sort of stupid about it, but I already miss him. I really wish I could just hear his voice.

Typing quickly, I tell him about the plane, the shuttle ride, and my confrontation with Joy and Christian. I talk a little more about Joy, purposely leaving out the part when she offered to let him sleep in her bed. And I mention meeting Gigi and Angela.

"They seem like normal people," I write, "and that's saying a lot, after what I've seen so far."

After I reread what I wrote, I hesitate at the end. How do I sign off? *Sincerely*? *Your Friend*? Both of those sound stupid, fake. Not how we'd really say good-bye to each other.

I can't quite figure out why this is bothering me so much. Billy is Billy. Home is home. And I—well, I'm a contestant on one of the most popular reality shows on television. The way I end an e-mail tonight can't be half as important as the way I begin my first day here tomorrow.

Yawning, I type, "Love, Nora" and press SEND.

To: Nora Henderson **norahenderson@naca.edu**
From: Billy Watkins **billythekid@westonhighschool.edu**
Subject: Re: I'm here

Nors—

Hey kid—good to hear from u. Glad u made it there in 1 piece. Hope the flight wasn't bad. Sux you don't have ur phone—I'd love to hear ur voice.

U aren't missin much. Ur dad and I hit up the truck rally after you left—brought the smoker on the trailer. Pretty fun, but everyone asked about u. Everyone's rooting for u down here. Especially me.

Can't wait to see u on TV. Write back soon.
Billy

Contestant Interview

Nora Henderson

Producer (P): So, Nora, tell me, how are you feeling so far about your living arrangements?

Nora Henderson (NH): Um, they're fine . . .

P: It seems like you're having some trouble with your roommate.

NH: [hesitation] No, no. It's okay. We're a little different, that's all.

P: That's all?

NH: [shrug] Sure.

P: Nora, you can be honest with me. These interviews are a chance for you to vent your frustrations. To tell the truth.

NH: But [looks at camera] aren't these being filmed?

P: Of course. Everything is filmed. It's a television show.

NH: [long pause]

P: Nora?

NH: Sorry. [hesitates again] No, like I said, everything is fine. Joy seems *great*.

P: And there's nothing she's done to annoy you? To bother you?

NH: Of course not. We're roommates. I'm sure we'll be best friends in no time.

CHAPTER *three*

Jerk Ain't Just a Type of Chicken

"Are you finished yet?" I yell at the closed bathroom door.

A moment later, Joy emerges, followed by a cloud of perfume and wearing a smug smile.

"It's all yours."

"Thanks a lot," I grumble, glancing at the clock.

It's the first day of classes and I have approximately twenty minutes to get showered, dressed, and across campus to orientation. I gave up the hope of makeup and a blow-dryer about ten minutes ago. At this point, I'm just hoping I can brush my teeth in time.

"See you in class," Joy says sweetly, grabbing a disgustingly large designer bag off her desk chair and sweeping out of the room.

Just when I think I can't dislike her more, she figures out a way to prove me wrong.

Fifteen minutes later, I'm sprinting along the brick path

that weaves through the academy grounds. Wet clumps of hair cling to my face, and the collar of my shirt is soaked. I hope orientation doesn't involve a lab component because if I get anywhere near sharp implements, I might attack my self- ish excuse for a roommate.

BEEP. BEEP.

I jump into the grass just as a black golf cart, sleeker than any I've seen before, flies up next to me. I take one look at the driver and groan.

Wonderful. Just my freaking luck.

"Morning."

Christian's hair is perfectly combed, his shirt and pants pressed and wrinkle-free. He's holding a cup of coffee in one hand and the steering wheel in the other. He gives me a once-over.

"So. How are things?"

"How do they look?" I snap, pushing the wet strands of hair off my forehead.

"Damp. Disheveled. All around, pretty sloppy," he muses, cocking his head at me.

"Thanks. Thanks a lot."

I start walking faster, attempting to get away from him as quickly as possible. Christian paces me and I try to ignore him.

"You know, if you just asked nicely, I'd be happy to give you a ride."

I glare at him. "I'm not asking *you* for *anything*, and if I did, it sure as hell wouldn't be *nicely*."

He accelerates briefly, then shifts into park. By the time I reach him, he's rotated his seat to face me. I think about taking that hot coffee he's holding and pouring it all over his impeccable designer shirt.

"Look," I say, rolling my eyes, "I realize you're having a blast making me feel like crap and wasting my time, but I'd like to get to class as quickly as possible."

"If you don't get in, you're going to be late."

"I am *not* getting in a vehicle with you."

"Why not?"

"Because!"

I say it with conviction, but a voice in the back of my head is raising a meek objection. *"You want to be on time, don't you? It's the first day,"* it says.

"All right, suit yourself."

Christian pushes on the accelerator and begins to pull away.

Dammit. The last thing I want to do is rely on this jerk for anything.

"Wait."

He turns to look at me, his left eyebrow raised. "Yes?"

I come around the side of the golf cart and slide in beside him. From the corner of my eye, I can see him looking at me expectantly.

"Just go," I grumble, crossing my arms over my chest.

"I didn't hear 'please.'"

"You're right, you didn't."

"Ah, I love it when girls are surly in the morning."

Moments later, we're flying across the tree-lined grounds. I hate to admit it, but this *is* a much faster way to get to class in the morning. If I had unlimited cash at my fingertips like he clearly does, I can see how one of these would be an intelligent investment.

"How did you get this thing, anyway?" I ask, running a hand over the glossy dash.

"It was delivered this morning."

"No, I mean, we aren't allowed to have cars or bikes or anything. How did you get it approved?"

He shrugged. "I didn't."

I shake my head. Figures.

"So, you're an only child?" Christian asks. He has one arm resting across the back of my seat. I scoot further away from him.

"How do you know that?"

He shrugs. "Obviously someone isn't sizing up the competition like I am. Besides, if you ever get to the end of that packet Benny gave us, you'll find profiles on all of us."

I just nod, not sure what to say. I'm surprised that he's had time to read through any of the information, let alone gotten through the whole stack. I figured he would have spent all his free time partying with Joy and the rest of the *Gossip Girl* cast.

We glide up to a bike rack in front of a white columned building. Christian shifts into park and pulls the key from the ignition.

"Thanks," I say, practically choking on the word.

"Don't mention it." He slides out from the driver's seat. "I'm often coming to the rescue of damsels in distress."

He pulls a messenger bag from the rack behind the seat. I grab my books and hurry behind him.

"I wasn't in distress."

He grins. Even his teeth are perfectly straight and annoyingly white. "Sure you were. Just admit it. I saved you."

I snort. "You do understand I have legs, right? I would have made it here on my own."

"Maybe." Christian pulls open the door. "I guess we'll never know."

He gestures for me to enter the building. Annoyed, I grip my books harder and stomp past him.

The lecture hall is a vast, high-ceilinged room with seats like a movie theater and a huge screen in front. A data projector is running a slide show of colorful photographs—all different types of foods from various foreign countries:

Pints of beer at an English pub.

A tray of rising bread dough in a French bakery.

Barrels of spices at a Turkish bazaar.

I see Angela and Gigi waving at me from one of the middle rows. Breathless, I collapse into the seat next to them. Gigi raises her eyebrows.

"Did I just see you walk in with Preppy McPrepperson?"

I glance back at Christian. He's sitting next to Pierce Johnson, whose eyebrow ring and multiple tattoos are on full display. They're both laughing when Christian glances up, meeting my gaze. He winks.

Quickly, I turn away and shake my head.

"Just a coincidence," I mutter, digging a pen out of my purse.

The lights begin to dim and a heavy woman in a bright-blue suit and silk scarf walks across the front of the room to the podium. I recognize her right away and, from the way the crowd falls silent, everyone else does, too. Kathryn Svincek is more than just the President of NACA, she's also the head judge of *Taste Test*. Everyone remembers her for her honest critiques and sharp tongue, made sharper somehow by her sophisticated accent.

She raises both her hands for quiet, despite the fact that no one's uttered a word since she hit the stage.

"Hello," she says into the microphone. "And welcome to the North American Culinary Academy!"

There is some polite applause and she looks around appraisingly as though checking to see who isn't clapping.

"I trust that you've found your quarters adequate."

There's a more enthusiastic response this time. I look back and see Joy, who has a disgusted expression on her face. What could Her Highness be upset about now?

Ms. Svincek begins to discuss the history of the academy— how the greatest chefs in the nation wanted to found a school for the most elite young cooks around the country, how the school has partnered with the International School of Cuisine in Paris since its inception.

"And here you are—a new generation of food lovers committed to creating the finest dishes and the tastiest concoctions. Likewise, the professors at NACA are equally committed to assisting you with your studies."

The Academy faculty files out onto the stage, their tweed blazers and stern expressions both a little cliché and totally intimidating. They stand in a long line as, one by one, they introduce themselves. Some are doctoral professors; others are professional chefs or nutritional scientists.

"We are, of course, missing a very important member of

the NACA community," Ms. Svincek says, her voice a little wobbly. "My late husband, Ronald, was an integral part of the NACA faculty and was instrumental in developing this reality program. The entire NACA and *Taste Test* community is indebted to him. May he rest in peace."

There is polite applause and Ms. Svincek wipes her eyes. It must be difficult for her to come here every day, knowing that her husband can no longer enjoy what he worked so hard for.

"Well, moving along. All competitors," she continues, clearing her throat, "are entering their final semester of high school. The classes you take at the academy will satisfy English, science, and history credit requirements needed for graduation. Please remember, however, that these are *college-level* courses. We will expect the same amount of discipline and will hold you to the same standards expected of our traditional first-year students. In return, your time at the academy will ensure you a spot in one of many prestigious culinary programs.

"But only one," she booms, her volume increasing, "will be leaving here with a full ride to ISC-Paris and a check for $50,000."

She beams as the crowd breaks into joyous whoops and hollers.

When we leave the lecture hall a few minutes later, we're handed an updated class schedule. Three times a week we have Modern World Cuisines, Classic Techniques, and Flavor Foundations. On Tuesdays and Thursdays, we attend longer labs for Chemistry of Cooking and Tools of the Trade. I've never been that into school, but here, with *these* courses, I feel sort of excited about going to class.

"So, you guys want to grab a coffee before class?" I ask, suddenly needing a jolt of caffeine. Gigi peers at the schedule in her hand.

"We've got, what, an hour before Modern World?"

"Yep."

"Sure." Angela nods. "Sounds good."

The three of us start toward the exit just as Christian is walking out. He holds the door open for us with a flourish. I roll my eyes.

But once Angela and Gigi have walked through ahead of me, the jerk proceeds to let go of the handle. Without warning, the whole door flies backward, almost smashing me in the forehead. I struggle to push open the heavy plate glass and ignore the people around me as I stomp past the golf cart.

"You're a jackass," I hiss at him.

Christian, who's already sitting in the front seat, gives me an appraising look. Pierce is in the passenger's seat. He looks from Christian to me and back again.

"What's up with you two?" he asks with a grin.

"Nothing." Christian shifts the golf cart into reverse. "That's the problem. See, I've been trying to let her down easy, man, but she keeps asking me out. I'm just not interested in making a commitment. It's too early in the competition to be limiting my options."

"You are unbelievable," I say, crossing my arms. Christian starts to pull away, giving me a little wave.

"See you later, Nora. And remember—it's not you, it's me."

"That. Guy. Sucks," I say slowly, drawing out each word.

Angela puts a hand on my shoulder. "Let's go get that mochaccino."

You'd think a walk across campus to Cyber Cup would be enough to calm me down, but I'm still fuming as I flop down at one of the little round tables.

"All right, girl. Spill it." Gigi hands me my steaming coffee and sits down across from me.

"Spill it? I just got it—can't I drink some first?"

Angela rolls her eyes.

"Seriously, Nora? What is the deal with you and Christian? Seems like an awful lot of drama for two people who barely know each other."

I shake my head. "He's just such a jerk—he thinks the rules don't apply to him and that he can just treat people however he wants."

"Uh, I recall the word 'jackass' being thrown around," she points out.

"He slammed the door in my face!"

"We know, we were there."

"And he started it with those comments about my dad's restaurant and hillbilly food! Who does he think he is?"

"Okay, okay." Angela sets her mug down. "Look, we're not saying he isn't a jerk or anything. It just seems like you two have it out for each other. Either that or . . ."

She trails off, a hint of a smile playing her lips.

"Or what?"

"Or you're nursing that big crush he accused you of."

"Whatever," I scoff. "He wishes!"

"Probably." Angela narrows her eyes. "He seems like the type who would appreciate a few groupies. From what I've heard, he has some already."

"Surprise, surprise."

"Look," Gigi says, licking some whipped cream off her spoon, "don't take it too seriously. Have you ever thought that Joy and Christian might be targeting you? You know, like a tag-team kind of thing? Clearly they know each other from before—maybe this is just a game to them."

"Yeah, but what would they be targeting *me* for?"

"To mess with you. Try to get you to crack before the competition even starts. Maybe they figure they've found someone they can get all worked up and stuff. Try to get in your head so you choke in the arena, or something like that."

"Yeah, maybe . . ."

For the first time today, I actually start to relax. I take a satisfied gulp of my coffee as, and a few seats away, a couple of girls get up from the computer they were sharing.

"Want to go online while we're here? I need to check my e-mail."

Angela shakes her head.

"Nah—I've got to run to the campus store and get my mom a NACA T-shirt. I promised I'd stick one in the mail as soon as I got here."

"Actually, I might join you," Gigi says, pushing out her chair. "I want to see if they can order me a copy of Professor Grenski's book."

"Okay, cool—I'll see you guys in Modern World?"

They nod before bundling themselves back up and

bracing for the cold walk ahead of them. I make a mental note to have a producer take me to buy a coat as soon as I have a chance.

"I'll save you a seat," Angela calls back to me as they head out the door.

I settle into the comfy leather armchair in front of the flat-screen monitor. When I log on, there's an e-mail from my dad.

To: Nora Henderson **norahenderson@naca.edu**
From: Judd Henderson **smokesignals@ncbbq.org**
Subject: Re: Hey Dad

Glad to hear you got there okay.

Love you,
Dad

Leave it to Dad to literally interpret the phrase "short and sweet." I glance at the clock on the wall. With the few minutes I have left, I decide to attempt a spur-of-the-moment reconnaissance mission. I pull up a search engine and type in "Joy Kennedy-Swanson." A few dozen results pop up.

"Laura Kennedy-Swanson made first State Representative from Manhattan."

"Kennedy-Swansons honored for contribution to remedy homeless crisis downtown."

"Estate for Sale: Kennedy-Swansons sell posh penthouse."

And then, at the very bottom of the screen, there's a link for a New York gossip magazine. I click on it and I'm transferred to a flashy page with photos of celebrities and fluorescent head-lines. I scroll down until I find a handful of pictures of Joy.

There's one of her standing with two former presidents and who I can only assume are her parents. Another of her on the beach with an actress I recognize. A few more shots that don't mean anything to me. Then one catches my eye.

I take a closer look at it and blink. It's a picture of Joy and Christian. They're standing with two men, both of whom are wearing sunglasses. They sort of look familiar, but I'm not positive *how* I know them. Then I read the caption below the photo.

"Party on the High Seas: The Hamptons Twilight cruise was overflowing with high-profile guests celebrating socialite Joy Kennedy-Swanson's 18th birthday. Pictured below are the birthday girl, Taste Test *series judge Holden Prescott, culinary phenom Thomas Van Lorton, and his seventeen-year-old sous-chef son, Christian Van Lorton."*

Jackpot.

Unless you've been living under a rock for the last few years, you'd know the 411 on Holden Prescott. At twenty, he was the head chef at One Love, New York's only Jamaican fusion bistro. Now, at twenty-three, he has two restaurants bearing his name, is a regular *Taste Test* judge, and probably hasn't actually *cooked* anything for a few years.

But he's far more well known for hitting the party circuit. From what I've heard, he's slept with half the show's former contestants—and, by the way, his hands are cupping Joy's hips in this picture, I think it's safe to say that she's his latest conquest.

I sit back in my chair and stare at the screen. I'd bet a hundred bucks—no, a *thousand*—that Prescott the Player is the only reason Princess Joy is in this competition at all. I should have known there were strings to be pulled. The idea of Joy cooking is almost laughable. She's probably never eaten anything that isn't room service.

But on top of all of that, I've finally figured out why Christian Van Lorton's name sounded so familiar to me the first time I heard it. And now that I know, I have every intention of exposing him for the Legacy Loser he really is.

Contestant Interview

Christian Van Lorton

Producer (P): So, Christian? How are you adjusting? This must be a really different environment from what you're used to.

Christian Van Lorton (CVL): Meaning?

P: Well, you must have a much more glamorous lifestyle in New York. I mean, what with your father's restaurant and television appearances and all those parties . . .

CVL: [shakes head] Not really. I spend most of my time in the kitchen.

P: It must concern you, though, that your fellow contestants will eventually realize who you are.

CVL: And who is that?

P: The son of a famous chef.

CVL: So?

P: So, there are some preconceived notions that come along with that.

CVL: Look, man, I'm just here to cook and to win. Everyone has their own baggage to deal with.

P: And your "baggage," as you call it, must include coming out from behind the shadow of a celebrity family member. A family member who is known for doing exactly what you aspire to do.

CVL: Are we done here? I have class.

P: You just might want to prepare yourself, Christian.

CVL: Prepare myself for what?

P: For the backlash.

CVL: [mumbles something unintelligible, leaves room]

To: Billy Watkins **billythekid@westonhighschool.edu**
From: Nora Henderson **norahenderson@naca.edu**
Subject: Re: Re: I'm here

Billy—

So, today was full of surprises. Remember Tommy Van Lorton, the chef? He had that show on Food TV—*Taste of New York*? Well, apparently this Christian guy, one of the contestants, is his SON. Crazy, right?

And Joy, my roommate—well she's got some kind of thing going with Holden Prescott. I mean, I don't have proof of that, but I found these pics on the Internet—they were looking pretty cozy.

Honestly, between Christian's family tree and Joy's love life, I feel like everyone's got a leg up on me. Why is it that I've always gotta fight harder than anyone else for what I want?

I hate that you guys went to the rally without me—that makes me miss home so much!

Talk soon,
N

CHAPTER four

Photo Shoot? Try Photo Firing Squad!

"Christian Van Lorton!" I hiss into Angela's ear.

She jumps a little as I slip into the seat next to her. Gigi glances over at me, her eyes narrowed.

"What about him?"

"Don't you recognize the name?"

Angela looks at me like I'm an idiot.

"Um, yeah. *It's Christian's name.* Duh."

"Yes, I realize that, Captain Obvious. I mean, doesn't it sound *familiar* to you? Like you've heard it before?"

She shrugs.

"Sounds like the name of a condiment. Or an investment firm."

"How about Tommy Tornado?"

Gigi rolls her eyes. "Of course. *Everyone's* heard of Tommy Tornado."

I wait for the connection to sink in. A second later, her mouth pops open in surprise.

"No WAY! Is that—? That's his DAD?"

Angela's eyes widen. "You're kidding!"

I'm about to launch into an explanation just as Professor Michaelson clears his throat and gestures to the notes on the screen in front of us. Unfortunately, it looks like he's planning on taking his sweet time lecturing about feasts in the sixteen hundreds. Halfheartedly, I scribble some notes about mead and preserved meats, trying not to look at Christian, who is sitting on the other side of the room and seems engrossed with the lecture. By the end of class, though, I'm so distracted that I probably look like some kind of addict, tweaking out of control and unable to focus on anything but my fix.

When the three of us finally head back to the dorm for lunch, I speed through an abbreviated version of Joy's story before diving head first into Christian's. His dad, Tommy Van Lorton, is about as successful as it gets in the food world. Besides having his own TV show, he's a big time restaurateur with setups in LA, New York, Chicago, and Miami. He just opened a food-themed casino in Las Vegas. Rumor has it that he'll replace Donald Trump as host of the next season of *The Apprentice.*

But aside from all that, Tommy is best known for the women he dates—Victoria's Secret models; hot, young actresses; and the like. Entertainment news shows are constantly talking about who he is dating now and who he might be dating next.

Gigi shakes her head.

"Tommy Tornado. Wow. I can't believe we didn't make the connection."

I shrug. "Most people don't think of him by his last name—he might as well be Madonna or Cher."

Angela chews her lower lip.

"You know, I'd heard he had a kid working at his Manhattan joint, Diamonds and Spades, but I've never met Christian before."

"Well, clearly he's met Joy before, and obviously his dad knows Holden Prescott. The four of them looked pretty cozy in that picture."

"It's shady, all right." Gigi nods. "Do you think we're the only ones who've figured out the connection?"

I shake my head. "I doubt it. I mean, obviously the judges, the producers—all of the powers-that-be *must* know. They do a lot of research about our backgrounds and stuff. If I found the picture in two minutes, they definitely know. Not to mention Joy and Pierce and the rest of his entourage. I'm sure they just love being around a Celebu-Chef's kid."

"True." Angela looks pensive. "So, now what?"

"What do you mean?"

We've walked into the dorm lounge and she climbs up onto a high-backed bar stool.

"I mean, really, what difference does it make? He's a Van Lorton. He's privileged and snooty. We already knew all of that."

"Right, but that doesn't make him a good chef," I argue.

"Maybe not." Angela doesn't look convinced. "But we haven't even done any of the press events yet. I bet there'll be tons of coverage about Christian following in his dad's footsteps. Like father, like son, and all that crap."

Something sort of shudders in my chest—either my heart is sinking or my bile duct is flaring up.

"You're right." I shake my head. "It makes for a good story—famous father, brilliant son. If anything, it'll make him *more* popular."

But as I pick at my salad a few minutes later, Gigi eyes me with interest.

"Look, I know you aren't giving up yet. So what's the plan?"

I sigh, piling my lettuce on one side of my plate.

"I don't know. I was just thinking it would be nice to get some ammunition, you know? Something to hold over his head, something to make him stop being such a jerk."

"Yeah, that'd be sweet." Gigi nods enthusiastically.

I look out the window at the courtyard. Christian and Pierce are surrounded by a flock of giggling girl contestants. I guess they're doing something right, since the boys seem to be enjoying it.

"You know what?" I say, still looking outside. "I don't think we're giving this enough thought."

"What do you mean?" Angela asks, sipping her soda.

"I mean that the context is wrong but the idea is right."

"Huh?" Gigi looks confused. I lean in a little and lower my voice.

"What if what Christian needs is to be exposed? To be embarrassed, humiliated, made a complete fool of?"

"Couldn't hurt."

"Exactly. He seems like the type to use his fame—or his dad's, anyway—to get what he wants, be it notoriety or attention or—"

I glance back outside. Now one of the groupies is sitting on his lap.

"—or an easy hookup."

"So?" Angela asks.

"So, there's got to be *something* that would knock him off that pedestal he's put himself on. *Something* that will get him to shut up when he seems most obnoxious and full of himself. A guy like Christian with an ego like that just needs to be forced back down to earth."

When I walk to hair and makeup a few hours later, the excited energy from my earlier plotting transitions back into raw nerves. Filming doesn't start until tomorrow, but tonight we have our first group photo shoot. There's a spread we're doing for a magazine and some advertisements that are going to show up on city billboards. I have to say, the idea of my face being on the side of a building is pretty cool. Of course, the actuality of my six-foot-tall head with inch-wide pores and softball-sized nostrils is a whole other thing entirely.

It's sort of surreal walking down the Forbidden Hallway for the first time. The same guards are keeping watch, but I can hear voices calling out over each other and the faint whirr of a blow-dryer. A door to the left of the arena is slightly ajar and I pull it open.

Inside, it's total mayhem. There are rows and rows of salon-style setups with big mirrors, bright lights, and about a hundred cans of hair spray. Off to one side, multiple racks on wheels are weighed down with hangers of bright fabric and shiny material. There are makeup artists, hair stylists, and fashion designers—who would have thought a cooking show would need so much backstage beautifying?

A man wearing skinny jeans and a furry jacket is scurrying around the room like a very panicked, very trendy rat. Seeing me, he stops in his tracks and covers his mouth with one hand.

"Oh, I can see it now. Country girl goes glam."

He hurries toward me, his tan face creasing into an excited smile.

"You're Nora, right?"

"Um, yeah . . ."

"I knew it!" He grabs one of my hands and examines it. "Down to the bitten nails! Girl, you're a project and a half, that's for sure!"

Embarrassed, I pull my hand away and shove it into the pocket of my jacket.

"Now, now, don't be shy. We have to notice all the little things that make you *you* . . . so that we can change them and make you *fabulous*!"

He steers me toward a chair, talking a mile a minute. Somehow, I manage to get that his name is Bryce Houser and he's "*the* stylist to the culinary stars."

"You know Buddy Pearson?" Bryce asks, wrapping a plastic cape around my neck. He leans in conspiratorially. "He was a three-hundred-pound loser living with his mama when I met him. Now look at him—dropped the weight, dyed the hair, and he's hosting that sushi show on the Raw Network. *And* I hear he's going to be the next *Bachelor*!"

"So." He steps back, putting a finger to his lips. "Here's what I'm thinking—you need some kind of signature look. Something that makes you stand out. Without that, there's no reason for you to be here at all, right?"

"Right," I echo. Up until this moment, I haven't given any thought to what I want my image to be or how I want it to change.

"Okay, let's take a closer look . . ."

Bryce swivels the chair to face the mirror and drops his head just above my shoulder. We both stare at my face.

"You're a very pretty girl, Nora. Look at those cheekbones! I know a few clients who would *kill* for that kind of definition. And talk about a heart-shaped face. You're a regular chip off the Reese Witherspoon block."

He puts a heavily be-ringed hand on each of my shoulders.

"I'm thinking some cocoa-colored liner to play up those huge blue eyes. And, obviously, we'll need to spray tan. But nothing too Oompa-Loompa. And those eyebrows—honey, are they some kind of homage to Brooke Shields? They have *got* to go!"

Gently, he loosens my ponytail. My hair tumbles over my shoulders, happy to be free from its elastic hair-cuffs for once. It's weird seeing it frame my face—it makes me look older. More serious.

"Tell me, Nora, how do you feel about blond?"

I swallow. My hair's always been dark chestnut. My dad used to tell me how much it looked like my mom's when she was younger, and I felt like it was some sort of link to her.

Bryce is watching my face and he can see my apprehension.

"Okay, maybe that's a little extreme. How about some nice highlights then—some honey strands, a kiss of sun here and there?"

He starts pulling sections up and away from my face. I think about how much I want to win this thing. As the saying goes, image is everything. I take a deep breath.

"Sure. Highlights are great. Let's go for it."

"Fab!"

Bryce looks thrilled and, seeing his excitement, I start feeling a little thrilled, too.

But my smile falters a bit as a burly woman with spiky hair and multiple facial piercings approaches holding a bowl and brush. *I'm sure she's great*, I tell myself. *Just because she obviously enjoys pain doesn't mean she wants to inflict it on me.*

As Spike not-so-gently divides and conquers my unruly hair, I watch the chaos swirl around me. I recognize most of the nearby girls from the contestant profiles. I try to match names with faces, to remember what I'd read about them.

There's a beautiful black girl named Coral with huge dark eyes and cropped hair. She's quiet despite her surroundings, reading a book whose title I can't see. I remember that she's the one who got an early acceptance to Harvard, but deferred it to compete here. Talk about intimidating.

To her left are two blond girls, Abby and Amy, practically carbon-copy cutouts of each other. They're gossiping back and forth while two makeup artists struggle to apply lipstick and eyeliner to their moving faces. I remember one of them was sitting on Christian's lap at lunch. A lurch of nausea flies through me.

There's Kelsey, who speaks five languages; Emily, whose parents died in an earthquake; and Jennifer, who lost her hearing when she was five. It occurs to me that everyone has a story that can be condensed down to a caption, a blurb, and that's all I know about them. I can't help but wonder how different each of them is from the short paragraph I've read. If they're judging me by mine, they think I'm the "daughter of a successful barbecue entrepreneur who's won many notable culinary awards."

I've gotta say, I'm not sure how notable it is to win First Place for Pig Butt Texture in Doody's Regional Pork-Off.

"Looking good, looking good." Bryce comes over to the dryer I'm planted under and checks the progress of my highlights.

"We'll rinse these in just a minute. But first . . ."

He reaches over and picks up a small pot of honey-colored wax. I've been dreading this the most. Joanie helped me wax my eyebrows once before and they were red and swollen for a day and a half. But, in the world of television, I guess it's better to look like a burn victim than Bert from *Sesame Street*.

When I look in the mirror an hour later, I have to admit that the transformation's pretty amazing. I turn my head from side to side to examine the effect of the subtle caramel-colored highlights. It really *does* look like I've been out in the sun for a few days. The spray tan booth wasn't exactly the most comfortable ten minutes of my life and I think I'm a little too orange, but Bryce assured me that it'll look normal on TV.

"Wow."

I look up to see Joy standing behind me.

"What?" I say defensively, pulling off my cape.

"Nothing." She shakes her head, but doesn't move. "I'm . . . surprised."

"What, you thought I couldn't clean up nicely?"

"Oh no, not that." She bends down a bit and inspects her eyelashes in the mirror before glancing back at me. "I know that Bryce can perform miracles. He's been working with my family for years. I guess I'm just surprised that you let him change you so much. I mean, hell, the only thing you had going for you was that 'regional redneck' thing. Now even your *own* kind won't root for you."

I bite down hard on my inner cheek and force myself not to tackle her. Instead, I get up and walk around to the clothing racks, trying to calm my breathing. What the hell did I ever *do* to this girl, anyway? I have to remind myself that if I'm patient, I'll expose her for the fake that she is. I just need to see if my suspicions about her and Prescott are right.

I notice a gauzy black dress hanging at one end of the rack, paired with lacy patterned leggings and shiny black cowboy boots. A note pinned to it says, "Photo Shoot One—Nora H." I run a hand over the dress. I've never worn anything so low-cut, so clearly meant to show off "the goods"—which I'm really not a huge fan of showing off. I don't exactly subscribe to the "if you've got it, flaunt it" mantra.

"Is this—this is what I'm wearing?" I ask one of the wardrobe assistants speeding past.

She glances at me and the dress.

"You Nora?"

"Yes."

"Then, yep, it's yours. Dressing rooms are over there." She gestures to a bank of curtained cubicles behind us.

It takes me a few minutes to get the leggings on right, save for the inevitable wedgie. The boots are tighter than the ones I brought from home, but something about them is comforting; they are the only thing I'm wearing that feels remotely familiar.

Outside the dressing room, I feel exposed. What Joy said is getting to me, regardless of how much I want to ignore her. This stuff *isn't* me—it's just a trendy costume to hide my rough edges. But that's the point, right? No one needs to see dirt under my bitten nails, now tipped with French manicured acrylics, or my imperfect smile, now whitened with an ultraviolet light. For the first time in my life, I'm camera-ready. I just have to fake the confidence I need to pull it off.

I stand up a little taller, turn the corner, and proceed to run directly into something—or someone.

"Shoot, sorry!" I mutter, rubbing my arm where it met something hard—an elbow, I think. The roadblock turns around to look at me. It's Christian. He's wearing a tight black T-shirt and dark jeans. I try not to notice how tight they are, too.

"Sorry," I repeat, looking down. I attempt to slide past him but he follows me into the hallway.

"You look . . . different," he says. I tug up the neckline of my dress.

"Joy already beat you to it," I snap. "I don't care if I'm a sellout."

"I wasn't going to say you're a sellout."

"Right. Then what *were* you going to say?"

He shrugs. "That you look sort of hot."

I choke on a surprised breath. By the time I stop coughing, Christian's already walked away, leaving me red faced and speechless for the second time today.

"Contestants!"

Ms. Svincek stands with her hands on her hips, flanked on both sides by two of the other judges. Kenneth Mason is the head chef at 80/20, one of the most successful restaurants in Los Angeles, and Gloria Bouchon is the dean of admissions at the International School of Cuisine in Paris. Standing just behind them is none other than the illustrious Holden Prescott. I scan the crowd to find Joy, hoping to see a chink in her armor. But once I spot her, she's yawning, looking a little bored.

"The photo shoot for *Foodie Magazine* will take place in the empty space next to the arena," Ms. Svincek calls out. "We've set up a studio for our esteemed guest photographer, Jean St. Jean, to work in."

She smiles at a small white-haired man to her left before looking back at the crowd more sternly.

"Monsieur St. Jean has decided to take pictures of you in pairs. Your partners have already been assigned—when you enter the room, you'll find your names listed on the wall. Find your partner, discuss some possible poses and be ready for your turn when it comes."

She sweeps out of the room without so much as a "good luck" or even an introduction to the other judges. I guess we're just expected to know who they are—not that any of us don't.

Crossing the hall, the boys and girls merge together into one herd of sparkly, freshly shaven, heavily made-up opponents. The guys have neat haircuts and designer clothes. The rest of the girls, the ones I haven't seen, are dressed similarly to me—trendy dresses and high-heeled shoes. I feel like I'm walking into an issue of *Teen Vogue*.

On the back wall of the large room, there's a poster-sized sheet of paper with two columns. I hover in the background while people push forward to find their name on the list. As they pair off and head away from the wall, I inch up close enough to read the names.

I find my name two from the bottom. My eyes move across the page. I blink hard when I see the name opposite mine, hoping it's just my imagination. When I open my eyes, it's still there.

Oh, for the love of—

"Howdy, Pard'ner."

Christian sidles up to me as though wearing chaps and spurs. I guess I should have seen this one coming.

"So, I'm thinking a nice, cozy couples shot," he muses. "Maybe you can sit on my lap—or I can sit on yours?"

I give him a dirty look. "Not likely."

"Do you have a better idea?"

"Not yet. But I will."

I spin on my heel and head in the opposite direction. I'm not spending one extra second with Mr. I-Think-I'm-So-Hot-Why-Don't-You-Undress-Now. I'd rather eat my own arm.

I find Gigi over to one side of the white-sheeted set. Her long hair has been twisted into complicated ringlets and her eyes are framed in glitter. She grins at me as I get close.

"Nice partner."

"Nice makeup," I shoot back.

She elbows me in the side. "Hey, I don't know what you expected. I mean, everyone's seen you guys arguing. What did you think would happen? They want an interesting picture. They want a dynamic."

"Yeah," I grumble. "I guess so."

She shoves me lightly. "So give them one! Seriously. Remember what we were saying earlier? About humiliation? Now's the time! Think about it—these pictures are going to be *everywhere*. You can't waste an opportunity to make him look like the jerk he really is."

I watch the other partners pose in a variety of interesting ways—girls lifting up boys and boys holding girls on their shoulders. Angela carries a diminutive Aaron Hale, no more than a hundred and forty pounds wet, like a bride over the threshold. When Gigi and Dillon make it up there, he crouches down on the floor, grinning like an idiot, while she climbs on top of his back and stands there with her arms crossed triumphantly.

Everyone may be choosing a fun pose, but I need something different. Something that will be so funny, so ridiculous, that Christian will wish he never messed with me.

Inspired, I rush toward him and grab his arm. He cocks one eyebrow.

"I thought you were done speaking to me."

"I just wanted to tell you what pose we're doing."

"And explain to me why it is that I'm just going along with your choice of poses?"

"Because you owe me."

"For what?!"

"For telling people I'm stalking you."

He smirks. "I don't think I said *stalking*, exactly."

"Whatever. Just do what I do."

When they call our names, we reach the middle of the set and I turn so that my back is facing Christian's.

"Now move your legs apart a little—shut UP!" I warn him, as he opens his mouth.

He grins, but pretends to zip his lips. Jean St. Jean comes out from behind the lens and nods.

"Yes, that eez pair-fect. Stand just like zat."

I take a deep breath as he moves back to the tripod. As though in slow motion, I watch his finger inch its way across the top of the camera. Just when it hovers directly above the button, I swivel around to face Christian and aim a kick right at his manhood, stopping just short of a direct hit.

I watch the monitor as the picture flies up onto the screen. Me, red faced and determined with my leg in the air. Christian, eyes wide with fear and both hands covering his crotch.

To: Nora Henderson **norahenderson@naca.edu**
From: Judd Henderson **smokesignals@ncbbq.org**
Subject: <None>

Nora,

Billy tells me you're a little stressed about the competition. I just wanted to remind you to keep your chin up. Remember what I said before you left, North Star—you're just as talented as anyone with some fancy culinary pedigree. In the end, we all live, eat, and breathe the same way. You may win some, you may lose some—but, no matter what, you need to stay true to yourself. Cook how you live—like a firecracker ready to ignite.

Love ya,
Dad

Contestant Interview

Angela Moore

Producer (P): Well, Angela. It seems like you're settling right in.

Angela Moore (AM): Things are going pretty well.

P: And it seems like you and Nora and Gigi are becoming quite close.

AM: [nods] Yeah, they're great. Easygoing. No drama.

P: Then, I'm sure Nora's talked to you about her feelings for Christian Van Lorton.

AM: [raises eyebrows] Feelings?

P: Angela, you and I both know that pretending to kick someone is just another way of flirting.

AM: [laughs] Then you don't know Nora. She hates that guy!

P: Really? She *hates* him, huh? Did she use those words?

AM: Well, not *hate*-hate. I mean, they're obviously both very competitive people.

P: Well, competition can often spark the best kinds of chemistry. We've certainly seen it happen before.

AM: [rolls eyes] Look, the only kind of chemistry you're going to get from Nora and Christian is the oil and water kind. Or the gasoline and fire kind. The two of them need to stay far away from each other or they might spontaneously combust.

CONTESTANT INTERVIEW

Giada "Gigi" Orsoni

Producer (P): Giada, tell me—

Giada Orsoni (GO): [interrupting] It's Gigi.

P: Of course. Gigi. So, what has Nora Henderson told you about her relationship with Christian Van Lorton?

GO: What relationship?

P: Well, like I was saying to Angela, a crush is often masked by other emotions—anger and hatred being the most popular.

GO: If you say so.

P: Okay, then. What about you?

GO: [crossing legs] Well, *I* sure as hell don't have a relationship with Christian.

P: But you must have *some* feelings about someone like him, with his background and all.

GO: [shrugs] Not really.

P: You're telling me that it doesn't bother you that someone with that much power—given who his father is—and that many doors already open to him is competing with you for a scholarship he doesn't need?

GO: [looks down] Well, when you put it that way . . .

P: Seems a little unfair, doesn't it?

GO: Trust me. If I've learned anything, it's that life isn't fair. I guess I'll just have to beat him.

P: And you think you can do that?

GO: Sure. Why? Don't *you* think I can?

P: [pats GO's shoulder] Why not, Gigi? It's like they always say. Everyone loves an underdog.

CHAPTER *five*

You Gotta Fight! For Your Right! To Sauté!

I'm definitely going to puke.

Every time it occurs to me that tonight is episode one, our first challenge, a wave of nausea comes over me. We've done all the press stuff—the conferences, the interviews, the photo ops. But the competition officially starts tonight and the thing that really matters—the cooking—is what's going to make the difference between who stays and who goes.

If there's a bright side to the last hectic few weeks, it's been Christian's absence from my life. Ever since I pretended to kick him in the junk at the magazine photo shoot, he's stayed as far away from me as possible.

I smile at the memory. I'll never forget the look on his face. And the judges? They LOVED it. They thought that the picture embodied everything the competition is about. Ms. Svincek even said that they might use it as the official show photo on the website.

The only thing is—well, after the initial shock wore off, Christian didn't seem too bothered by the whole thing. The idea was to humiliate him, but instead he played it up as if it had been his idea in the first place. He even suggested a few more takes, but Monsieur St. Jean said it wasn't necessary: "Zee first one 'olds zee element of surprise."

So I haven't had to say so much as "get the hell out of my way" to Christian since. A few times he's been in the doorway of my room, talking to Joy, but as soon as I approach, he abruptly leaves. I have a hard time believing it was that easy to shoot him down. I know he's up to something, has something up his sleeve to get me back for the "kick heard 'round the arena."

Regardless, I've had to put all that stuff out of my mind today and concentrate on what I'm going to cook tonight. In some ways, the first challenge is the most important one of all. It separates the beginners from the "professionals"—we'll know by the end of the night who really deserves to be here.

My strategy is simple: cook what I know. There are certain dishes that all good cooks have in their arsenal. Usually you've got some "old faithfuls"—some good standby dishes that are sure to please, if not impress. Then there are your showstoppers, the recipes that look beautiful and taste delicious. I've got a handful of both. I've been cooking almost as long as I've been walking, and I've grown up in the most popular roadside restaurant in eastern North Carolina. I know what people like to eat and I know what makes them come back. And *that's* what I need to show the judges, no matter what the challenge ends up being.

If someone were to bottle the nervous energy in the space outside the arena doors, they'd have the bestselling sports drink known to man. It's funny to see the nervous habits people have, the rituals they do. There are a handful with ear-buds in, murmuring lyrics along with the songs. A bunch of girls chatter to each other a mile a minute. Me, I lean up against the wall and stare at the ceiling, trying to clear my mind and not smudge my camera-ready makeup. I smooth my hands over my TASTE TEST signature chef's jacket and take a deep breath.

"Ladies and gentlemen."

An armed officer greets us, holding up a hand for quiet.

"A few moments from now, you'll be escorted into the arena. Be sure to empty your pockets of all items before walking through the metal detectors."

"Metal detectors," someone mutters. "Are you kidding me?"

"The metal detectors are here for your safety. As are the cameras, the motion sensors, the security detail, and every other precaution we've taken. You're a hot commodity and we pull out all the stops to keep you safe."

He turns to open the door.

"Welcome to *Taste Test*, chefs. Good luck."

With trepidation, with excitement, with terror, we head into the arena.

Initially the lights are almost blinding. It takes a second to understand that they are actually being reflected a thousand times over by the mirrorlike finish on the brand-new stainless-steel appliances.

As my eyes adjust, I can see dozens of stoves, restaurant-sized refrigerators, and different gadgets that I've never used before. In a back corner, there's a pantry the size of my bed-room at home. Jars of condiments and bottles of olive oil gleam on metal racks. Huge bucket-like containers say things like SEA SALT, ALMOND MEAL, and CHINESE FIVE-SPICE POWDER.

This place is like a cooking wonderland.

"Please, everyone! Find your places!"

The director, Marcus, a wiry man with a bushy mustache, hurries through the crowd of contestants, pointing to *X*s of tape on the tiled floor. I glance around as people start moving forward to find their assigned stations. Gigi is a few paces away, diagonal from me. Angela is on the other side of the room, plopped right between Christian and Joy. I give her a sympathetic smile.

"We'll begin filming momentarily, starting with the intro-ductory address for episode one. Make sure the tape on the floor is evenly positioned between both your feet."

As Marcus passes me, he stops, backs up a bit, then yanks my left leg away from my right. I stumble a little bit and catch myself on the counter. I guess they take the whole blocking thing seriously. You'd think we were on Broadway or something.

"Okay . . . marker." He sits back down. "And . . . ACTION."

This is it? No coaching, no "get ready, it's happening now"?

Nervously, I run a hand through my hair and watch as the judges, dressed in crisp suits, enter through a door on the right of the arena. They assemble in front of us, stony faced and silent.

"CUT!"

The director mutters something to his assistant, then nods. "Okay, let's try it again."

The entire first hour continues like this—minute-long bursts of filming, followed by endless adjustments and retakes. I'm beginning to understand why being an actor is such hard work. My feet are starting to ache and my neck could use a good massage.

I try not to move too much—every time one of us changes position, we have to do another take. It's pretty tedious and I find myself itching for the actual challenge. The good news is that, once we start cooking, there won't be multiple takes. Instead, half a dozen camera men will crowd around us like paparazzi, trying to catch every sizzle and bubble in every pot and pan.

"We need you to stand in two lines, facing each other. Line up accordingly—Dillon, to the left. Kelsey, to the right. Lawrence, to the left . . ."

Marcus directs each of us to one side or the other until we're standing in two equal rows. His assistant hands out aprons monogrammed with our names and the *Taste Test* logo.

"Each of you will take one slip of paper."

I watch as Holden Prescott walks slowly along the line, waiting for each person to reach into the clear glass bowl he's holding. Is it just my imagination, or does he stop a little bit longer in front of Joy? She smiles at him, practically salivating. When he walks away from her, I think I see her eyes flash something hard—anger, maybe? Jealousy? When she notices me staring at her, though, she blinks and shoots me a dirty look. I grin back at her sweetly. A dozen jokes race through my mind about her and Pants-Off-Prescott.

He gets to me and I remove a piece of paper from the bowl. We aren't allowed to look at what they say yet. Instead, we stand impatiently until the last person from each row has chosen.

"The words on these slips of paper," Ms. Svincek begins, sweeping an arm over the group of us, "are words that represent what it's like to live and compete in the world that is *Taste Test*. Using your designated word, and the ingredients at your disposal, you must create something that represents the emotion or power that word holds for you. You will have"—she glances at her watch—"one hour to complete your dish. Let's start the clock please."

A large, electronic countdown clock on the wall above us flashes "1:00:00" in red.

"And . . . BEGIN!"

The air around me combusts into a mixture of crumpling paper, clanging pans, and feet clamoring toward the pantry and freezers. I wait until almost everyone has fled the arena floor before opening my little white paper and reading my word.

Unsure, I read it again.

My word is "insomnia."

I don't want to look like a moron just standing here and wasting time. But the words "drawing a blank" have never been so applicable to me in my life.

How do I cook the inability to sleep? What can I possibly make that will represent this word in a way that's both clever and delicious? I feel the panic rise in my chest. Unable to do anything else, I head for the pantry. The shelves have been ravaged by the time I get there, but my mind is clinging to an idea that I can run with.

Caffeine.

The one cure for lack of sleep.

The one thing that can jolt you back to a functional state.

And caffeine means two things, at least in my world—coffee and chocolate.

I find a variety of coffee beans in vacuum-sealed sacks and choose a dark Kona blend. Nearby, there are two or three brands of cocoa. I pick the one with the highest percentage of cacao.

I haven't figured all this out yet, but one thing's for sure—I can't just make a cup of espresso or a chocolate cake. I need to pull together some kind of main course. Something that reflects me and the word I've so unfortunately drawn.

The kitchen is emitting everything all at once—heat, steam, yelling, cursing, flames, and, most obviously, friction. Two guys, Patrick and Jason, are already in a heated debate over whose saucepan is whose. The cameras crowd around them like hungry lions.

I let ingredients run through my mind as I set up my station.

Coffee . . . cocoa . . . *cayenne.*

A dry rub! Perfect.

But what about meat? I'm sure the good cuts have already been claimed. I open the refrigerator closest to me and scan through what's left. On the bottom shelf, I see two untouched packages of baby back ribs.

Bull's-eye.

Anyone who's ever competed—runners, swimmers, dancers—knows that you get into a zone where it's not about what you think, but what you do. Your hands and feet move as though they are controlled by some inner force. Only a few minutes in, I feel that zone take over for my thoughts. It's not about Christian or Joy or Prescott or anything else right now. It's not even about me. It's about the food. Time doesn't exist. I work in a way that's almost automatic, like what I'm doing is the only thing I could, or should, be doing at all.

I've just portioned my ribs onto the judges' plates when the timer runs out. I look around me at the hands rushing to finish things up, the faces dripping with sweat. There are still pots on the stove and pans in the oven. The judges seem unimpressed by the half-finished appearance of some of the plates. I sprinkle on a last dusting of chili powder before pushing my dish to one side of the counter.

The judges begin making their rounds, stopping at each plate. They scrutinize the appearance of the food first before tasting it. There are a lot of steaks, a lot of red meat in general. I'm glad I didn't even try to go in that direction, and I'm even gladder that I'm the only person who made a pork dish. Since it's so easy to overcook, I'm sure people were afraid to screw it up on the first shot. But, for me, cooking ribs is like brushing my teeth. It's a daily occurrence.

It's interesting to see what the judges like and what they aren't blown away by. Madame Bouchon described Joy's lobster bisque with roasted corn and potato shreds as "decadent and comforting at the same time." Unfortunately, Gigi's play on a deconstructed Waldorf salad doesn't seem to please anyone. Prescott practically spit out his mouthful, then complained about the "inedible texture and lack of seasoning."

"Now, this is what I'm talking about." Chef Mason smiles, looking up from Christian's dish. He's taken sea bass and roasted it with fennel and beets, then topped it with a microgreen salad.

Ms. Svincek takes a bite and looks equally pleased.

"Well, well, well. We have a contender here, folks."

Christian looks directly at me and winks. I want to slap that smug expression off his stupid, too-handsome face.

"Nora Henderson." Gloria Bouchon gives me a nod. "Can you tell us about your dish?"

I take a deep breath. I try to forget about the cameras that are trained on my every move and the challengers waiting for me to screw up.

"Well, my word was 'insomnia.' When I think of lack of sleep, I think of how to remedy it. For me, that's caffeine."

I wave a hand over the platter.

"I've prepared baby back ribs with a coffee-cocoa-cayenne dry rub and three-chili macaroni and cheese."

One of the director's assistants moves forward and starts unceremoniously sawing apart the ribs.

"Am I just supposed to . . . pick it up?" Madame Bouchon asks, sounding a little disgusted.

"Um . . . yeah . . ." I feel a stab of panic—why did I think that these people in their nice clothes would want to gnaw on pig bones? I watch as each of them takes a bite. Then another. Chef Mason is the first to speak.

"Strong aroma. Nice crust on the meat. Is this a recipe you've made before?"

"It's an adaptation of my dad's dry rub. He owns a barbecue restaurant in North Carolina."

Somewhere in the arena, I hear a snort of laughter. I can feel my face redden.

"Well, Ms. Henderson," Chef Mason says, smiling, "you've certainly made good use of your time today."

"I agree." Ms. Svincek nods. "Excellent flavor and texture, Nora. I would imagine that, as the competition progresses, you'll be someone to watch."

They liked it.

I'm *someone to watch.*

I exhale slowly, a bubble of giddiness inflating in my chest. It only deflates when I remember what's still to come.

The Elimination Table is the viewers' favorite segment of the show and the one the contestants dread most. We all have to sit on uncomfortable stools in front of a long stainless-steel table while each of the judges grills us on the techniques we used or choices we made. It's grueling and nerve-racking, which is why it makes such good television. The show draws it out longer and longer every season; the competitors are hunched over in pain by the time they're excused from the arena.

"Now." Chef Mason speaks first, his voice is deep and resonating. "This Elimination Table will be different than others you've seen in the past. In fact, it will change *everything* about this season from here on out."

My heart stutters a bit before picking up where it left off, a little harder and a little more quickly.

I guess we should have expected something like this. Every first episode has a surprise, a change in the show that serves to shock the audience and trip up the competitors. Once, they brought in three alumni from *Taste Test UK* to compete against the new contestants. Another time, they had each competitor cook for a famous celebrity chef, who in turn chose the winners—and losers. I can only imagine what they've decided to do this time.

I glance at Angela, who shrugs, then at Joy, who is examining her fingernails in the halogen lights. Against my better judgment, I look over at Christian, too; he's staring straight ahead, his face blank.

Like *he* has anything to worry about, anyway. I'm sure Daddy's reputation will keep him in until the end.

"As you already know," Chef Mason continues, "an elimination challenge requires someone to be excused from the show. To be eighty-sixed, if you will."

Chef Mason's face is serene, expressionless.

"This time, however, we aren't eliminating one contestant."

He takes a breath and time seems to stutter to a halt.

"We're eliminating four of you."

There's a shifting in the air around me, as though everyone's stopped breathing entirely. My head is spinning. Four people?! The idea of *one* elimination is nerve-racking enough—but *FOUR*? Hell, there are only twenty of us here in the first place!

Gigi is sitting beside me and I can't resist turning to look at her. Her eyes mirror what I feel, what everyone seems to be feeling—shock, horror, and, most of all, fear.

The crew adjusts their cameras and Marcus leans forward in anticipation. The judges take their seats and Ms. Svincek gives us a smile that can only be called menacing.

"Let the interrogations begin!"

DIRECTOR'S NOTES

Challenge One

These guys are in—try to catch reactions on camera—can be a brief shot, no prolonged excitement. Encourage hugging.

Joy Kennedy-Swanson
Emily Myers
Nora Henderson
Pierce Johnson
Christian Van Lorton
Kelsey Dison
Dillon March
Angela Moore
Aaron Hale
Coral Bishop

Bottom Six (in)—hold for a longer reaction, camera trained. Will be interviewed individually post—Elimination Table.

Malcolm Letterman
Gigi Orsoni

Lawrence Simon
Jennifer Berrymore
Jason French
Patrick Atchley

Bottom Four (out)—these guys are outta here. Film longest moments, preferably shots with tears or visible anger. Encourage emotional reaction.

Walter Warwick
Sky Norman
Abby Johnson
Amy Brenner

To: Nora Henderson **norahenderson@naca.edu**
From: Billy Watkins **billythekid@westonhighschool.edu**
Subject: How'd it go?

1st challenge was last nite, right? Tell me everything.

B

To: Billy Watkins **billythekid@westonhighschool.edu**
From: Nora Henderson **norahenderson@naca.edu**
Subject: Re: How'd it go?

Well, I'd tell you—but then I'd have to kill you. LOL. Lemme put it to you this way—there's gonna be a lotta drama. The show's just started and this place has already become soap-opera worthy. I dunno if I'm coming home with a scholarship or a Daytime Emmy!

N

CHAPTER six

Spy-cing Things Up

"Wow, that was intense," Aaron mutters.

"I can't believe what Svincek said to Walter," Emily says to no one in particular. "She was harsh!"

Malcolm kicks a rock, launching it several feet in front of the group.

"What the hell right does Prescott have to interrogate *me*? When's the last time *he* cooked something instead of posing for magazine covers?"

The walk back to the dorm is completely different from the walk down to the arena a few hours ago. Some people are red faced, tear stained, and stuffy nosed. Others are grumbling or shaking their heads in disbelief. Most, though, are like me—silent. And everyone can't help but observe the glaring, most obvious change—that there are four less of us heading upstairs. Four people who won't be back to their rooms tonight. Four of us whose double rooms just became singles in a matter of minutes.

When the judges announced the elimination times four, it was like the atmosphere of the whole contest transformed. Each of us, no matter how sure we were about our dishes, felt as though there were a target on our backs. Even Joy, the queen of supposed self-confidence, started chewing the inside of her cheek, trying to mask her worried expression.

The panel asked each of us questions, but never gave praise—only harped on the mistakes they perceived in what we had done. Had I thought of brining the meat before I grilled it? Did I consider a coarser grind for the coffee beans? A few times, it took all my practically nonexistent self-control to bite my lip, nod, and stay quiet.

But the worst part . . . the worst part was the handful of devastated people told to say their good-byes, that they'd been "eighty-sixed from *Taste Test.*"

Don't get me wrong—we all expected eliminations. Everyone knew they were coming, knew they were inevitable. But our chances of being eliminated that first night were far greater than we could have imagined. What made it all the more painful was that the contestants who were cut were actually selected from the bottom *ten*, as decided by the judges. So, not only did four people have to go home, but six more got to stay here knowing that the judges thought their food was bad, just not quite bad enough.

And Gigi was one of those six.

The bulk of us take the stairs to the second floor and I keep my eyes trained on the back of Christian's head a few steps in front of me. I bet *he's* feeling cocky as hell. When the judges voted on which dish was the winning one, Christian's was hands down the favorite.

You know what pisses me off the most, though? It's the fact that I don't know if my dish was number *two* or number *ten* on their list. If I let it, that fact will drive me crazy for a long time; it's a whole lot easier to just spend my time hating Christian Van Legacy and his Merry Band of Bourgeois Brats.

I pause at my door and fumble with the key. I want to take a shower before I go check on Gigi. She seemed to take the judgment in stride, but I know I'd be upset if a judge told me my dish was "a sad example of deconstructive gastronomy," whatever that means.

"Good game."

I turn to find Christian behind me, holding out his hand to shake mine. I stare at it, narrowing my eyes.

"This isn't baseball," I retort, turning away again. I'm not usually a sore loser, I swear, but I am *so* not shaking his hand right now.

"I wish I could have tried your ribs; they looked delicious."

I roll my eyes. "Obviously not delicious enough."

"I wouldn't say that."

"Wouldn't you?" I turn back around, my hand on my hip. "Are you here to gloat? Mission accomplished. You won—this time. Next time you won't be so lucky."

"Oh yeah?" He grins at me, eyebrows raised. "What does that mean?"

"It means I'm just getting started," I say, leaning into him. Our faces are barely an inch apart. "And I have no intention of letting you win again anytime soon."

"Right." He takes a step back. "Well, I'm looking forward to your attempt to dethrone me. I'm always up for some comic relief."

I swing the door open and, with a last glance at his triumphant expression, proceed to slam it in his face.

"Good night, Nora."

His words are muffled, but I can hear the smugness in them. I pick up a pillow and throw it precisely at the place where his face would have been.

When I knock on Gigi's door, I try to forget my own frustrations. I think of all the things I'd want to hear if I were in the current "bottom six."

"What doesn't kill you only makes you stronger."

"This too shall pass."

"You can always just pretend to kick someone in the balls. It made me feel a hell of a lot better."

As the doorknob turns, I take a deep breath, preparing myself for the swollen eyes and inconsolable tears.

"Hey, Nora. What's shakin'?"

I blink.

Gigi is in her pajamas, holding a huge bowl of popcorn. Behind her, Angela is sprawled out on the floor and the TV is blasting a high-speed car chase scene. I look at her again, trying to see if she's just hiding how she's really feeling. She looks back at me like I'm a nut job.

"Dude, why are you staring at me?"

I shake my head. "I don't know. I—I guess I thought . . ."

"That I'd be a sobbing mess lying on the floor in a pool of my own vomit?"

"Not exactly. No vomit, anyway."

Angela looks up from the magazine she's flipping through.

"Trust me, I was thinking the same thing—I even brought her tissues." She gestures to a box of Kleenex on the desk. Gigi laughs.

"I'm fine, guys. Seriously. Don't worry about me. Tomorrow's another day, and all that crap. I should have known better than to do a salad, anyway."

"Wow," I say, impressed. "Can you be me when I get voted off? I'd like to have *someone* react rationally, since I know I won't."

She rolls her eyes. "You have nothing to worry about. You won't get voted off anytime soon. They loved you."

"Not so much—not enough, anyway."

"Sucks that Christian won, huh?" Angela says, taking a sip of her soda.

"Yeah." I can feel my lip curling. "He was nice enough to stop by my room to gloat."

"Bastard," she mutters. "I really wish there was some way for someone besides us to see what an arrogant prick he is."

"Don't you think people see it all the time?"

Gigi shakes her head.

"I doubt it. The guys think he's cool, the girls think he's hot, and the judges think he's talented. We're pretty much the only ones who've got him pegged for what he really is."

I grab a handful of popcorn and settle into the denim beanbag chair in front of the TV. A muscular, half man–half robot attacks a bus on the screen.

"You know, what pisses me off the most is how obvious it is to me—to us—that he's a total prick. It's practically written on his forehead or something."

"Well, we can't exactly write it on his forehead . . ." Angela scoots a little closer. "But we *could* write it somewhere else."

"I'm not tattooing his butt, if that's what you're getting at."

"Shut up, perv. I was thinking more along the lines of his door."

I meet her eyes. We both turn to look at Gigi.

"You got markers?" I ask her.

"All different colors."

She digs out a box of art supplies from under her bed.

"Wanna go now?" she asks eagerly.

"Nah, we should wait—at least until after ten so that the hall cameras don't catch us."

"Good call."

It's actually closer to eleven when we tiptoe past the elevator to the boys' wing. I look at my friends doubtfully and whisper, "I don't even know what room he's in!"

Angela moves ahead and beckons for us to follow her. A second later, we stop in front of a door labeled CHRISTIAN AND PIERCE RULE! GO HOME NOW AND SAVE YOUR DIGNITY!

"Unbelievable. Who *writes* that?" Gigi whispers.

The rest of the door is plastered with pictures of bikini-clad models and beer ads. We uncap our markers and, without so much as a glance at each other, begin to scribble all over the smiling bimbos and their perfect tans.

SQUEAK!

My Sharpie skids across the glossy paper with a horrible squeal. Angela snorts, then claps a hand over her mouth.

"Stop it!" I mutter through clenched teeth.

Just then, we hear the sound of footsteps coming from the

other side of the door. The three of us jump back and press our bodies up against the wall. Moments later, the footsteps fade away and we hear the unmistakable sound of a creaking mattress.

"Let's make this quick," Gigi whispers, drawing a green mustache on a redhead in a sailor-suit bikini.

"Okay, just one . . . more . . . thing . . ."

I scrawl, *I don't date Legacy Losers!* coming out of a big word bubble near a model's mouth. Angela underlines the word "Legacy" with her purple marker.

"All right, let's get outta here."

We break into a sprint, slipping on the marble tile in our socks. As I start to turn the corner, I hear the unmistakable whir of the elevator rising and the muted ding when it arrives on our floor. Angela keeps running, but Gigi and I skid to a stop. Our rooms are too far down for us to make it without being seen.

Just as Angela reaches her door, the elevator opens. Two people enter the darkened hallway as she slips into her room. Gigi and I quickly move back into the shadows.

I feel a surge of panic. *Please, please don't let them come this way.* One glance around tells me that we've got nowhere to hide, unless we want to wake up a male contestant and beg for asylum. And, as a general rule, it probably isn't a good idea for two girls to show up at a guy's door around midnight. Silently, Gigi leans forward to peek around the corner. I try to tug her back.

"Gigi, no!"

"I just want to see . . ." She sucks in a breath. "You're not gonna believe this."

"What? Who is it?"

"Joy."

"So?"

"And *Prescott.*"

My eyes widen. "No *way!*"

"Look!"

Tentatively, I take a peek.

Joy, wearing one of her skanky sequined dresses, is standing with one bronzed leg crossed over the other. Prescott is leaning into her, an arm propped on the wall. I strain to hear their conversation.

"You know I thought your dish was the best, baby," Prescott purrs. "I just didn't want to throw us under the bus. We can't risk being exposed, you know that."

"How is your voting for me to win a challenge going to expose us?" Joy pouts.

He curls a finger under her chin. "Who cares about the first win, anyway? It doesn't even mean anything."

"Um, it could have meant me being *eliminated* tonight!"

Prescott shakes his head. "I'd never let that happen."

Joy looks unconvinced until he puts his other arm around her waist and pulls her close. He says something that makes her smile and she nuzzles his neck. Slowly, she tilts her head back and starts to kiss him.

"Ugh!" I duck back, rolling my eyes at Gigi. "They're making out."

"Shocker," she whispers sarcastically. She nudges me over and takes another look. Furrowing her eyebrows, she leans further forward.

"Gigi," I hiss, "you're going to get us caught!"

"Nah," she says and looks back at me. "They're far too into each other at this point. We could probably walk right past them."

"Let's not test that theory, please. We just need to wait them out."

Waiting, however, turns out to be pretty boring. Within a few minutes, we're practically climbing over each other to view the live Skin-a-Max movie taking place in our dorm.

"You're stepping on my foot!" I mutter.

"Sorry!"

Gigi shifts her tiny body a little.

"You know, this looks really bad," I mutter.

"I know—I wish someone would walk out and catch them!"

"No." I shake my head. "I mean this—us. We look like complete psychos."

She shrugs. "We can't help that they've chosen to do this on *our* floor. There are lots of other places to go—elevators, couches, kitchen tables . . ."

"Yeah, I get the idea."

She jerks her head toward the other end of the hall. "How about I see if the stairwell's unlocked—maybe we can go down to the first floor and back up the other side?"

I shrug. "I guess that's the only good option at this point."

She takes off, sliding a little in her socked feet. I turn my attention back just as Prescott pulls away from Joy. He holds her at arm's length and lowers his gaze.

"Now, you just have to trust me. I'll take care of everything."

Joy looks down. "I don't know, Holden. I—I just—"

"Baby, listen." He tucks a lock of hair behind her ear. "It's a foolproof way to keep you in the competition."

"Okay, okay," Joy says, crossing her arms. Prescott smiles at her and pushes the elevator button on the wall.

"I knew I could count on you. You're the best."

He leans down and gives her a swift peck on the cheek. She looks peeved.

"Don't you want me to come with you?"

"No." He shakes his head. "You need to stay here. What if your roommate wakes up and you're not there?"

"So what?"

"So you should try to protect your innocent reputation."

He reaches down to grab her thigh before disappearing in the elevator. Once the doors close behind him, she turns on her heel and heads for our room. A few moments later, Gigi is behind me, breathless. She bends over and props her hands on her knees.

"No. Dice," she heaves. "Downstairs. Door. Locked."

"I can't believe you just missed that," I whisper loudly, pointing to the now empty hallway.

"What, they left? Boo, that's no fun—things were just starting to get good!"

"Yeah, well, listen to this—Prescott said something to Joy about taking care of everything—"

"Um, I can think of a *dozen* things he wants to take care of for her. Like her tonsils, evidently."

"Gross. Stop it. Seriously, I think something's up with that guy—I mean, something shady, you know?"

"What are you talking about?"

I tell her what I heard—about Prescott telling Joy to trust him, about how he said it would keep her in the competition.

"Yeah, but think about it. It might just be something stupid, like giving her an idea for a dish," Gigi points out.

"Maybe—but what if it's, like, I don't know, a secret plan or something. Like a conspiracy!"

"A conspiracy?"

"Yeah." I nod emphatically. "Like an evil plot to take over the show and . . ." I trail off, at a loss for what an evil plot would entail when reality TV is involved.

Gigi stares at me, shakes her head, and starts walking toward her room. "Nora, do you hear yourself?"

"What do you mean?"

"I mean I think you're becoming some sort of paranoid weirdo or something. I don't think a TV chef is out for world domination."

"Yeah, I guess." I look at the wall clock, starting to feel a little stupid. "Maybe I'm just tired."

"Maybe you're just shocked that your roommate's a full-blown harlot."

"Nah." I grin wickedly. "I'm not shocked by that at all."

As we head back to our rooms, Gigi glances over her shoulder at Christian's room. "Man, I wish I could be there in the morning when he opens his door!"

"I know, right?" I grin at her. "Priceless."

Our vindication is short-lived, even when the phrase "Legacy Loser" seems to travel around the dorm like the best kind of inside joke. Part of the letdown is because of the stern lecture all the contestants receive from the production staff about vandalism and destruction of property. Words like "misdemeanor" and "immediate dismissal" were thrown around.

I didn't dare look at the girls until we were walking out. When I finally did, Angela was fixated on her shoes and Gigi looked a little green.

Despite all the drama surrounding the door graffiti, our next challenge is occupying my mind more than my criminal activity. I start brainstorming recipes but nothing feels right—I need a sounding board, a person to bounce ideas off of. Up until recently, that person was always Billy. He'd listen patiently while I rattled off lists of ingredients and directions, cooking methods and temperatures; then, when I'd finished, I could tell just by the cock of his head or twist of his mouth which recipes he liked best. It's strange—I know his face better than my own, but, somehow, I can hardly picture it in my mind.

I decide that, as long as I'm Billy-less, I should take advantage of my new friends' cooking expertise. Between classes, I stop by Gigi's room, but she isn't there. When I don't have any luck finding Angela either, I pull on my only sweatshirt and head outside for a walk. I need a distraction and if I can't be around my friends, I need to get away from the dorm, the cameras, and the competition. I have to admit, too, that the cold air actually feels good. Everything seems sparkly and fresh, like clean laundry.

It isn't until I'm a few feet away that I see Christian, bundled up in a ski jacket, sitting on a bench. He's scribbling furiously in a notebook and I stop for a second, mesmerized by his intensity. He glances up and sees me before I have the wherewithal to hurry past him.

"Nora?" He seems surprised. I look down.

"Hi. Sorry, I was just—"

"You wanna sit?"

I blink hard.

"Uh . . . no. That's okay."

"What's wrong? Don't want to get too close to a 'legacy loser'?"

Something inside my stomach twists hard.

Does he know it was me? Is he bluffing?

Either way, if I run from him now, I'll look totally guilty. Reluctantly, I inch toward the bench and glance at his notebook, covered in writing.

"What's that? A journal?"

"No."

"No?"

"Did I stutter?"

I feel a prickle of irritation.

"Dude, you're writing in a notebook. I could call it a diary but, last time I checked, you weren't a twelve-year-old girl."

I'm surprised when he laughs.

"It's not a diary or a journal. It's a strategy log."

"Lemme guess—chess team? No, I got it—it's Dungeons and Dragons, right?"

He rolls his eyes. "It's where I write stuff about cooking— recipe ideas I have, how long it takes to cook something, ingredients I need for new dishes . . ."

"Oh."

A strategy log, huh? I wish I weren't, but I'm actually impressed.

"So, you ready for tonight's challenge?" he asks, watching me.

I shrug. "Sure. I guess so. It's not like I have a—a game plan or anything." I gesture to his notebook.

"It only helps so much. I have no idea *what* we'll be cooking, just like you."

"I think that's the most nerve-racking part," I admit, sitting down next to him. "That I never know what's coming."

"I know," Christian agrees. "I mean, it could be anything— you can't possibly strategize. You just have to hope you're good enough to win."

I bristle at that, not sure if he's trying to insult me or make me nervous.

"Well, it's nice to know you aren't using your connections to get a leg up on the competition," I say, my tone a little icy.

"Ah, yes." He looks at me, eyes narrowed. "People like *me* would really rather cheat than win legitimately. You know, last time I checked, my dishes speak for themselves. It's not my fault they're better than yours."

I glare at him.

"*Better* is a highly debatable evaluation of your work. I can't think of anything more cliché than poached sea bass."

"The judges seemed pleased."

"Maybe they were." I shrug. "But that kind of Contemporary Cuisine 101 crap isn't going to get you any further than the next few challenges. Eventually they'll realize what you really are."

"Oh yeah? And what's that?"

His unruffled facade is beginning to give way. I narrow my eyes.

"A daddy's boy who gets what he wants. A chef's kid who is using his father's reputation and wealth to get him something he could already have. Why the hell would you need a scholarship, anyway, Christian? It's not like you can't afford to go to Paris."

"Maybe it's not about that."

"Not about what."

"Not about what I already have. Not about money. Maybe I want something more."

I scoff. "Of course you do. Guys like you—you're never happy with what you've got. You always want what *other people* have. Well, fortunately, you can't steal talent."

"You know what, Nora?" He stands up. His breath looks like smoke in the freezing air. "If you stop wasting so much time hating me, you might actually have a chance to win this thing. As it stands right now, you'll be lucky to get through the next challenge."

He turns and starts toward the dorm, his notebook tucked under one arm. I'm frozen in place on the bench, mouth hanging open. I don't know how he manages to keep leaving me speechless, but it's getting really old really fast.

Strategy Log—Challenge Two
Southern Recipes

Ingredients I know are in the pantry—
 Cornmeal
 Black-eyed peas (dry though—would need to soak.
 Check on soaking beans beforehand—cassoulet
 later on?)

Ingredients I know are in the walk-in—
 Buttermilk
 Bacon
 Swiss chard—Collards? Can I interchange
 these?

 And what to add? Bacon, ham
 hocks?
 Preference—regional?

To Do—
~~Ask Nora for opinion?~~
See about chicken-fried steaks—Timing? Tenderness?
Is there fresh corn? Frozen acceptable—no canned!

If this doesn't get under her skin, I don't know what will.

CHAPTER seven

Powder Keg

When the judges walk into the arena, there's one obvious difference between tonight and the last challenge—they are smiling. Grinning, even.

Somehow, that worries me more than a frown ever could.

"Welcome back, competitors," Ms. Svincek says. "I trust you are refreshed and ready for tonight's challenge."

There's a murmur throughout the kitchen. It reminds me of the buzzing around a beehive—sort of frantic and filled with energy.

"Tonight, you'll have the opportunity to do something very special—work with one common ingredient using different techniques and your own style."

Chef Mason wheels in a large cart covered with a sheet. The top looks lumpy and awkward, like there's an elementary-school science-fair volcano underneath. With a flourish, he removes the cloth. A pile of brightly colored bell peppers spills out of a large bushel basket.

"Your task is to create a dish that will appeal to the mainstream American audience using bell peppers, an ingredient that is readily available year-round. It needs to be something viewers will be able, and will want, to cook at home. Whoever wins tonight will have his or her recipe featured on the *Taste Test* website."

Around me, people are already restless. I see a few of them eyeing the open pantry. Others are inching their way toward the freezers. When the clock starts ticking, everyone takes off.

This time, I don't trail behind them. I'm in the thick of it, getting jostled by the crowd of people. It's a madhouse. Two hands reach for one can of green chilies, sparking the first argument of the evening. Most people are gravitating toward the predictable—corn tortillas, cumin, black beans. The obvious choice is Mexican or Tex-Mex or something like that. I snag a bag of semolina flour and slip back out of the pantry.

We've got ninety minutes this time instead of sixty, but I don't feel any more secure. I know the second I do, something will change. Besides, this time the judges will be walking around to talk to us and watch our technique more closely.

After I prep my pasta dough, I start slicing my peppers lengthwise, working to mimic the width of fettuccini noodles. My dish is one I've made a thousand times at home, one that Joanie and my dad always request on their days off. Along with the red peppers, andouille sausage and grilled chicken are sautéed in olive oil and garlic. Throw together a simple alfredo, and you've got Chicken Pasta Nora—at least, that's what Dad calls it.

The nice thing about making something so familiar, so second nature to me, is that I can actually take the time to look around at other people's work. Next to me, Harvard Coral (that's how I think of her, at least) is finely chopping her peppers and adding them to a bowl with grated cheese. Across the room, Angela is roasting hers over an open flame. She gives me a quick salute and I shoot her a thumbs-up.

"Well, isn't that nice?"

Prescott comes up behind me and leans against the counter.

"I think it's wonderful to see contestants supporting one another. Making friends."

I give him a forced smile before turning back to my cutting board.

"So, tell us about your dish, Nora." Chef Mason peers over my shoulder. "You've got a good julienne on those peppers."

As the judges move toward Coral's station, I notice Joy heading for the communal sink. When she sees the line of our fellow contestants, all holding empty pots, she rolls her eyes and stomps across the kitchen to the other sink—the one reserved for that side of the arena. I narrow my eyes. Leave it to my selfish roommate to think that she's too good to wait her turn like the rest of us.

Stop it, I tell myself. *Wasting time hating Joy isn't going to help anyone. Especially not you.*

I redirect my attention to my dish, which, if I'm not careful, could easily become tough and decidedly un-delicious. I cube the cold butter for my alfredo, then flip my chicken breasts in the grill pan. Realizing I still need to boil the pasta water, I glance over at the closest sink, where Coral is busy shucking her oysters. Hmm. Well, better to steal Joy's idea and use the sink on the other side than risk a fishy water bath for my fresh fettuccini. Pasta pot in hand, I head across the kitchen.

I'm only a few feet away from the sink when someone blocks my path.

"What do you think you're doing?"

I look up. Christian's staring at me, his arms crossed.

"Getting water," I say, stepping to the side. He moves to block me again.

"What's wrong with *your* sink?"

He points to the one closer to my station on the other side of the arena.

"It's filled with crustaceans."

I try to move again, but he's like my shadow. I glare at him.

"What's your deal, Van Lorton?"

"Oh, breaking out the last names now, are we?"

"Look, I'm going to fill this pot with water. Get out of my way."

"No." He shakes his head. "Not a chance. Use your own sink, Henderson. There are rules here."

"Rules? About the sink?"

"No, rules about trespassing."

"*Trespassing?*" I look at him incredulously.

As we stand there arguing, Angela passes by holding a saucepan. She puts one hand on her hip and shakes her head.

"Christian, can't you stop being an idiot for once?"

"Or what? You'll join the 'I Hate Christian' club, too?"

"I don't need to join." She smiles sweetly. "I'm a founding member."

"Just forget it," I grumble. "Thanks, anyway, Ang."

I spin on my heel and stomp back toward my station. Jeez, who really cares which sink we use? And besides, aren't some rules meant to be broken?

BOOM!

The explosion happens so fast that, for a second, I think I've just imagined it. It's the roar of something unrecognizable that has me drop to the floor. I look around; in between the kitchen stations, I see three or four other people in similar positions. I can hear the overwhelming sound of what I think is rushing water and someone moaning.

"Judy." I hear a man's voice—Benny, I think—call out to the assistant producer. "Call security. Have them send in the EMTs."

Slowly, I pull myself to kneeling and look over the counter. Half a dozen people are crowded around something—or someone—lying on the ground in front of the sink. The faucet above them looks like a half-peeled banana, the metal folded back on itself like skin. Water is gushing out into the basin and onto the floor, along with steady streams that are spraying in all directions.

Two paramedics enter through the double doors and race across the room. I start to move over toward my station, but I'm unable to tear my eyes away from the portable stretcher they've laid across a counter. Seconds later, I watch in horror as the men lift Angela up onto the stretcher and carry her toward the doors. She's holding one hand against her shoulder. Blood has seeped down the sleeve of her shirt.

"Oh my God—Angela!" I tear off my apron and run toward the door, with Gigi right on my heels. A production assistant holds an arm out to prevent us from following them to the ambulance.

"Guys, she'll be okay. It's an arm injury—we think she just needs a few stitches."

I try to push him away with little luck. "I want to go with them—she shouldn't be alone."

One of the producers, Monica, joins him. She gives us a sympathetic smile. "Ladies, are you telling us you're ready to leave the competition?"

I stand up a little straighter.

"You can't be serious," says Gigi incredulously.

"If you don't finish your dishes for the judges, you forfeit your spot and you'll go home. Period."

"But—but what about Angela?"

"I'm sure Angela would want you to do your best to win." Monica pats me on the shoulder. "Come on, girls, let's finish up. She'd want you to go on without her."

Reluctantly, I walk back to my stove and halfheartedly adjust the burners. All around me, people are talking quietly— the low, incoherent hum of shock. That's when Joy's voice rings out loud and clear.

"What a total inconvenience. Now my dish is completely overcooked."

I turn to stare at her. As though a movie screen has lowered in front of me, I see Joy just as she was last night—draped all over Prescott and completely enamored. I see Prescott, too, holding Joy's chin and kissing her hard—just before he urged her to trust him to take care of everything.

I blink, trying to take stock. Joy broke the rules to use the other sink. Joy was the last one to use that sink before Angela. That sink just exploded in Angela's face. And Joy is standing here, indignant and unharmed. I can feel my lip curl up with rage and I start to move toward her. It takes Joy a second to notice me, but when she does, she throws her shoulders back and narrows her eyes.

"What?" she asks defensively.

"You know what," I practically growl, walking around my station and out into the open arena.

"Nora . . . ," Gigi says quietly.

Joy tosses her hair over her shoulder and turns her back to me. Before I realize what I'm doing, I've crossed the space between us. I reach out and grab her arm, a little harder than I mean to.

"Oww!" Joy whips around and glares at me. "What is your *problem*?"

"*You* are my problem."

"You better get your hands off me."

I squeeze harder and feel her flinch beneath my hand.

"Someone is hurt, and all you care about is your precious dish. You are the most self-centered, back-stabbing, two-faced—"

"All right, that's enough." Benny pulls the two of us apart, but Joy refuses to back down. She reaches over Benny's shoulder, grasping for me.

"If you ever touch me again, I swear to God, I'll sue you so fast, your backwoods, white-trash head will spin," she shrieks.

I lunge for her just as a director's assistant yanks Joy to one side, forcing her to the opposite end of the set. I run a hand back through my hair, which is now sticking up in multiple directions. Benny has his arms crossed and is looking down at me. Angry Santa-Shrek is a pretty scary sight.

"Nora—you know better. You all signed a no-contact clause—physical force equals elimination."

"But, Benny, it's her fault! I know she did it, I know she—"

Gigi grabs my shoulder and smiles at Benny.

"She's just upset, Benny. It won't happen again."

I open my mouth to protest, but Gigi squeezes harder and I wince.

Benny still looks skeptical. He glances at his watch and sighs. "All right—but you've had your warning, Nora. You won't get another one."

As he walks away, I turn to stare at Gigi and she shakes her head.

"You want to tell him that Joy blew up the sink when you have absolutely *no* proof? It'll be her word against yours, Nora. And she has a judge who'll back her up."

We stand there, silently, looking at the exit as though we can still see Angela being rushed through it.

"Do you—do you think she's okay?" I ask quietly.

Gigi shakes her head.

"I don't know. It . . . it was a lot of blood."

"The production guy—he said she'd just need a few stitches. That it was just her arm . . ."

"Let's just finish up so we can get the hell out of here. Maybe then we can figure out a way to get to the hospital."

"Absolutely." I nod. "I'm not above hitchhiking in a time of crisis."

During the inevitable lull between Judging and Elimination, all anyone can talk about is what happened to Angela.

"Did you see what it was?"

"I didn't even know she was hurt."

"That sound—it was like a bomb went off!"

"She was bleeding so much!"

Only Gigi and I sit quietly, watching the time creep by on the clock above us.

The judges agreed to give us five extra prep minutes tacked onto our remaining time, so everyone scraped together a hasty version of the dish they originally intended. No matter the recipe, no one was really happy with the end result—ingredients had hardened or overcooked and a perfect meal just wasn't possible.

On top of that, the judges tasted our dishes without us there this time. None of us has a clue what any of them think about what we've made, not like we could have defended ourselves even if we did. Rule one—no talking back during judging. You know, I actually thought it wasn't possible for me to be more nervous than I was at the last challenge. I was really, really wrong.

Just before we line up in front of the judges, we get word that Angela will be back in the dorm tonight. According to one of the set techs, a washer—that metal donut thingy inside a faucet—had corroded or something, forcing the whole end cap of the unit to blow off when the water was turned on. I don't buy it, not for a second—those faucets are brand new and meticulously inspected by the crew before being used. Not to mention—I mean, I don't know much about plumbing, but why would a rusty piece of metal make a faucet blow up?

The entire time I'm waiting to go into Elimination, I'm focused on Joy—her movements, her facial expressions, her posture. Her face is blank, unconcerned. I bite down hard on my lip.

I know she did it—I know she did *something* to that sink, something that caused that explosion. There's just no way for me to prove it. At least, not yet.

In the darkened surroundings of Elimination Table, the judges somehow look older. I don't know if it's the powerful spotlights or the deeper shadows, but Ms. Svincek's forehead creases are extra pronounced, despite an obvious brush with Botox. Even Prescott looks a little haggard. I wonder what his girlfriend thinks of him looking a little less like a playboy and a little more like Hugh Hefner.

"We'll begin with our three favorites," Ms. Svincek pipes up, smoothing the skirt of her burgundy dress. "First, we have Kelsey Dison's spicy fajita casserole."

Kelsey's reddish curls bounce with her excitement. She runs her tongue over her full set of old-school metal braces.

"We loved your use of the pepper as a key component—the layers were distinct and flavorful. Well done."

Kelsey gives the judges a silvery smile and I think I see Svincek wince.

"Next is Christian Van Lorton."

"Of course," I mutter to Gigi. She pinches my arm.

"Christian," Madame Bouchon begins, "your Southern fried steak with red pepper relish was like a trip to the Deep South. Tell me, how did you come up with such a specific regional dish?"

I stare at him, mouth gaping involuntarily. Southern fried steak? Red pepper relish? It's like he walked into my gran's house on a Sunday afternoon and took a page out of one of her cookbooks.

He glances over at me smugly before looking back at the judges.

"I've found myself inspired by the different regions and cultures represented on this season of *Taste Test*."

"How fascinating," Madame Bouchon gushes.

I wonder how fascinating it would be if I projectile vomited all over her hideous paisley dress . . .

"Nora?"

My head snaps up. Oh God, did I really puke on her? Panicked, I run my eyes over the blue-green fabric. Nope. It looks heinous, but that has nothing to do with me.

"Nora, your red pepper pasta was not only delicious; it was full of texture and cost-effective. When thinking of the audience, you really made your food accessible. Bravo. We've unanimously given you the highest marks—you are tonight's challenge winner!"

The group applauds politely and the clapping rings in my

ears. Ms. Svincek moves forward to shake my hand and I feel a little dazed. I actually won a challenge—the challenge I *told* Christian I'd win. As I accept a hug from Gigi, I look over her shoulder at him. He's wearing a little half smile. It's actually, sort of . . . well, sexy. Not that I'd ever admit it out loud.

The three of us—Christian, Kelsey, and I—shuffle out of the room, leaving the rest of the contestants behind to face Elimination. It's a different experience—being at the top, I mean. The publicist takes some pictures of the three of us for the website. She poses us strategically—since Christian's the tallest, he stands in the middle.

"Now put an arm around each girl," she says.

I force myself not to look at him. I feel his hand slide along my shoulder, then down to my waist. I feel a surge of warmth rise up my neck and into my face.

Back in wardrobe, I shed my chef's jacket in favor of a pair of jeans and a long-sleeved T-shirt. I came down here tonight in slippers and I'm grateful for it now. They feel like little furry hugs as I slide my feet into them.

I hang out in the hall, waiting for Gigi, hoping that she's again safe this week. I don't think I could take any more bad news tonight. Every now and then, I hear a high-pitched laugh—Madame Bouchon—or Chef Mason clearing his throat, which he does every time he's about to say something not-so-nice.

"So, do you think Ms. Svincek wears a wig?"

I jump, then turn to see Christian behind me. He is smiling. "If it's not a wig, she must be going through a massive amount of hair spray."

"Oh, I'm sorry." I cross my arms. "Are you lost? This is *my* side of the hallway."

He rolls his eyes.

"You know, you could say thank you," he says, leaning against the wall directly across from me.

"For what?!"

"Uh, for saving you from the shard of metal that apparently lodged itself in Angela's shoulder. That could have been you, you know."

"Whatever"—I shake my head—"you just wanted me out of 'your' kitchen."

Christian shrugs. "Rules are rules."

He pauses for a second, looking at me.

"Congratulations, by the way. For the win and all."

"Thank you," I say, looking down at my shoes. I've always been a little uncomfortable taking compliments.

"Wow. Weird."

"What?"

"A genuine sign of appreciation without even a *hint* of sarcasm."

I can't help but smile a little. "It happens every now and then."

I scuff the fluffy toe of my slipper against the tile floor. "It's probably pointless to keep waiting here. They could be in there for hours."

"Probably," he agrees. His face sobers a little. "Have you heard anything else about Angela?"

I shake my head. "I wonder if she's back yet."

"She might be. You wanna go up and see?"

"With *you*?"

Christian runs a hand through his hair. "Well, I can walk about ten feet behind you if you want—but eventually we'll end up in the same place."

I blink. I'd planned on waiting for Gigi and we'd go up together.

"Why do *you* want to visit her, anyway?"

"I'm not *completely* void of emotion, Nora, regardless what you may think. Even Legacy Losers have hearts."

I hesitate for a second, and he shoves his hands in the pockets of his hoodie. "Just forget about it. I can go by myself."

I shake my head slowly. "No, I'll go. I want to see her."

We're silent as we walk upstairs and through the second-floor corridor. A few feet from Angela's door, we both reach out to grab the handle. As our hands touch, I feel a jolt of heat run up my arm and down into my belly. I try to ignore it.

Angela is propped up on her bed, surrounded by a half dozen pillows. Under the thick strap of her tank top, a large bandage covers her left shoulder. There's no blood in sight and she gives us a weak smile.

"Wasn't I talking to you two right before this happened?"

Christian grins. "If I remember correctly, you told me to stop being an idiot."

Angela cocks her head. "And if *I* remember correctly, you were giving *this one* a pretty hard time about using that sink. Good thing for Nora, huh?"

She gestures to her arm, which makes me feel even worse. I sit down on the edge of the bed.

"Did they ever figure out what happened?" Angela asks, "with the faucet, I mean?"

"It was a washer," Christian explains. "Something about corrosion or something."

She nods. "Yeah. That's what they told me, too. I gotta say, though—I've never heard of rusting metal turning a sink into a time bomb."

My thinking exactly.

"Don't worry about that right now," I say, standing up. I pat her good shoulder. "Get some rest. I know Gigi will come by when she gets out of Elimination."

"Wait—they're still at E.T.?" She looks from me to Christian. "Which of you won?"

I bite my lip, trying not to smile. She lets out a little whoop. Christian ignores us both and hands Angela a prescription bottle from the nightstand.

"Take a painkiller, enjoy yourself. Milk the sympathy card for all it's worth—I'll send Pierce over to give you a nice back rub."

I give him a disgusted look and Angela shakes her head.

"Thanks for the offer, but I don't think so."

"A sponge bath then?"

I bend down to give her a gentle hug before yanking Christian out of the room by his shirt sleeve. Once we're through the door, I smack the back of his head.

"Hey—what the hell?" Christian yelps. "What was that for?"

"Because you're a pig—a *sponge bath*? Really? That's disgusting."

He shrugs and smiles. "I think it would cheer her up."

"Why would *that* cheer her up? Sponge baths remind me of old people."

"Wow. Well, whatever turns you on, I guess."

"Oh, shut up."

I don't know if he meant to—I don't know if I even *wanted* him to—but Christian ends up walking me to my door. When we both realize it, there's this weird pause. Him, shuffling his feet. Me, picking at my acrylic fingernails.

"So, anyway." I busy myself unlocking my door. Once I hear the click, I turn back around. "Um, see you tomorrow?"

"Sure." He shifts his weight from one foot to the other. "Congratulations again."

"Yeah, thanks."

Ding ding.

The nearby elevator doors slide open and we step apart. I hadn't realized how close we were standing to each other. I look up at his face and he opens his mouth to say something. Then he looks down and away.

"I'll see you later."

"Right. See you."

For a second, I watch as he walks back down the hall toward his room. His body blends and fades into the crowd of people exiting the elevators and coming in from the stairwell. I duck into my room and close the door; for a second, I just stand there, breathing hard, my hand still on the doorknob.

What sticks with me—what I fall asleep thinking about and wake up remembering—is how it felt watching Christian walk away from my room. How it seemed like he'd forgotten something. How, for no clear reason, I felt sort of disappointed.

To: Nora Henderson **norahenderson@naca.edu**
From: Billy Watkins **billythekid@westonhighschool.edu**
Subject: Where'd ya go?

It's been a few days since u wrote—everything ok? I know ur busy and all. Things are the same around here—first episode premieres tomorrow, so ur dad's hooking a TV up in the dining room so we can all watch. Can't wait to see about this drama u talked about.

Billy

To: Benny Friedman **benny.friedman@tastetest.com**
From: Nora Henderson **norahenderson@naca.edu**
Subject: Recipe for the website

Benny,

Here's the recipe for my dish. I'm really excited about it being on the website.

Listen, I just want to say I'm sorry again about the whole Joy thing. I was just really upset about Angela. It won't happen again.

See you at the next challenge.

Nora

Nora Henderson's Red Pepper Pasta

2 tablespoons butter, melted, plus 1/4 cup, divided

1 tablespoon olive oil

1 cup red bell pepper, thinly sliced

3 cloves garlic, minced, plus 1 clove garlic, crushed, divided

1/2 cup andouille sausage, diced

2 cups grilled chicken, diced

salt and pepper to taste

1 cup heavy cream

1 cup Parmesan cheese, freshly grated

6 cups cooked pasta

¼ cup parsley, chopped, to garnish

Directions:

In a 12-inch skillet, heat 2 tablespoons butter and olive oil over medium-high heat. Add bell peppers and 3 cloves minced garlic. Sauté 3 to 5 minutes or until vegetables are soft. Add andouille and sauté 3 additional minutes, stirring occasionally. Add grilled chicken and season to taste using salt and pepper. In a saucepan, melt ¼ cup butter over medium-low heat. Add cream and simmer for 5 minutes, then add 1 clove minced garlic and cheese and whisk quickly, heating through. When sauce is thickened, remove from heat and incorporate with 6 cups of your favorite cooked pasta. Top with chicken/sausage mixture. Sprinkle with parsley and serve.

Contestant Interview

Angela Moore

Producer (P): Angela, thanks for meeting with me so late. Obviously, we're incredibly sorry for everything that happened to you tonight. How are you feeling?

Angela Moore (AM): Okay. [yawns] I'm in a little bit of pain, but nothing major.

P: Well, I know there is only so much you can say, considering that you saw very little before the sink—er—broke, as it were.

AM: You mean exploded?

P: [shifting in chair] So, tell me, what *do* you remember? Any sputtering from the faucet? Any sounds that were out of the ordinary?

AM: I don't think so. Maybe. [puts hand to head] I'm sorry, I'm really tired.

P: Of course. Well, it was wonderful getting to know you, Angela. [hands AM an envelope]

AM: What's this?

P: Your dismissal papers.

AM: [eyes wide] My what?

P: Obviously we'd love for you to be able to stay and compete. But your injury is going to prevent you from cooking for at least a week, maybe two, while it heals.

AM: No, I—[frantic] I can do it. I don't need to be excused from classes. And I'll compete next week—

P: [holding up hand] I'm afraid the decision's already been made. [stands up]

AM: [tears in her eyes] I—I don't know what to say. I didn't do anything wrong.

P: Just get some rest. Don't worry. We won't make you pack up your stuff until tomorrow.

CHAPTER *eight*

Keep Your Friends Close

"They WHAT????"

Angela looks down at her hands, then back up at us. Her eyes are sad, but she isn't crying. Not anymore, anyway.

"At least I've got my friends back home. A life I can return to. Hopefully I can make up the work I've missed and still pass the semester." She sighs and fiddles with her sling.

Gigi shakes her head, looking as furious as I feel.

"That's total CRAP, Ang! I mean, it's not your fault you were hurt—it was an accident!"

Or not, I think.

"It's okay, guys. I've sort of accepted it. I'll really miss you, though."

Watching Angela leave makes me all the more sure that Judas Joy and Prescott the Prick are responsible for what happened to her. It kills me that I don't have a way to prove what my scheming ho-bag roommate did—and now one of the really decent, deserving chefs has been sent home for no reason.

Unfortunately, I don't have a spare second to think about my roommate's extracurricular activities. I've been slammed this week with school work—a report on medieval grilling practices, a multimedia presentation about the difference between electric and gas stoves, not to mention the usual amount of homework and notes. I also have to finish my dessert recipe for Flavor Foundations and I still haven't decided which direction I want to go in. I've come up with some cool ideas with sea salt and caramel, but I don't know if that's too played out. Back in my room after our evening lab, I plop down in my desk chair and stare at the blank computer screen.

What about raspberries?

Oranges?

Kiwi?

Clink.

I look up, but I don't see anything. Probably just the heat clicking on. I start to type.

Clink. Clink.

Oh, please don't let that be a mouse or something. Joy will have a conniption. While it would be fun to watch her jump up on a chair like a lunatic, I'll be the one that has to deal with the little vermin.

Clink. Clink-clink.

This time I see the pebbles hit the window pane before they land on the sill. I slide open the screen and look down.

"How's it going?" Christian asks, peering up at me. He's wearing a heavy hooded sweatshirt and has a football tucked under one arm.

"Um, I'm not sure if you realize this, but *you live in this building.*"

"You busy?"

"If you're asking if I want to throw the football, you've lost your mind."

"Of course not," he scoffs. "Everyone knows girls can't play football."

He ducks as I throw one of his pebbles back at him.

"Come on, I want to show you something."

I glance at the clock. "It's getting late."

"What, scared of breaking the rules?"

I'm not scared of anything. "Okay, okay. I'll be down in a sec."

A few minutes later, I find him perched on a shoulder-high brick border along one side of the building.

"Please tell me we're going somewhere indoors," I say, shivering.

"Of course."

He jumps down next to me. His cheeks are pink from the cold, which makes his eyes even bluer.

"So, where are we going?"

"Follow me, Your Highness. We wouldn't want to keep Your Ladyship cold."

"Shut up."

He leads me around to the back of the dorm. The area is overgrown and surrounded by scrubby bushes and a few years' worth of dead leaves. I take careful steps and pray that there aren't any snakes like back home.

"Here it is."

I look up to see a door cracked open, golden light seeping

from the room behind it. Christian motions for me to go first.

Tentatively, I step inside.

The room is as warm as the light looks. I turn around in confusion. It's a kitchen—not a regular house kitchen and not the arena kitchen either. More like the one at a restaurant or cafeteria. It actually reminds me a lot of the setup at Smoke Signals.

Christian's leaning against the wall behind me, arms crossed.

"It's the original dorm kitchen. The basement of this building was a dining hall before they gutted it for the show's renovations."

"How did you find this?"

He gives me that smile—the one that makes him look like he's keeping a secret.

"I've made friends with some of the security guards. You'd be surprised how far a few rounds of poker will get you."

"Of course." I walk between the well-used cooktops and tray racks, the double-door fridges and wall-mounted broilers. "You know what this reminds me of?"

"Home?"

I turn to stare at him. "How did you—?"

"That's what I thought, too, the first time I came in here."

He runs a hand along the counter.

"It doesn't really matter how big the restaurant or how fancy the food—the back of the house is the same no matter where you are. Same splattered stoves, same banged-up pots." He pushes himself up and sits next to a stack of cutting boards. "Don't you think?"

"I guess. I mean, I've never really been in any other restaurant kitchens besides my dad's. But, yeah, it's just like his."
I touch the lip of an extra-large sheet pan. "Just like what I'm
used to."

"It's weird, you know," he says thoughtfully. "Like, the
arena kitchens are nice and all, but they're nothing like working in a real kitchen."

"I know, right?" I'm shocked that he, of all people, sees
it that way. "It's nice to have the perks, but why bother?
You're never going to use a state-of-the-art mandolin slicer
again—you'll probably never need to."

"If you can't do everything you need to with a good knife,
you shouldn't be in the kitchen at all."

We sort of stare at each other for a minute, as though baffled that we could have this opinion in common. For the first
time, I notice the slight bump on the bridge of his nose, the
shadow of stubble along his jawline. There's something about
those little imperfections—I don't know, they make him seem
more human. More . . . palatable.

"Anyway." He jumps off the counter and walks over to the
fridge, swinging the door open with a flourish.

It's completely stocked—butcher-paper-wrapped packages
of meat and bags of every fruit or vegetable I've ever seen.
Then I notice the bottles of oils, vinegars, and spices lining
the counter closest to the stove.

"Jeez, are you making dinner for the whole building?"

He shakes his head. "I figured we needed a place to practice
that's more private than the common areas. Everyone's been
staying up until two in the morning, trying to get time in the

dorm kitchen upstairs. If we work down here, we won't have to worry about that anymore."

"We?"

"Yeah, sure. Me, you, Pierce—maybe Gigi. Unless you don't want to."

"Are you serious?"

He rolls his eyes. "No, I just made the whole thing up to mess with you."

Let me get this straight. Christian found a private kitchen and he's willing to share it? I look at him warily.

"Why?"

"Why what?"

"Why would you want to offer this up to *me,* or anyone for that matter?"

"Are you saying you don't want to use it?"

I shrug. "I can use the dorm kitchen like everyone else."

"Oh, okay. Great. Well, you enjoy that. I think they have a shift free between 4 and 5 a.m."

I sigh. "All right, all right. I see your point."

"You really have trouble saying 'thank you,' don't you?"

"No," I say, defensively.

"Then just accept this for what it is—me being nice."

"Okay . . . well, then, that's really cool of you, I guess."

I don't know if I'm supposed to hug him or shake his hand or what. I settle for an awkward high five and I feel like I'm about eight years old. He sort of laughs and shakes his head.

"So, how about a little one-on-one—me and you? We can finally break out the big guns."

"Um—isn't that what we've been doing? It's sort of the point of the show, Christian."

"Oh, are you saying you don't have any tricks up your sleeve?"

"Okay, I see how this is going to be. Fine. You're on."

After some heated negotiations, we decide on a beef tenderloin cook-off. We start pulling stuff out of the fridge and Christian hands me a bottle of Worcestershire sauce.

"Hey, I heard about Angela," he says. "That really sucks."

I nod. "Yeah, it does."

"When does she leave?

"She had until tomorrow, but she took off this morning. I can't blame her—I'd want nothing to do with this place if they screwed me over like they did her."

He shrugs. "I mean, honestly, pretty much everyone gets eliminated at some point. She got the shaft, that's for sure, but it just sped up the inevitable."

"She could have won, you know. If she'd had the chance."

Christian doesn't say anything to that. We work in silence, the only sound the slight whir of the running refrigerator. It's more soothing than I ever realized appliances could be.

I'm about to sear my filet when I remember I made plans with Gigi to watch a Jacques Pepin special for Modern World Cuisine. I check my watch—I'm supposed to be in her room in fifteen minutes. Maybe I can reschedule with her for tomorrow. I wipe my hands on my apron and untie it before walking toward Christian.

"Hey, I need to run upstairs really quick."

"Yeah, right," he scoffs. "I'm not falling for that one. How do I know you don't have some special barbecue spice blend stashed away that'll blow my tenderloin out of the water?"

"What, you think I smuggled in some magic tenderizer or something?"

"You wouldn't be the first one to try it."

I roll my eyes. "I'll be right back down."

"No cheating!"

"I don't need to." I smile. "I could win with my eyes closed."

I run around the side of the building, pulling both hands up under my sleeves to keep out the biting cold. By the time I make it to Gigi's room, I'm just beginning to thaw. I lift my hand to knock when I hear her voice through the heavy wooden door.

She sounds angry, yelling about "judges" and "preparedness." I jump as something hard slams against the other side.

"Look," she says, her words muffled, "I'm doing the best I can. I don't know what you want from me."

There's a long pause.

"Don't you think I know that, Mom? Don't you think I *want* to make it until the end? I'm not doing this on purpose!"

Whoa. I can't believe her parents would *call* here. The only phone calls we're allowed to get are if there is an emergency at home or something. And making Gigi feel like crap about being in the bottom of the competition isn't exactly an emergency.

I straighten up when I hear her bang something else—I assume the receiver—down. I listen for a second before knocking lightly.

At first, there's no response. I go to knock again when the door swings open.

"Hey."

Gigi's eyes are swollen and red, her face splotchy. I don't say anything, just follow her into her room.

"Are you okay?"

"Yeah." She gives me a watery smile. "I'm sorry. I'm . . . just a mess."

"Don't worry about it."

I sit on the bed while she paces in front of me, wishing once again that I could talk to Billy. He's way better than I am in a crisis. He can always make someone laugh, even when it's the last thing they want to do.

"This whole thing is just so much pressure, you know?" Gigi is saying. "I mean—like, there's no way to make everyone happy. You want to win, but the competition's intense. You're not good enough no matter what you do. And then you're in the bottom *again* and you feel like crap and everyone tells you that you aren't good enough, anyway . . ."

She trails off and sniffs hard. I shake my head.

"No one thinks you aren't good enough, Gigi."

"You're wrong. There are *definitely* people who think I'm not good enough. They just happen to be related to me."

"Well, those people have *no idea* what it's like to fight for your right to be here. To be proving yourself every day, surrounded by amazing chefs."

"But it's just so easy for you." She flops down next to me, wiping her eyes. "You're always in the top three. It's like you're in some sort of secret club I can't break into."

I shake my head. "It's not like that. I promise you. You have so much talent."

Gigi closes her eyes.

"This place is like a pressure cooker waiting to explode. I feel like there's never any relief. Can't we just, like, watch a movie or something? Forget about cooking and competing and all that crap for a while?"

"Of course. Of course we can do that." I smile at her. I remember the last time I'd had an argument with my dad, Billy put on a ridiculous Adam Sandler movie and spent two hours trying to catch popcorn in his mouth. By the time the credits were rolling, I could hardly remember why Dad and I were fighting at all.

That's what I need to do for Gigi—I need to make her forgive and forget, the way Billy always does for me.

Then I remember Christian waiting downstairs.

"Um, do you want me to go pop some popcorn or something?" At least then I'd be able to explain the situation to him.

"No, I'm good." She settles against the wall and starts flipping channels. "Ooh! *Heart Belongs*! I love this movie—Brad Boxer is such a freakin' hottie, don't you think?"

What am I supposed to do now? I look at Gigi, who's smiling at the screen. I sigh.

"He's all right, I guess. I think I like Levi Gregory better."

"Levi Gregory—no WAY!"

"Brad Boxer has a funny shaped head."

She rolls her eyes at me. "You are disturbed, Nora. You know that, right?"

"Yeah, I know."

I pick up a pillow from the floor and lodge it behind my head. I'll just explain everything to Christian tomorrow. I'm sure he'll understand.

"I said I'm sorry."

I can barely keep up as Christian leaves class the next day. He didn't show up at breakfast and ducked into Flavor Foundations at the last minute. It doesn't take a genius to know when someone's avoiding you.

"I told you, don't worry about it," he mutters.

"I didn't realize—I didn't think you actually cared if I—"

He stops abruptly to face me. "Nora, it's fine, it's done. Let's move on."

"Okay," I say, brows furrowed. "If you're sure."

"I'm sure."

"Well, great—I'm glad you aren't mad."

"Look, I'll see you later, okay?"

He hurries away, leaving me standing alone in the middle of campus and feeling like a total jerk.

It isn't until our challenge two days later that I manage to corner him outside the arena doors while he's tying on his apron.

"Can we please talk?"

"Sure. What do you want to talk about?" He doesn't look at me.

"This sucks, you know? I feel really terrible about the other night. I mean, I thought we were becoming . . . friends or something."

Something in his face hardens, like a veil of stone lowering over his blue eyes.

"Nora, you know how things are. Here one minute, gone the next. Don't kid yourself."

He brushes some flour off his jeans with one hand.

"We're here to compete and to win. I've been pretty good at that lately. And you've been keeping up with me. But that's going to change tonight."

"Excuse me?" I take a step back.

"I think you heard me."

"So, I hurt your feelings and you're going to try to *punish* me?"

Christian gives a cold laugh and looks at me like I'm demented.

"Trust me. You couldn't hurt me or my feelings if you tried."

He walks a few steps toward the arena doors before turning to look at me.

"Get ready for the fight of your life, Henderson. You're about to find out what losing feels like."

I put both hands on my hips and narrow my eyes. "Is that a threat?"

He steps forward and gives me a knowing smile.

"Nope. Not a threat. Not a promise, either. It's a fact."

"Right." I finish knotting my apron strings. "You want a battle? It is *so* on."

A production assistant opens the door and beckons us with one hand.

"C'mon, you two. We're about to start."

"May the best chef win," Christian says, holding his hand

out. Grudgingly, I reach out to shake it, but he quickly pulls away and runs it through his hair instead.

"Smooth move," I say, rolling my eyes.

He grins as he opens the arena door.

"You ain't seen nothin' yet."

To: Billy Watkins **billythekid@westonhighschool.edu**
From: Nora Henderson **norahenderson@naca.edu**
Subject: Re: Where'd ya go?

Billy—I'm so sorry. I've been totally swamped with classes and the challenges and all this strategizing. It's like the only way to win is by being ruthless—which I can do, I guess, but it just feels like a whole lotta BS.

What did you guys think of the first episode? Live up to your expectations? What did Dad say?

Miss you!
Nora

CONTESTANT INTERVIEW

Christian Van Lorton

Producer (P): Christian, Christian, Christian. What a battle tonight! I could practically cut the tension in that room with a butter knife.

Christian Van Lorton (CVL): Yeah, I guess it was a little intense.

P: A little? Hell, I thought Nora Henderson was going to blow a gasket when she saw your dish.

CVL: [shrugging] It's not my fault she didn't think of something a little more impressive than butternut squash ravioli.

P: Well, the judges still seemed to like it—she got second place.

CVL: [scoffs] A distant second. It was nothing compared to a cassoulet. That girl couldn't cook French cuisine if she tried—besides the obvious—French fries, French toast, stuff like that.

P: So tell me—is it true what they say?

CVL: What are you talking about?

P: That you only hate the ones you love?

CVL: [shaking his head] Are you crazy? That girl is a *psycho*. You saw her when she went off on Svincek tonight. I'm surprised you guys are letting her near the knives at this point.

P: I'm pretty sure she's harmless, Christian. And it seems like you guys have some pretty obvious feelings for each other.

CVL: Feelings of dislike, maybe. [leans back in chair] Nora Henderson is trying her hardest to be a force in this game. What she doesn't get is that I'm just getting warmed up.

P: So that's all this is to you? A game?

CVL: Of course. I'd be stupid to think it's anything else. In the end, there will only be one person left. And that person is going to be me.

CHAPTER nine

And Your Enemies Closer

"Too much pepper?"

I take another bite of Gigi's sautéed bok choy and shake my head.

"No, it's not that—I think it needs another layer of flavor. Have you thought about adding sesame oil? Or saffron?"

"Ooh, sesame oil!"

She rummages through the refrigerator and finds the small glass bottle. Shaking some on, she looks at me. "So, you're *sure* Christian doesn't mind that we're in here?"

I shrug. "Just because he found this kitchen doesn't mean it belongs to him. It's as much ours as it is his, right?"

"I guess." Gigi props herself up on the counter. "I just sort of feel bad, you know? I mean, he bought all the ingredients we're using . . ."

"Since when to you care about how Christian feels? Besides, we can replace everything we use."

I turn away and chop my spinach, ignoring Gigi's reproachful look.

"I still can't believe last night," she says a few minutes later. "I mean, it's like someone lit a fire under you or something."

"I guess the whole pressure thing is getting to me, too," I say, starting on my garlic. I haven't told her about my argument with Christian before the challenge and I'm not planning on it.

"It wasn't just you—did you see Christian last night? He was a like a tornado up in that kitchen—and, holy crap, a cassoulet? In *three hours*? How is that even humanly possible?"

I just grunt and break apart a head of garlic.

"I mean," Gigi continues, "what's in one of those, anyway? Goose? Sausage? Dry beans? Sounds kind of gross."

"He used duck confit. And he soaked the beans for two days," I grumble, crushing the garlic with an unnecessary amount of force. "When they said we could prep ahead of time for this challenge, I thought it meant an hour before the competition. Otherwise, I would have pulled something like that weeks ago. I still maintain the rules weren't clear."

"Yeah," Gigi smirks, brushing past me to grab a hand towel, "I think everyone's *real* clear on how you feel about that whole situation."

I color slightly. I may have overreacted a little when I saw what Christian was doing. I may have even taken it too far—it's not like I'm proud of that. I wince as I remember demanding that the producers clarify the rules and regulations in our handbooks.

The worst part, though, was turning away from Benny to see the cameras hovering behind me. Why, *why* do I keep forgetting they are there? And, of course, I chose that exact moment to look at Christian on the other side of the arena. He was grinning from ear to ear.

So, screw it. Now we're in his beloved secret kitchen and I'll be damned if he kicks me out of it. Like I said, it isn't his to grant permission to use. We'll stay here as long as we want. In fact, I've been in here for hours, just so that I can tell him that to his face.

Of course, he hasn't shown up yet, but it's just a matter of time.

I purse my lips, thinking about Christian's cassoulet again. Everyone oohed and ahhed over his skill, his execution. I may have gotten second place, but the complexities of my sage butter sauce were hardly as impressive. It really frosts my cookies that he's so good. I didn't even know what a cassoulet *was* when I got here. For all I know, he was making them in preschool.

"Well, well. If it isn't Has-Been Henderson and her ever-present sidekick."

Gigi and I spin around to see Christian and Pierce standing in the doorway of the kitchen. Both of them have their arms crossed.

"What do you think you're doing in here?" Christian asks, walking toward us. He peers into Gigi's sauté pan. "Besides burning bok choy?"

Gigi narrows her eyes as he passes by, but I can see her looking back at her pan doubtfully.

"What do you want, Christian?" I ask, crossing my arms, too.

"I'm here to work."

"So are we."

"Uh, no. Not down here you're not."

I move my hands to my hips. "What ever happened to '*we need a place to practice*'?"

He shrugs. "You forfeited that privilege."

"Why, because I stood you—"

"Hey, Pierce," Christian interrupts. "Go ahead and grab that stock pot up there, okay? We can use it to start the base for the crab bisque."

"Um, excuse me." I glare at him. "I don't know if you noticed, but the burners are being used here. You're gonna have to come back."

Christian laughs. It's a brittle sound.

"Like I said, there's no 'we' anymore. You guys need to get out of here."

"This isn't your kitchen to control."

"But these are *my* ingredients. No food, no cooking."

"How about this, then," I try, moving my cutting board aside to lean against the counter. "How about we have a cook-off? Whoever wins gets rights to the kitchen."

"Why would I want to do that when I can just kick you out?"

I hesitate. "Uh . . ."

"Because," Gigi pipes up, "if you do, we'll tell everyone about this place and it won't belong to any of us anymore."

"Whatever. It's your time to waste. But I'm picking the dish."

"Fine. And we need to get someone to judge. Someone . . . impartial."

"Pierce is nothing if not a fair, unbiased person," Christian smirks, looking at his friend.

"Absolutely." Pierce nods, grinning. I shake my head.

"No way. It needs to be someone who won't win or lose anything by us having extra practice time. Like maybe Benny. Or another producer."

"So when are we doing this?"

I glance at my watch. It's almost noon. "How about tonight?"

"Great—the sooner I win, the more time I'll have to practice."

"You know, your overblown sense of personal ability continues to astound me."

"Well, if you have any intention of beating me, let alone anyone else, you might want to start believing in yourself a little bit more."

"Whatever. I don't need to pump myself full of affirmations the way you do—I'm here to cook, not to blow smoke up my own ass."

But, by the time dinner rolls around, I'm pacing the floor of my dorm room feeling completely inept. Gigi's lying on my bed, watching as I move from one side of the room to the other.

"Nora, you've gotta stop, you're making me dizzy."

I flop down in a chair and put my head in my hands.

"Why did I agree to this?" I moan.

"Because you're going to win!" Gigi sounds far more sure than I feel. She gets up and walks over to the table.

"Seriously, why are you suddenly such a wreck? You've competed against Christian before."

"Not one-on-one, though."

"What difference does it make?"

"I don't know," I say, shaking my head. "It shouldn't make any difference, but it does."

Christian and Pierce are already in the kitchen when Gigi and I walk in minutes later. Christian's pulling various utensils out of an undercounter drawer. I come around the center island and lean up against the stainless-steel surface.

"So, go ahead—what's the plan?"

"What plan?"

Christian's voice is muffled as he digs through a cabinet. He comes out holding a cast-iron skillet in each hand.

"Um, the 'what we're cooking tonight' plan?"

"Don't be nasty." He sets both pans on the counter and turns for the fridge.

"So, could you maybe tell me so that I can start prepping, too?" I ask his back.

He turns and looks at me. "Pancakes."

"What?"

"You heard me."

"You can't be serious." We've got hundreds of dollars worth of seafood and meat, the best ingredients money can buy, and he wants us to make *breakfast*?

"Why not?" he asks, coming toward me holding eggs and milk. "It's simple and easy to screw up. You make a good pancake, it shows that you know about cooking and baking, about temperature and timing. Pancakes show a lot of skill."

I shrug, fingering the cardboard carton he's put in front of me.

"Whatever. Let's just get this over with."

"My, my, why so negative? Realizing you've lost before you've even started?"

Bristling, I grab one of the skillets. "Not a chance. I'm the one with the advantage. I imagine the last time *you* had pancakes anywhere near you, it was from room service."

Gigi and Pierce, our moderators, decide that we should have twenty minutes to prep our batter and ten to cook our pancakes. Pierce stands in front of us like that token girl at a drag strip who starts a race by waving a scarf. He's got a serious expression that looks odd—I've never seen him without a smirk on his face.

"All right. You know the rules. Thirty minutes for a complete dish. No funny business."

I roll my eyes as he waves a dish towel in the air.

At first, the kitchen is pretty quiet—the only sounds are the cracking of eggs against the lips of bowls or whisking dry ingredients into wet ones. As five minutes pass us by, though, the sense of urgency seems to increase. I watch Christian out of the corner of my eye. He's thrown a few slices of bacon in his skillet.

"What the hell is that? I thought we were just doing pancakes." I reach to grab his skillet off the stove and he swats my hand away.

"How else do you expect me to get bacon grease, genius?"

he shoots back. "I'll throw the meat away when I'm through with it."

"You're so full of crap," I grumble, turning back to my bowl. After the whole "cassoulet" nonsense, I don't trust him as far as I can throw him. He's one of those contestants with a perpetual strategy up his sleeve.

Or, in his case, in his girly diary thing.

I decide to make my butterscotch banana pancakes, which are practically a food group at home. I grab a bottle of white vinegar and pour a couple teaspoons into a pint of milk. Christian gives me a funny look but I just ignore him. When you're out of buttermilk, sour milk is just as good. A *real* cook would know that.

I try not to watch him, but, since we're sharing the stove, it's hard not to pay attention to Christian as he cooks. Up until now, our competitions have required us to be about fifty feet apart. Now we're actually sort of working together. There's something to be said about the chemistry of a kitchen—it can be clockwork and it can be a disorganized nightmare, depending on who's working in it.

"Behind you," I say, sliding past him.

"Hot pan," he calls out, pulling his skillet off the stove.

It's almost like a dance. Like it's choreographed—a tango without touching.

"All right, sixty seconds!" Gigi calls out, tapping her watch. I flip my last three pancakes onto a plate, admiring the slightly crunchy caramelized surface. A few feet away, Christian is removing his with a spatula. I arrange a couple of banana slices along the edge of the plate and sprinkle the whole thing with confectioner's sugar. Christian douses his pancakes with a healthy dose of maple syrup and I chuckle under my breath.

"Something funny?" he asks, eyebrows raised.

"You know what they say about syrup . . ."

"Oh, and what's that?"

"That it's a mask for what the pancakes really taste like."

"Oh, Nora." He shakes his head in mock sadness. "How awful that you were never taught about flavor enhancement. I guess I shouldn't be surprised."

"What's that supposed to mean?"

"Oh, nothing. Just that the only flavors you are used to are lard, lard, and more lard. Oh, and Crisco."

"You know what, you are completely full of—"

"TIME!" Pierce calls out cheerfully. I glare at Christian as we pass our dishes over to our friends.

"Remember," he says to Pierce, "if you can't find Benny, and don't try too hard to do that, look for a girl that's not a contestant. Preferably a blond with huge—"

"I think he gets the idea," Gigi cuts him off. She yanks Pierce toward the door, calling over her shoulder, "We'll be back."

As they head outside, it occurs to me that we never really considered what Christian and I would *do* while we waited for them to come back. I start by ignoring him, busying myself with cleaning my area and putting things away. Unfortunately, it only takes a few minutes before the stove is wiped down and the counters are spotless. I cross my arms and lean up against the fridge.

"We need to season the cast iron," Christian points out. "And do the dishes."

"Right. Okay."

We're standing side by side, rubbing melted shortening into the skillets when I realize he's looking at me. I ignore it at first, but a minute later, he's still staring and I'm starting to feel a little twitchy under his scrutiny.

"What?" I finally snap, still looking at my rag and pan. "Is there something you want to say or are you just trying to make me uncomfortable?"

"Am I making you uncomfortable?"

I feel my cheeks get hot. "No."

"Then why'd you say it?"

"Whatever. Forget it."

We fall silent for another minute.

"So, where were you, anyway?" he asks. His hands, submerged in dishwater, look sort of green.

"Where was I when?"

"You know." There's an edge to his voice. "The night you didn't show."

"Oh." Right. *That* night. "I was with Gigi."

He sort of grunts.

"What does that mean?"

"Nothing."

"I . . . Gigi had this big fight with her mom. I didn't—I couldn't leave her."

Christian shrugs. "I don't particularly care one way or the other."

I turn back to the dishes. "You wanted to know why. That's why."

"Well, thanks for that, then. Your life if just *so* fascinating to me, a play-by-play is truly appreciated."

I throw down my rag and glare at him. "Why do you have to be such a jerk *all the time*?"

He starts laughing.

"What the hell is so funny?"

"You—trying to be all tough and serious. It's sort of adorable."

"Whatever. You're a complete lunatic. I seriously think you might be bipolar."

"Could be." He shrugs. "Maybe I just get under your skin."

"Is that your motive? Do you want to get under my skin?"

"If I *wanted* to get under your skin, I could do a lot more than stare at you."

"Oh, really? I don't think it gets much worse than that."

I feel him move a little closer. He leans in and murmurs, "Maybe I want to get under *something*, but not necessarily your skin. Maybe just under these jeans." He tugs hard at one of my belt loops and I feel my stomach turn over on itself.

"You're disgusting," I mutter, stepping away from him. A shiver sends the threat of goose bumps up and down my body. I try to remind myself that he's obviously trying to make me squirm—that he's not actually flirting with me, no matter how real it feels.

Christian smirks a little, his tongue tucked inside his left cheek like it's holding in a secret. "You're so easy to read, you know that?"

"What are you talking about?" My brows knit together.

Slowly, he runs his palm along the inside of my forearm. Before I can take a breath, and despite my best efforts, the goose bumps manage to set up shop and build franchises.

"I'm talking about the way you fold into yourself when I'm getting to you," Christian continues, squeezing my shoulder with one strong hand. "It's like you're trying to make yourself smaller or something. You get all hunched over, your eyebrows furrow—it's like you're the hunchback of North Carolina. Minus the hump."

I know I should be pissed about being compared to Quasimodo. Instead, I'm embarrassed that I'm so transparent— and a little flattered that he's paid enough attention to me to notice how my body reacts when he's around.

"Besides," his voice breaks through my thoughts, "you could be a little more grateful."

And just like that, we're back where we started—Christian and his Enormous Ego.

"*Excuse* me?"

"There are plenty of chicks here who are dying to have this much time alone with me."

I roll my eyes. "You know what, Casanova? You can do these dishes all on your own. If I have to stand near you for one more *second*, I'm either going to throw up on you or throw something at your head."

We're facing each other, both of us glaring, as the door flies open. Gigi bursts in, panting, holding an empty plate; Pierce is just behind her. I'm disappointed when I see his plate's empty, too.

"So?"

"So," Gigi says breathlessly, "it was—it was—"

"It was what?" I ask impatiently.

"A tie," Pierce supplies, his face still pink from the cold.

"What?" Christian and I say in unison. I glance at him and he's almost as flushed as Pierce.

"What do you mean a tie?" I ask, staring at Gigi in dismay.

She just shrugs. "We tried, guys, we really did. Benny couldn't choose. We found a production assistant—female," she says pointedly at Christian, "and she couldn't make a decision, either. Finally, we just put the plates out in the lounge and got everyone who walked by to try them."

"And?" Christian asks.

"And the only consensus is that they were both really good."

I groan, leaning back against the sink. How can this possibly be happening? A tie. That doesn't solve a thing. Christian looks just as pissed as I feel.

"So now what?" I ask him. He eyes me, then shakes his head.

"I don't know. You want to do this again?"

"Not particularly."

"Should we try a custody agreement?"

"A what?"

"You know—you get odd days, I get even days. Something like that."

I roll my eyes. "Forget it. Can't we just—you know—share or something?"

Christian grimaces a little. "You mean, cook in here together? You can't be serious."

"I mean, we could just work around each other. I'll tell you when I want to use it and you'll do the same. We'll make it as democratic as possible."

"And you think that will work?"

"Doubtful," Gigi mutters.

"Sure. Why not?" I say, shooting her a dirty look.

"All right then," Christian says slowly.

"Good. Then it's settled."

Christian sets down his towel and wipes his hands on his apron before untying it. "Well, just as a heads-up, I'll need the kitchen every day from six to nine—right after dinner, preferably."

"What?" I sputter, blinking rapidly. "Christian, you can't be serious."

"Can't I?"

"You'd be taking almost all our evening free time. You can't just claim it."

He shrugs then grins at Pierce. "Sure I can. And if you want to be in here, you'll just need to work around me."

Without another word, he walks out of the kitchen and into the cold night, Pierce on his heels. I look at Gigi and she shrugs. Then I notice the sink full of still-dirty dishes. I groan.

"Surprise, surprise. He's left us with his mess to deal with. What a jerk."

Gigi, her face half-amused, half-sympathetic, grabs a sponge.

"I guess you should have known better than to bargain with the enemy."

"I guess so," I reply. I stare down into the basin of the sink, where the cloudy dishwater ripples along the edges of the plates and pans. "I have to figure out a way to beat this guy. I swear to you, if he wins this thing, I'll never get over it. And he'll never let me forget it."

Gigi pats my arm and smiles.

"Just remember, Nora—he's got to have a weakness. Everybody does."

Judges' Notes: Kathryn Svincek

Episode Four:
LOSING MY RELIGION

Cooking for nuns from
Our Lady of Prayer Convent

Challenge Ingredient—Chicken

<u>IN</u>

Joy Kennedy-Swanson	needs to work on texture
Emily Myers	moist chicken, good flavor
Nora Henderson	spicy, full-bodied flavor
Pierce Johnson	sophisticated palate, good texture/crust
Kelsey Dison*	nice caramelization, good flake
Christian Van Lorton	a little bland but well structured
Gigi Orsoni	excellent work, a beautiful and complex dish
Aaron Hale	good temperature, nice sear

BOTTOM FIVE

Dillon March   slightly undercooked

Lawrence Simon   trying too hard, overcooked

Jennifer Berrymore under-seasoned, undercooked

Jason French   little more than take-out

Coral Bishop   strong plate presence, less impressive finishing
            sauce

OUT

Malcolm Letterman Ugh. Just . . . Ugh.

* challenge winner

Judges' Notes:
Kenneth Mason

Episode Five:
TAKE MY BREATH AWAY

Cooking for officers of the 81st airborne division

Challenge Food—Airline Chicken

<u>IN</u>

Joy Kennedy-Swanson	*decent piccata, Prescott convinced she's a prodigy*
Emily Myers	*great Marsala*
Nora Henderson*	*fantastic Cajun marinade—top three, for sure*
Pierce Johnson	*under-seasoned but well cooked*
Christian Van Lorton	*as always, excellent—well-composed roulades*
Kelsey Dison	*sweet, sugary finish complemented chicken*
Jason French	*needs to commit to a vision, but good overall*

BOTTOM FIVE

Gigi Orsoni   heavy on the sherry, not my favorite dish

Aaron Hale   works hard, doesn't improve—lacks talent?

Coral Bishop   needs a sense of place in her dishes

Jennifer Berrymore   great idea, horrible implementation

Dillon March   No follow-through

OUT

Lawrence Simon   bad taste, bad texture, bad everything

* challenge winner

JUDGES' NOTES: GLORIA BOUCHON

Episode Six:
EVERYBODY WAS KUNG FU FIGHTING

Challenge Ingredient—Soy

IN

Joy Kennedy-Swanson	salty, needed spice
Emily Myers	good, solid kung pao
Nora Henderson	strong palate, well-composed flavors
Pierce Johnson*	balance of sweet and sour, impressive
Christian Van Lorton	good use of umami
Gigi Orsoni	commits to a flavor and follows through

BOTTOM FIVE

Aaron Hale	unfamiliar with ingredients
Jason French	bland food, uninteresting dishes
Kelsey Dison	consistently mediocre
Coral Bishop	trying too hard to look sophisticated
Dillon March	lacking creativity

OUT

Jennifer Berrymore   unprepared and frequently careless

* challenge winner

JUDGES' NOTES: HOLDEN PRESCOTT

Episode Seven:
EVERYBODY WANTS TO RULE THE WORLD

US diplomats challenge
Sweden and New Guinea
Challenge Ingredient—Potato

IN

Joy Kennedy-Swanson	perfect in every way
Nora Henderson	unimpressive, I say out, but I'm outnumbered
Christian Van Lorton *	chip off the old block
Kelsey Dison	ugh. brace-face. Okay au gratin, I guess
Pierce Johnson	decent twice-baked, heavy on the salt

BOTTOM FIVE

Jason French	bisque tastes like glue

Gigi Orsoni   someone, please tell me why this
                  chick's still here???
Aaron Hale   inedible and ugly food
Emily Myers   nice rack, horrible dish
Dillon March   decent searing, not great plating

OUT

Coral Bishop   I've never had a steak that bad
                  before. I'm actually sort of impressed.

* challenge winner

CHAPTER ten

Burn Notice

"Earth to Nora . . ."

Four more challenges and still tied.

"Hey, Nora. Yoo-hoo!"

How is it possible that he just keeps getting better?

"NORA!"

Gigi's voice, amplified by her cupped hands, manages to break into my thoughts. I shake my head.

"What? Sorry—I was—thinking."

She rolls her eyes and picks up her backpack. "I was just asking you what you think tonight's meeting is about."

Before class this morning, we'd all received a hand-delivered message from the judges, saying that they'd be holding a gathering in the arena tonight. I shrug and doodle in the margin of my notebook.

"Who knows? Something they want a reaction about, I'm sure. Whatever it is, I bet it's being filmed."

"Well, duh. They film everything."

One thing we've all learned over the last few months is that the show comes first. It doesn't matter if we're pulled out of bed at five in the morning, like we were for the Air Force challenge. It doesn't matter if we're up until two in the morning cooking for diplomats from foreign countries. All that matters is that they get the best shot and compose the perfect story line.

It's funny—we take all these courses to prepare us to cook, but no one ever talks about how to deal with the show itself. And since Christian and I are locked in our own raging battle, the uncomfortable spotlight is too often on us.

The Nora vs. Christian story line has become a key part of the show, and it doesn't help matters that we're consistently tied for challenge wins. Even though we're still weeks from the finale, people are already projecting that we'll be in the final three. Part of me is flattered, I guess. Obviously I want to make it to the end. But another part of me, the bigger part, feels uncomfortable under the constant scrutiny. Honestly, I'm starting to dread challenges—class is one of the only times I feel free of the burdens that come along with the show.

After Tools of the Trade, I head to my room to finish working on my report—*Microplanes, Zesters, and the Best Ways to Garnish*. Joy isn't home again, not that I'm surprised. I found out from Bryce that her dad rented her an off-campus apartment for the rest of the semester and she had it cleared with production. Something about her asthma and the building's ventilation system. What a crock.

I guess now she and Prescott have a place where they can meet to hatch their brilliant plans. Like last week, when two of the microwaves shorted out for no reason. And the day that there weren't any meat cleavers in the knife blocks, and we were working with porterhouse steaks. I can't give 'em credit for creativity, but they get bonus points for inconvenience. I guess everything is fair game for their twisted attacks, not just the challenges themselves.

And still, I can't prove a thing. I feel my hackles rising just thinking about it. Ms. Svincek and the other judges, Prescott included, just keep saying that all good cooks need to be prepared for accidents, for imperfection.

"Sometimes things just don't work out as planned."

Yeah, no kidding. Like when your roommate turns out to be a scheming ho-bag, your friend gets sliced open by a shard of metal, and a guy (a friend? an enemy?) decides to turn a rivalry into an all-out war.

The walk down to the arena tonight feels sort of eerie. On challenge nights, there are people everywhere; tonight, there are only a couple of production assistants coming in and out of the metal double doors. Once we get inside, we cross the floor and join the rest of the contestants in the seating area. Christian and Pierce are sitting right up front, so Gigi and I find seats up near the control room. I want to keep as far away from the two of them as humanly possible.

Moments later, Chef Mason stands in front of us, his hands behind his back and a smile on his face. Despite the dim lighting, I notice that Joy is still missing—surprise, surprise.

"Contestants, thank you for meeting us here. On behalf of the other judges and myself, we'd like to say congratulations for making it this far." He claps loudly and the rest of us feel compelled to follow his lead.

Abruptly, the door behind him flies open. Joy flounces in carrying her Louis Vuitton clutch and wearing huge sunglasses, looking like a celebutante fresh out of rehab. Chef Mason waits for her to take a seat, an expression of thinly veiled disapproval on his face.

"*Anyway*," he begins again, giving her a pointed look, "now that you've been reduced to half the original group, each and every one of you should feel proud of the strides you've made here. You are all great chefs, chefs who will do many grand things, I am sure."

In the background, I watch a few tuxedoed men start wheeling in carts laden with food—a huge carved ham, trays of canapés, a tower of petits fours. I'm baffled—are we doing a surprise challenge? Are they going to make us work a cocktail party or something?

"Because you've been working so hard," Mason goes on, "we'd like to invite you to kick up your heels for a bit. Relax, enjoy yourselves. Get a chance to mingle with each other and some of our invited guests."

At that, he steps aside and Ms. Svincek, Madame Bouchon, and Prescott walk out from the shadows, accompanied by a dozen or so people. As I start to recognize them, my eyes widen. There's Tressa Jackson and Jacob Warner, two of the past *Taste Test* champions. The man in a silver satin shirt is Jamie Boyle, a British chef who has a live cooking show out of Las Vegas. Two of the head bakers from *Makes Cakes* are wearing their signature cupcake aprons. Everyone up there is either a television star or a famous chef in their own right.

"Please." Ms. Svincek motions for us to join them on the floor. "Come and say hello. Introduce yourselves. Have a mushroom puff."

At first, most of us are pretty hesitant—I mean, this is the equivalent of an aspiring musician meeting their favorite band. How do you talk to your idol face-to-face? But once Jacob pops open some champagne off camera and swears the contestants to secrecy, we start to relax. About an hour in, someone turns on the sound system. Within a few minutes, people are dancing to '80s music and attempting to do the moonwalk.

"This was my favorite night of the whole season. Not a lot of people can say that they slow-danced with the hottest new chef in Miami and took a Jäger shot with the host of *Food Fixes*."

I turn around to see Tressa behind me, watching a chef in front of us trying to break dance without breaking his back.

I smile at her and hold out my hand. "Nora Henderson."

"I know who you are." She shakes it and smiles back. "You're a great chef. I've been rooting for you since the beginning."

"Really?" I say, surprised.

"Really. I think you're talented."

"Wow. Thanks. That . . . that means a lot."

We continue to watch the people around us dance. I notice Christian with his arm around a blond woman who's got at least ten years of life (and five inches of chest) over me. I feel my lip curl involuntarily.

"Do you know who *she* is?" I ask Tressa.

"Carolyn Cleveland. Don't you recognize her?"

I shake my head. "She can't possibly be a chef."

Tressa laughs. "Not quite. She's the Butt-Naked Baker. She has a show on SEXY, the cable network."

"And is she . . . naked? On the show, I mean."

"Um, I'm pretty sure she's sans clothing by the end of every episode."

"Jeez." I roll my eyes. "And of course Christian's sought her out right away."

She eyes me for a second before looking back at Carolyn. "What's the deal with you two, anyway?"

"Who two?"

"You and Christian. You guys go out or something?"

"What?!" I almost spit out my miniquiche.

Tressa shrugs. "You can't fake chemistry. Remember Bret from my season, how he and I used to fight like crazy during challenges?"

"Yeah, sure. You would always be battling each other for first place. I think you tied more than once."

"Exactly." She smiles at the memory. "And the reason it was so intense was because we were hooking up offscreen every chance we got."

I almost drop my plate. "Wow. Uh, I never would have thought that."

"That's the thing." She takes a swig of champagne. "You can always tell the ones that are messing around off camera. They're the ones who're fighting hardest on-screen."

"Well, not in this case."

Tressa smirks. "Don't worry, there's still time."

She pats my shoulder before walking back toward the bar cart, leaving me standing there feeling a little nauseated. Warily, I look over to where Christian was sitting moments ago with Naked Baker Barbie. She's still there, draped over one of Eat TV's new game show hosts, but Christian's nowhere to be seen.

I start to walk around the perimeter of the kitchen, smiling and saying hello as I pass people. A few minutes later, I spot him standing in a nearby alcove, and he's not alone—there's a tall, broad man with dark hair standing in front of him with his back to me. Nonchalantly, I start piling appetizers on my plate.

"What the hell do you want from me?" Christian asks. He sounds tired, weary almost.

"Just listen," the man says. "You wanted to come here and be the best and win the whole damn contest—and yet, you're making dishes a first-year *line cook* could pull together. What the hell is up with that?"

"I don't know if you've noticed," Christian replies icily, "but I've won almost every challenge so far."

"Yeah. *Almost* every one. It could be every *single* one if you worked a little harder."

Christian starts to walk away. Abruptly, he turns back around.

"Look, you didn't even want me to do this. I don't know why you're *here* right now. Was it just to tell me that I'm not good enough? Because, honestly, I've been hearing that from you my whole life. You didn't need to fly up to Connecticut to remind me."

And at that, he stomps out into the arena. I turn back to watch Tommy Tornado straighten his tie before walking back under the bright stage lighting. Seems that the golden boy isn't so perfect in the eyes of his famous father after all.

Christian disappears through a set of side doors and I feel a surge of satisfaction. If anything is going to throw him off his game, it'll be this. Obviously his dad is the last person he wanted to see. I force myself to ignore the twinge of sympathy in the back of my mind as I follow after him into wardrobe.

At first, I'm pretty sure he's bolted. A minute later, though, I hear the sound of a shoe scuffing itself repeatedly on the concrete floor, as if it were being swung back and forth like a pendulum. Silently, I walk around a heavily laden rack of clothes. Christian's sitting in a barber's chair on the other side, staring into the mirror, but not at himself. I lean against a nearby stool.

"So, your dad's here, huh?"

He looks up at me briefly, then back down again. "It would appear so, yeah."

I put my hands in my pockets and rock back on my heels.

"I guess you weren't expecting that?"

Christian sighs and rubs his brow with one hand. "Look, Nora, are you planning on just standing here and asking me stupid questions all night? Because I have to say, if that's the case, I'd really rather you go."

"What, you can dish it out but you can't take it?"

"Seriously, can you back the hell off?" His voice is almost a growl. "Do you just want me to feel worse than I already do?"

"I don't know. Maybe."

"Yeah, I can tell."

"Can you really blame me, Christian? You've been nothing but nasty to me for—well, pretty much since we met."

"Let's not stop that now, then. Don't let the door hit you in the rear on the way out."

I roll my eyes. "Look, don't let your dad's attitude ruin your whole night."

"Easier said than done."

"Fine." I lean against a nearby pole. "But you're being a big baby."

He's out of his chair so quick that it startles me into stepping back. I watch his face, which is now twisted up with something more than anger, something more like pain.

"A *baby*? Tell me—if your father showed up here after *forbidding* you to come at all, after telling you it was a waste of time, how the hell would you feel?"

"I—"

"And when he gets here," he continues, ignoring me, "he proceeds to tell you all of the things you're doing wrong, just like he does at home. Just like he does at work. Just like he's always done."

For one uncomfortable second, I think he might actually cry.

"Look." I reach to touch his shoulder, and then think better of it. I shove my hands in my pockets instead. "I'm sorry. I didn't—I didn't realize it was such a big deal."

He doesn't say anything.

"Seriously," I try again. "Why don't you come back out

and enjoy some brie pillows or whatever the hell they've got out there?"

He shakes his head.

"I can't think of anything more I'd rather *not* do right now."

"Well, you don't have a choice. Besides, don't they have some announcement they're making? If they're eliminating you for your gigantic ego," I elbow his side, "you should probably be there to take it like a man."

Despite his best effort not to, I watch him start to smile.

"Come on." I grab his hand and drag him toward the door.

"Let's bust out of here instead," he suggests. "We can go down to the basement kitchen. I'll cook you something fantastic."

"We can't, I told you. We have that announcement thingy."

"Who cares?"

"I do. And you should too. I'm not going to let you sacrifice your spot on the show because of your egomaniacal father."

He cocks his head. "You know, Henderson, you're actually a decent person when you want to be."

I grimace. "Don't get used to it. It's only because you're acting so pathetic. I'm taking *pity* on you."

"Then I should probably enjoy it while it lasts, huh?"

He's so close, I can see the flecks of gray in his blue eyes. As he's standing there, looking down at me, I'm reminded of how on the day I left Weston, Billy had the exact same expression on his face.

How I thought that he might kiss me before I was gone for good. How I actually wished he would.

"Come on, let's go," I say hastily, turning away from him.

My cheeks are blazing and I force myself not to look back as we walk back into the arena. Somewhere, deep inside my head, I hear Tressa's voice from before.

You can't fake chemistry.

Don't worry, there's still time.

Guest Chef One-On-One

Tommy Van Lorton

Producer (P): Welcome, Mr. Van Lorton. It's quite a privilege to have you here with us tonight.

Tommy Van Lorton (TVL): That's *Chef* Van Lorton.

P: Of course. Well, Chef, you must be exceptionally proud of your son, Christian. He's won almost every challenge so far.

TVL: Sure, he's doing all right.

P: Better than all right. He's blowing away the competition. With the exception of one or two others, that is.

TVL: [crossing legs] That's what I told him tonight. He needs to stop dicking around, if you'll excuse the term, and pull out the real tools from his arsenal. All this cassoulet nonsense. Who even eats that? Why make something no one even recognizes?

P: [blinking] It showed his talent. Everyone was very impressed.

TVL: [rolls eyes] That doesn't mean they want to *eat* it. I tell Christian this all the time—he needs to be more aware of his audience. His fans. People want food you can make at home, not froufrou French crap.

P: He did appeal to the home viewers with the Southern fried steak recipe from a few weeks ago.

TVL: [scoffs] Yeah, and he didn't win that one, did he?

P: Well, no . . .

TVL: [standing up] Exactly! [bangs fist on table] You can't settle, buddy. You can always do better.

CHAPTER *eleven*

Don't Hate the Player, Hate the Game

When we reenter the arena, Christian's face is a frozen mask; it doesn't betray a single emotion. Once we're immersed in the crowd again, though, he starts smiling and chatting with a few people. I stop by a table and pick up a flute of champagne. I consider gulping it down but take a small sip instead.

The last thing I thought I'd be doing tonight is making Christian feel better. I'm surprised at how good it made me feel, too.

"Meet me in the basement in thirty minutes."

I almost jump, feeling his breath on my neck. The tendrils of hair straying from my ponytail tickle my skin and a chill runs through me. I turn to look at him, unsure of what to say, but he's chatting to one of the women from *Suddenly Suppers*. Something he said must be hilarious because she's laughing hysterically. He looks at me and winks. I feel my heart plummet into my stomach, and an inexplicable, delicious nervousness spreads throughout my body.

I look around for Tressa, hoping to pump her for details. How did things start with Bret and her? Had she hated him at first? Did he have a huge ego? Did she find herself wanting to hit him one second and thinking about kissing him the next?

"Ladies and gentlemen, may I have your attention?"

Ms. Svincek is cupping her hands around her mouth like a megaphone.

"If you would be so kind, we're going to have a photograph taken to commemorate the occasion."

Positioning forty people for a group shot turns out to be the equivalent of brain surgery. The judges want to be up front. All the girls should be clustered together. No, the boys and girls should alternate. By the time the picture is actually taken, most of us want to strangle each other.

As people start to disperse, Christian's dad staggers over to him, clearly drunk.

"C'mon, son. How about a photo with your old man?"

Tommy leans over and taps the photographer on the shoulder.

"Hey, buddy—mind taking one of my son and me?" I see him slip the guy a hundred-dollar bill. Christian rolls his eyes.

"Dad, this is really unnecessary."

"Nonsense." Tommy stands with his chest puffed out, waiting for the flash. Defeated, Christian stands next to him and gives a halfhearted smile.

"Perfect," his dad slurs, throwing an arm around his son's shoulders. "The master and his protégé."

Jeez. No wonder Christian wanted to come here—at least then he wouldn't be stuck hearing stuff like *that* all the time.

"All right, Dad, that's enough." He untangles himself and starts to walk away. Tommy grabs his arm, hard.

"Listen, you ungrateful—"

"All right, contestants!"

It's the first time I've ever been happy to hear Prescott's voice. Tommy Van Lorton looks like he might collapse in a heap; Christian manages to loosen his grip and, instead, steadies his father as he teeters back and forth.

"As promised, we have a little announcement to make. A little twist, if you will."

Unable to help it, some of us groan. The last "twist" forced five of us out of the competition for good on the very first episode.

Seeing our displeasure, Prescott holds both hands in the air. "This twist does not involve eliminations. Well, not directly."

How comforting. I feel all warm and fuzzy inside.

"For your next challenge, *Taste Test* is no longer an individual competition. It's a competition for pairs. Tonight, you will be assigned a partner. A partner who you will be working with in classes, in labs, and in the arena to prepare the best possible dishes that reflect each of your strengths. The pairings are strategic and final."

Chef Mason herds us into a cluster close to Ms. Svincek, who's perusing a clipboard with a pencil in her mouth.

"Okay," she says slowly, looking at us over the rims of her glasses. "Once you've been assigned, please meet with your partner briefly to arrange some times to work together throughout the next week. In the restaurant of life, you know, we are only as good as the chefs around us."

I can't help but roll my eyes. Nice philosophy. Are we going to start hugging now?

Svincek goes down the list, calling out names. As the pairs are announced, people start breaking away from the group. Some of them are chatting animatedly, heads together, eyes bright. Others aren't so enthusiastic. A few have their arms crossed, looking anywhere but at each other.

I think of the last time we were paired up, and I shoot Christian a surreptitious look.

"Nora Henderson and Giada Orsoni."

I blink. Really? I look over at Gigi and she's grinning, so I can't have just made it up in my head. I start walking over to her.

"And, last but not least . . . Joy Kennedy-Swanson and Christian Van Lorton."

I freeze as Joy practically sprints toward Christian and throws herself into his arms. He looks a little surprised, but not as much as Prescott, who looks more than just taken aback. He looks a little pissed.

"All right, everyone. Get to know each other. Strategize. Come ready to fight for your spot. And remember—one pair will win and one pair will lose."

Translation—two of us will be out on our butts in a week.

"I can't believe they paired us up." Gigi is squeezing my arm. "I mean, they know we're friends and everything. You'd think that they would have kept us as far from each other as possible."

"Yeah, it's pretty crazy," I agree. I watch Joy cling on to Christian like a drowning rat with a donut.

"Are you even listening to me?" She follows my gaze. "Yeah, I bet she's happy about riding his coattails into a win."

I stare at Gigi. "You are a genius. Of course—that explains it!"

"Explains what?"

"A win—he paired Joy with Christian so she'll win." I turn to glare at Prescott. Gigi is looking at Joy now, her head cocked to one side.

"You know what? I thought you were paranoid about the whole Joy/Prescott master plan. But, I gotta say, this one's a stroke of genius. If they managed to arrange this—I mean, he'll literally take her to the top."

"What did you say about her on top?" I swivel back to look at Gigi.

She stares back at me, perplexed.

"Not on top. *To* the top. Nora, what's gotten into you? It's like you're possessed or something . . ."

As she trails off, I can see it. The bloom of recognition spreading across her face. Her mouth drops open a little, and then she starts to smile. She looks at Christian, then looks back at me.

The smile becomes a grin.

The grin turns into a laugh.

"You like him!" she crows. "You *like* him, like *him*. I can't believe I didn't see it before!"

"Shut UP!" I hiss, pulling her away from the rest of the crowd. "Seriously, please, don't say anything here."

"When did you—? How did you—? *Why* did you—?"

"I don't know." I shake my head. "I don't even know if I do or if it's just—I just don't know."

"Clearly. You can't even speak."

I shake my head. I need to figure out what I'm feeling before I try to explain it to anyone else. Right now, I can't even explain it to myself. All I know is that there's something happening between Christian and me. Whatever it is, it's totally unexpected and very, very real.

The night air is intensely cold and I find it impossible to catch my breath as I hurry around the side of the dorm. By the time I've made it to the back door of the kitchen, my legs feel numb and my nose is running. Fantastic. I'm sure I've never looked better.

Once I get inside, I push the loose strands of hair off my forehead and rub my hands together, trying to warm them. Exhausted, I sit down on the floor in front of the refrigerator, soaking up the slight heat of the running motor. Christian is late and, somehow, I don't even mind. I lean my head back and look up at the ceiling, trying to remember how exactly this happened. It went from hate to this—it went from war to this.

I close my eyes.

Can it all be blamed on chemistry, like Tressa said? Or does some of it have to do with my heart . . .

"Nora."

His voice is like a caress, a whisper. I smile.

"Nora. Wake up."

I love the way he says my name.

"Nora. You're lying on the dirty floor."

My eyes fly open. Christian is kneeling in front of me, his hand on my arm. I'm curled into a ball next to the fridge. I feel my hair matted against the vent, my cheek pressed against the unmopped linoleum. I can't even remember falling asleep. Hastily, I wipe a hand over my face and push myself up to sitting.

"What time is it?" I ask groggily.

"It's almost one."

"In the morning?"

"No, genius, in the afternoon. Yes, in the morning."

I yawn and look at him sleepily. He's smiling at me, his eyes crinkled in that way I've started to notice.

"Thanks for coming," he says, shifting to sit down next to me. "I'm sorry I didn't make it on time. I had a hard time getting away from my dad."

"Yeah, he seemed a little . . ."

"Drunk?" Christian supplies with a rueful smile. I shrug, but I don't say anything. It's his dad, not mine.

"He's sleeping it off in my dorm room," he continues, running a hand through his hair. "I feel bad for Pierce—my dad snores louder than anyone I've ever met. Way to go, Pop. Always a pleasure."

"I'm sorry. That sucks."

He shrugs. "Pretty crazy about tonight, huh?"

"You mean about our visitors or about the partners?" I ask, purposely not mentioning his dad again. He doesn't answer right away.

"I guess both. I was talking about the partner thing though. Didn't see that one coming."

I want to say something to him about Joy and Prescott. In fact, I open my mouth to do it—then stop. For whatever reason, I just can't. I don't know if it's that I don't trust him or if I'm embarrassed or maybe it's just that I think I might be wrong. Whatever it is, I can't say anything to him. Not yet, anyway. What I *can* say, though, is what he probably already knows.

"I don't think Joy's a particularly good cook."

He shrugs. "She's made it this far."

I don't respond. I can't really argue with that without saying too much.

"You excited about being paired up with Gigi?" he asks me.

"Sure . . ." I hesitate, then take a deep breath and pull myself up to look at him. "It might have been fun if they'd paired us up, you know?"

Christian looks down at his hands for a second and I can see the hint of a smile. When he looks back up at me, his expression is thoughtful.

"I guess that wouldn't have been a smart idea—putting the two of us together."

"Why is that?"

He reaches over and tucks a strand of hair behind my ear.

"Because there is absolutely no way I could concentrate with you right next to me all the time."

His face is close enough for me to count his eyelashes. I think about the times he's been this close to me before— times we were yelling at each other, times we were angry.

Somehow, this feels sort of the same—I'm just as hyped up on adrenaline. The only difference is that here, tonight, I'm not trying to get away from him.

He leans in a bit and his lips hover just above mine.

The memory enters my head like a bullet; Gigi's voice is in my ear as though she's sitting next to me:

"Have you ever thought that Joy and Christian might be targeting you? You know, like a tag-team kind of thing? Clearly they know each other from before—maybe this is just a game to them."

I jerk back, blinking rapidly.

What if she's right? What if this *is* a strategy, a trap—if he just wants me to like him so that he can screw with my head? How do I know that he and Joy aren't in on this whole thing together? One minute, he's totally rude and arrogant, and then the next, he's flirty and sweet. *Too* sweet. I can almost hear him laughing at my stupidity.

Ha, Ha! What an idiot! Actually thinking someone like me *would like someone like* her.

Christian reaches over and touches my cheek. He looks confused.

"What is it?"

"Look, I—I'm sorry," I stutter, moving further away from him. "I can't do this."

"Do what?"

"This. I—I have to get out of here."

"Nora . . ."

Before I lose my resolve, I scramble to standing and run for the door. I can't look at him, too afraid of what I'll see—his satisfaction that he "got to me"? His anger that I'm such a prude?

Quickly, I head out into the frozen night, trying my hardest to ignore the ache in my gut. In the end, I have to remember what is important: the contest. The scholarship. I need this. I can't throw away this chance, especially not on a stupid crush, or whatever this is. I pull my jacket tighter to me and hurry away. Away from the kitchen, away from Christian, and away from everything that, moments ago, had been so gloriously warm.

CONTESTANT INTERVIEW

Nora Henderson

Producer (P): What's on your mind, Nora?

Nora Henderson (NH): [shaking her head, distracted] Nothing. Sorry, can you repeat your question?

P: I asked you how you're feeling about the partners challenge.

NH: Oh, right. Well, good, I guess.

P: You feel confident paired with Gigi?

NH: Sure. I think we'll work well together.

P: And you feel like it's an even pairing?

NH: [confused expression] Yes . . . why, don't you?

P: Face it, Nora. You've got the talent. Gigi's gonna need to rely on you to pull her through the challenge.

NH: [rolling her eyes] Look, I get what you're trying to do.

P: And what's that?

NH: You're trying to get me to say that I think Gigi isn't a good chef, that she doesn't deserve to be here.

P: [shrugging] I never said that—but apparently that's the way you feel. Otherwise, why would you suggest it?

NH: [shaking head] Stop playing mind games with me. Gigi may not be the best chef in the world, but she works hard. She wants to be here. That's more than I can say for some of the other people that are still here.

P: Really? Like who?

NH: Just forget it. I'm tired of being manipulated by you.

P: Nora, I'm not trying to—

NH: I gotta get out of here. [removes microphone, leaves room]

CONTESTANT INTERVIEW

Christian Van Lorton

Producer (P): How are things going, Christian?

Christian Van Lorton (CVL): Fine, I guess.

P: Seems like you and your father have a pretty volatile relationship.

CVL: [shrugs] If you think so.

P: [eyebrows raised] Are you being difficult tonight on purpose?

CVL: [smiles] Maybe. How am I doing?

P: Pretty good. How about you tell me about how things are going with Nora?

CVL: [sighs] Let's try this one more time. There is NOTHING going on with me and Nora. Why can't you just drop it?

P: Because, every time the two of you are together, you seem so . . . intense. It's easy to think that the two of you are involved.

CVL: [rolling eyes] No. Trust me, now more than ever, I can promise you that Nora and I are *not* involved.

P: What do you mean "now more than ever"?

CVL: Just that we aren't having any sort of relationship.

P: Have you talked to her about how you feel about your father? How you feel about the show?

CVL: [rubs hand over face] And why would I do that?

P: It just seems that these things that are bothering you are the kind of things you might share with a friend. Or a girl-friend.

CVL: Jesus, can't you let it go? She isn't my girlfriend. We're not even friends. As far as I'm concerned, my life is none of Nora Henderson's business.

CHAPTER *twelve*

All Falls Down

"I still can't believe you just *left* him there."

"What was I supposed to do?"

Gigi shakes her head. "I don't know. Not *that*."

We're sitting at a table in the dorm lounge, poring over recipes we're considering for our partners challenge. Unfortunately, Gigi's been preoccupied with talking about me and Christian. I almost regret telling her about what happened.

"It doesn't really seem like you guys are fighting or anything."

"We're not fighting. We're just not talking."

"I don't get it. I mean, look, I'll be the first one to say he's a conceited pretty boy who probably sleeps with everything that has a pulse—"

"Does this rant have a point?" I interrupt.

"The point is—well, you said you were starting to like him or whatever. Or, at least you said you weren't sure. Are you telling me that now he isn't even worth your time?"

"It doesn't have anything to do with worth." I flip through my spiral, pretending to focus on a glazed pork belly dish. "I'm not here to make friends."

"Gee. Thanks."

"You know what I mean. This place isn't about connecting. It's about winning."

She shrugs, glances at her watch. "I need to get upstairs soon. I've got a production interview before dinner."

I roll my eyes. "Of all the things that drive me crazy, I hate those the most."

"Why? They're kinda fun. A good way to get in on some of the backstage dirt."

"Yeah, but they're always trying to instigate stuff. Get people mad at each other. Cause drama."

"That's true—they've asked me about you and Christian pretty much every time I've walked in there. And the whole Angela thing. And Joy . . ."

"And me and you," I add.

Gigi frowns.

"What about me and you?"

I wish I could reel the words back in. I shake my head.

"Nothing."

"Well, obviously not nothing. Otherwise you wouldn't have said it."

"I don't know. Who knows what they meant?"

Gigi isn't convinced.

"Nora, what did they say?"

I sigh. "It was stupid, something about the partners challenge."

"What about it?"

I look down, wishing I'd just kept my big mouth shut.

"About if I was mad we were paired up—since you haven't won a challenge yet . . ."

Gigi looks down. "Oh."

"I don't think like that, Gigi, I swear."

I reach across the table to grab her arm. She just shakes her head.

"Whatever. It's fine."

Abruptly, she stands and grabs her jacket from the back of her chair. "I really do need to go up for that interview."

"Listen, Gigi—"

"I said it's fine, Nora. I don't want to talk about it."

"Okay . . . ," I say reluctantly. "Well, I'm going to go work on that salmon roulade recipe in one of the labs. Do you want to meet me there after?"

She shakes her head.

"No, I've got a bunch of homework left to do. I'll just see you later."

I watch as she walks away and I want to hit myself. I am a *complete* moron. Why, oh, WHY can't I learn to shut the hell up?

A couple of our professors have offered us the lab kitchens when classes aren't in session, which gives me some other, more private options besides the dorm and the basement kitchen. But the worst part about cooking away from the dorms has got to be lugging my ingredients across campus. And considering how far the labs are from our building, it's a good thing I'm cooking fish and not a Thanksgiving turkey.

I try to ignore the vision of a quick, convenient golf cart whizzing me to my destination. If I don't stop thinking about him, this is just going to be more difficult and more awkward. Obviously he isn't going to get voted off anytime soon, so I need to push these feelings aside and learn to cohabitate and ignore.

I decide on the Chemistry of Cooking lab because it's furthest away from the dorms, so I figure there will be less of a chance of having to share it with anyone. When I get there, the lights are off and the late-afternoon sky bathes everything in cool blue light. I flip on one switch, then another. The ceiling fixtures flicker and come to life.

I spend almost an hour working. I try different filet knives, different cuts of fish, different fillings, but I've always had trouble with food architecture. My salmon slices aren't thick enough or my stuffing is lumpy and uneven. Instead of pinwheels, my roulades look like flat tires filled with bread-crumb glue. Ick. I'm not even going to bother to try to fix these—I think this is one recipe I'm going to have to scrap.

I take my time cleaning off the equipment and packing up what's left of my ingredients. There's no reason to rush back to the dorm, anyway—I'm avoiding Christian and now Gigi's probably avoiding me. Eventually, though, I force myself to heave my bags of stuff onto one shoulder. It's not like I can stay here and sleep on a lab table.

Just as I'm walking toward the door, though, it flies open. I take a step back. When he sees me, Christian's face screws up in a scowl.

"What are *you* doing here?"

"I just finished," I mutter. I want to get out of this room, which suddenly feels like a closet.

"Well," Christian says as he brushes past me, a reusable grocery bag in one hand, "good. I would prefer not to be disturbed while I work. Charles promised me I could have privacy in the lab."

"Don't you mean Dr. Anderson?" I raise an eyebrow. "I don't think a professor with a Cirrus Prize in food physics is in the habit of letting students call him 'Charles.'"

"He's a friend of my father's."

"Right. Of course he is."

"What is *that* supposed to mean?"

"Nothing." I shake my head and move toward the door. "Good luck with your recipes and stuff."

"You know, I really don't get you."

I turn to see him leaning against one of the lab tables, his jaw clenched. I sigh, crossing my arms.

"What don't you get?"

He rakes a hand through his hair. "I know that you and I haven't always gotten along or whatever. But the other night— I mean, one minute you're all over me and then you're running out the door. I don't know about you, but I can't downshift that fast."

"*I* was all over *you*?"

"Um, yeah—you were there, too, remember? Do you really need a play-by-play?"

"I never should have even *gone* there," I mutter.

"Why not, Nora? God, can't you just lighten up and have some fun? Be a team player?"

"We aren't teammates, Christian," I snap. "We aren't friends. We aren't . . . more than friends. We're competitors. We're supposed to be—professional."

I move to leave again when I feel his hand on my arm. With some effort, he turns me around to look at him. I can feel my heart thump rhythmically and a familiar blast of energy courses through me. My body reacts to his touch with a mind of its own.

"You may hate my guts most of the time," he says, looking down at me, "and I might think you're a giant pain in the ass. But you and I both know that there's something going on here—something worth trying out, at least once."

And then he kisses me.

A good first kiss is everything people say it is.

No. It's more than that.

For me, kissing Christian was like seeing the world through a whole new set of eyes. It was like I was there and I wasn't there. My body was operating under its own steam as I tumbled headfirst into the whole experience. It was a free fall, a nosedive. It was bungee jumping with my lips.

So, I can't explain why I pulled away.

And I really can't explain why I slapped him.

Christian yelps, taking a few steps back. We're both sort of panting and I've braced myself against the doorjamb. He rubs his jaw.

"What the hell, Nora?"

"I—sorry, it was a reflex."

"A guy kisses you and your first reaction is to *hit* him?"

"Apparently."

"Well, I guess that tells me everything I need to know."

He reaches a hand out to me as though we're meeting for the first time. Bewildered, I take it and he shakes it vigorously.

"Competitors it is. Nothing more, nothing less."

"Right," I say, the word sounding sort of hollow to me. I feel a little light-headed. Something somewhere deep inside me is pushing hard against the words "nothing more."

"Great," Christian is saying. "Now get the hell out. I want to cook without giving away my secrets to the enemy."

I give him a forced smile. "Uh, watch out for that one burner on the left, it flares up when you light it."

I don't look back at him as I hurry out the door and away from the lab, confused and nauseated.

When I get down the stairs and outside, I flop onto a bench and stare out into the darkness around me. My pulse is throbbing in my ears and my hands are still shaking. I touch my fingers to my mouth, and it's as though my lips are filled with their own electrical charge. When I close my eyes, I can still feel his mouth, soft and warm, against mine. For a second, I wonder if I've burned my tongue, if that tingling sensation is actually pain. It's sort of like fire, but sweet. It's a desire I've never felt before—one that has nothing to do with cooking or winning and everything to do with Christian.

"Holy crap."

I breathe the words, hoping there's no one around to hear me. It takes a few more minutes before I'm finally able to struggle back across campus, the burden of the stuff I'm carrying now secondary to the emotions I'm grappling with.

When I get back to my room, I somehow manage to unlock

the door without dropping my load. I stumble inside and finally let the bags, boxes, and containers spill from my arms onto the round wooden table in the center of the room. Letting out a big sigh, I flip on the overhead light.

"Turn that off!"

I jump a foot as Joy sits straight up in her bed, or at least what used to be her bed, glaring at me.

"What the hell are *you* doing here?" I stare back at her, horrified.

I haven't actually spent any time alone with Joy since Angela's accident and our on-camera confrontation. I feel the familiar sensation of blood boiling below the surface of my skin.

"This is my room, too," she sneers at me.

"Uh, since when?" I ask.

"Since I moved back in," she says sweetly. "I just missed you *so* much, I had to come back!"

With a dramatic huff, she flops back down and buries her head in the fluffy down pillows. I climb into my own bed, staring daggers at her back. I can't imagine why she decided to move back on campus, unless she was forced to. Maybe the other judges or Benny or *someone* finally realized what was really going on with her and Prescott. One can only hope.

By the time we're in wardrobe the next day, I hear her whining to someone from a nearby makeup station.

I pull on a pair of dark-blue boyfriend jeans and, as quietly as I can, slide my chair back until I can see Joy's shiny black hair twisted around a dozen hot rollers. A makeup artist is struggling to line her eyes while she blabs into her cell phone.

Her *phone*? How does she even *have* that?

"I know, Mommy," Joy is saying, "I totally agree. And once I win this thing, I'll be off to Paris and away from this godforsaken hole of a campus."

Rolling my eyes, I turn back toward my mirror and zip up my jeans. Leave it to Joy to find a way around the rules. Shaking my head, I walk away as she begins ranting about something else.

We find out a few minutes before the challenge starts that a bunch of the network bigwigs decided to watch tonight's filming. When the contestants walk into the arena, it's as though we're performing in front of a live studio audience— hardly a seat in the house is empty. On top of that, the kitchen itself has been totally revamped. Rather than the separate stations for each contestant, they've been combined into larger alcoves with room for two people.

"You ready?" I ask Gigi as she unties her knife roll and examines the blades. She gives me a half shrug.

"As I'll ever be."

I feel a cold, hard lump in my stomach. I forgot she was upset about what I'd said earlier.

"Hey, we're cool, right?" I give her a hopeful smile.

She looks at me, then looks away. "Yeah, we're cool."

"You sure?"

"Yeah," she says quickly. "Listen, I was thinking we should try something Indian. Tandoori spices, some richer flavors. No one's really tapped into that yet."

"That's a great idea!" I say, a little too enthusiastically.

Ms. Svincek takes the floor, clearing her throat into the microphone. The arena falls silent. I sneak a glance over at Christian. He's standing next to Joy, arms crossed. There's hardly a foot of space between them. The lump in my stomach grows colder.

"Welcome back," Svincek begins. "I hope you are as excited to work in tandem with your colleagues as we are to witness your work."

She pauses.

"We've had to make a slight change in the judging for this week. Chef Prescott will be unable to join us, so we are replacing him temporarily."

I look over at Joy, but she's staring at the floor. I wonder if this is why she is back in our room—did Prescott take off for good? Did they break up? Did someone discover what he was up to after all?

"Anyhow." Svincek picks up her ever-present clipboard. "Tonight's challenge will be judged by someone I think you will all be thrilled to meet."

Her cheeks are a little pink and there's a film of sweat on her upper lip.

"Rusty O'Neill, come on out!"

A tall, heavily tattooed man treads into the arena behind Madame Bouchon and Chef Mason, wearing biker boots and a leering smile. Rusty O'Neill had his heyday in the '80s glam-rock scene, but he's come back with a vengeance with his reality dating show, *Rock Steady*. I can't imagine he knows much about food unless it's chili dogs and body shots.

"Hey there, guys." He waves and takes his place next to Chef Mason.

"All right, now for the challenge." Ms. Svincek beams at Rusty. "In honor of Mr. O'Neill's talents and profession, each pair will be assigned one musical instrument. That instrument must inspire what dish you decide to cook tonight. There must be a clear vision that you can explain to the judges at Elimination Table and, of course, it should have that rock-star edge to it."

Madame Bouchon is already making the rounds, handing one person in each station a small envelope. Gigi rips ours open and pulls out a card with a picture sketched in black and white. It's a drum kit, complete with symbols and a cowbell. I point to the bell.

"Think that means we should make red meat?"

She elbows me and grins. "Nah, I've got a chicken dish that's gonna knock their socks off."

I feel a little bit better about things after that. Chef Mason sets the clock and has Rusty push the button for us to start. As the numbers begin to move, every twosome huddles close to strategize. We have an extra five minutes tacked on to our hour so that we can discuss what we want to cook. Gigi's sketching out a chicken dish on a piece of paper. Over her head, I watch Joy and Christian. He has one hand on her shoulder and she's laughing. I feel the distinct need to throw sharp objects in their direction.

Gigi and I ditch our Indian idea and decide instead on Chicken Napoleons—pounded chicken breasts cut into discs and pan-fried with a panko crust. We're going to layer the chicken with paper-thin chips made of crispy prosciutto, spinach, and Fontina cheese. The stacks will pile up at different heights to mimic a drum set.

Gigi starts searching for a meat mallet while I begin slicing cheese into coaster-sized pieces. I studiously look down at my hands and my knife, trying my damnedest not to watch Joy and Christian working. Any good chef will tell you that your partner in the kitchen is your right hand. It's one of the most important relationships you can have. So the idea of the two of them creating food together ties me in knots.

I remind myself that I'm the one who walked away from him in the basement kitchen, that I'm the one who slapped him in the lab. It doesn't make me feel any better—or any less jealous. Unable to resist any longer, I pretend to be checking the countdown clock and watch them from the corner of my eye. They're furiously chopping separate ingredients with almost identical speed.

How adorable. I may gag.

Whatever it is, though, a knife isn't enough for Joy. I feel a smug satisfaction as she crosses the room and pulls a food processor from a storage shelf.

Ha! *Amateur.*

"So, tell me about what you're making, ladies."

I turn to find Lusty Rusty leaning casually against our station counter, swinging a knife held between two fingers. I force myself not to grab it out of his hand. Gigi, on the other hand, bats her eyes like a lunatic.

"Mr. O'Neill, it's such a pleasure to meet you. I'm a *huge* fan!"

I stare at her, speechless. Since when is she a "huge fan"?

"Please, darlin'. Call me Rusty." He leans over with a sort of swagger. "I gotta tell you, you two girls are some of the cutest I've seen in here tonight."

I give him my most beatific smile as a flustered Gigi gestures to the chicken she's pounded flat between layers of plastic wrap.

"Would you like me to show you how to—how we do this?"

"Absolutely. Lemme just get an apron."

He carelessly tosses the carving knife into our sink with a clatter. Gigi grabs my arm, giving a little squeal. "I can't even believe he's actually talking to *us*!"

"Just don't flirt so much that you forget to bread the chicken."

She sticks her tongue out at me and I can't help but smile.

Rusty comes back, a black leather apron tied around his waist; he looks like a horror-movie serial killer. I try to ignore him as he asks some idiotic question about raw meat. Instead, I keep one eye on Joy while I start stacking ingredients into piles. She's stabbing at the keypad of the blender, but nothing happens. I try not to laugh as I watch her shake the base violently and smack the side a few times. I nudge Gigi.

"Not so perfect in Joyland."

But my partner is *far* too busy explaining the intricacies of bread-crumb variations to our rock-star judge to pay attention to me. I look back at Joy, whose face is bright red with frustration. She crosses her arms and glares first at the pantry, where Christian is rummaging through ingredients, and then out at the rest of the arena. And that's when she spots Rusty.

A slow smile spreads across her face. She puts one hand on her hip and smiles.

"Rusty, would you like to see how to make a rémoulade?"

To Gigi's horror, Rusty sidles over to Joy. She continues to grin and, as he gets closer, she leans forward on the counter in a beckoning pose. I want to puke.

"First, you want to make a basic mayonnaise," she says. She switches on the blender and nothing happens. Her smile falters and she tries again. Nothing. Gigi snorts back a laugh.

"Impressive, Joy," she calls out. "You are a real expert."

Joy glares at her as Rusty reaches over and tries to work the blender himself.

"I don't think this is gonna work out, honey," he says to Joy. Gigi seizes the opportunity to win back Rusty's attention.

"You know, a rémoulade is easy to whisk together." She walks over to Joy's station. "We can just dump these ingredients into a bowl."

She moves quickly, stealthily sliding between Joy and Rusty. Joy looks furious as Gigi reaches for the base of the blender.

"Um, *excuse me*, I really didn't ask for your help."

Gigi gives her a seemingly innocent smile.

"I just want Rusty to see how a real expert cooks."

"Thanks—if I see an expert, I'll let you know."

Rusty is leaning back against the stove with his arms crossed, looking exceptionally entertained as Gigi and Joy grapple with the blender. The cameras caught on about thirty seconds ago and are beginning to crowd around the commotion. Sighing, I put my knife down on my cutting board. I guess

I need to go get Gigi out of there before she does something she'll regret later. I've never really seen this side of her before. I don't know if this competitive flare is a good thing or not, but it's nice to see someone battle with Joy besides me.

I'm only ten feet away when Joy succeeds in pulling the blender from Gigi's hands. With a murderous glare at Gigi, she plugs it in for the second time. Gigi then reaches for the outlet and both girls are gripping the plug. I watch as one hand—I can't tell whose—pushes the START button on the base of the food processor.

And that's when everything goes dark.

CHAPTER *thirteen*

Playing the Blame Game

Back in Weston, my school used to lose power all the time. The building was built in 1949 and never renovated, so it wasn't exactly up to code when it came to the electrical needs of a twenty-first-century school. In the middle of class, the lights would flicker, then go out and everyone would scream as though a blackout transported them to the Amazon without a weapon. At first, this is sort of like that, except without annoying freshmen shrieking like little girls.

The cameras have battery backup, so there are tiny red lights blinking throughout the room. Someone close by fires up a gas burner; it gives off a dull gold light. I can see a few people running between where I'm standing and where Joy and Gigi were fighting only moments ago. I try to squint through the dark and figure out what's going on. Did we overload a breaker? It can't be hard to do in an older dorm, no matter how recently renovated it is.

I prop myself up against the counter and take a deep breath. It's just one more thing—every challenge now, something happens to throw us off our game. You know, I bet they did this on purpose. I'll bet the judges flipped a switch just to mess with us, to see how we'd react under pressure. I wonder if they'll taste half-cooked dishes and judge us on our progress. I really hope not, considering that will involve raw chicken in my case.

I've convinced myself that this is just another "twist" in the game, even after they bring in the flashlights. It isn't until they hand me one that I realize what everyone's beginning to see— in Joy and Christian's station, there's a figure slumped over on the tile floor.

Oh God. Gigi.

I take off at a full sprint. When I reach the alcove, though, I notice the shiny dark curls and expensive shoes. It's Joy who's lying motionless, surrounded by crew members trying to wake her.

My heart in my throat, I look around frantically until I find Gigi, crouched on the ground, tears streaming down her face. Rusty is standing next to her, looking pale. Kneeling down, I put my arms around her, watching as EMTs attempt to revive an unconscious Joy. I keep expecting to see her drag herself up off the floor and demand to speak to her attorney. Christian, his face waxy and pale, is gripping Joy's limp hand. I feel a stab of envy, then an immediate rush of shame. The last thing I should be right now is jealous.

I pull Gigi up and away from the scene. She's shaking so hard I'm afraid she might pass out herself. Most of the contestants have gathered close by, horror etching their faces. I can't see specific people, but I can hear someone crying in the dark. I can hear someone else whispering a prayer.

Once the paramedics have taken Joy out on a stretcher, the arena becomes strangely quiet. Those of us left just stare at each other in disbelief. As if timed by fate, the lights flicker briefly before blasting their bluish white haze over the room, the buzz from the fluorescent bulbs seeming deafening in the silence. We all stand there, blinking at each other.

"So, do you think she . . ." Gigi's voice is shaky. It cracks on the last word. I give her shoulders a squeeze.

"I'm sure she'll be fine," I lie. I'm really not sure of anything anymore.

"We were arguing, she grabbed the cord," Gigi babbles, becoming more and more hysterical. "She just kind of keeled over."

I support her body as it begins to shake with sobs.

"Giada Orsoni?"

We turn to see two officers in uniform standing behind us. They both have grave expressions on their faces.

"We need you to come with us, miss."

"Wh-what? Why?" Gigi is terrified, looking to me for help. I grab her hand.

"What is this about?" I ask the men, who proceed to ignore me. They pull Gigi by both arms away from me and toward the side exit.

"She didn't do anything wrong!" I protest.

The door slams shut behind them and I lean against the cold metal, wanting so badly to follow and forcing myself not to cry. I slide down to the floor and stare out into space, trying and failing to make sense of everything that just happened.

"You can't be serious."

Gigi looks down and away. She's sitting cross-legged on her bed, still in her pajamas. It's almost three in the afternoon.

"They think I set it up—that I was trying to electrocute her or something."

"B-but—" I sputter, unable to believe what she's telling me, "I mean, you didn't even—it's not like you wanted—"

"Nora, I spent two hours trying to convince them it wasn't my fault, that it was an accident. They need to review the tapes. I'm on probation until they make a decision one way or the other."

I want to throw something, to go confront the judges myself. Gigi is a lot calmer than I am.

"How's Joy?" she asks, her eyes concerned. I rub my forehead.

"Stable. Her parents flew in this morning. Benny's assistant came to the room to clean out the rest of her stuff."

"So, she's done then?"

I nod. "I'm not positive, but I think so."

"But, she's going to be okay, right? I mean, she was *electrocuted . . .*"

"From what the doctors said, she'll be fine. She's going to need to be monitored for a while before she can go home for good. Something about a heart arrhythmia?"

Gigi gazes out the window. The bare trees glisten with a shellac of ice. She looks back at me sadly.

"Joy can be a heinous witch—you and I both know that. But Nora, you know I'd never, ever—"

"Of course not," I interrupt, coming forward to hug her. "I know you wouldn't do anything to hurt her. None of us would."

"Apparently someone would." Her voice is muffled against my shoulder. She pulls away. "Clearly there is *someone* who wants people to get hurt, to get eliminated in any way possible."

I shake my head. "You know, Gigi, before this happened, I'd be the first person to agree with you. I've been saying since the beginning that there's something sketchy happening here—and that Joy and Prescott are behind it. But, Prescott's gone. For now, anyway. And Joy was the victim this time."

"I don't know . . ."

"Trust me. I was sure there was someone behind the accidents. But now? I'm starting to think that it may all just be a hideous coincidence."

Gigi looks skeptical. "Don't you think that is a little *too* convenient of an explanation?"

"What do you mean?"

"I mean, what if it doesn't have anything to do with Joy and Prescott? What if it's *someone else*? Someone who was banking on Joy and Prescott's shady relationship as their cover?"

"Like who?"

"Think about it—who was around Angela and Joy before both accidents?"

"A lot of people—all of us were around them."

"Yeah, but who was *closest* to them—who was there just before the accidents happened?"

I rack my brain for a link, a connection. Exasperated, Gigi stands up to pace the room.

"There is only one person who was around Joy the whole night, Nora. Only one person who stopped you from using that sink before it blew up."

Christian's face enters my mind like the sudden answer to an impossible question. I shake my head.

"No way."

"Yes way!" Gigi explodes. "Christian's station was right next to the sink—he had more time than anyone to mess with it. *And* he was Joy's partner—he was with her, in the same area, with plenty of access to food processors and outlets and whatever else he needed."

I squint a little, thinking. "But, that doesn't really make sense. I mean, Joy plugged in the cord the first time and nothing happened. It wouldn't even work. I really think it's possible that it's just a fluke. That this stuff just . . . happened . . ."

"I can't believe you're *defending* him—can you really say he didn't do it? Can you really say he's innocent?"

"I don't . . . I just don't think Christian would do this. I mean, he's—he's not that type of person . . ."

"Nora. Seriously? This is the same guy you pegged for a jerk the day we got here."

I take a deep breath. "I know. But that doesn't mean he'd try to sabotage the whole competition to win. Besides, Gigi, he's already winning!"

"Sure, maybe *because* of his sabotage—maybe he's doing a whole bunch of stuff we don't even realize. Like the cleavers the other week, remember?"

I do remember. I'd thought Joy was behind those. But, then, I thought Joy was behind a lot of things.

Still, as cocky as Christian is, I know he'd want to win because he was the best, not because he hurt other people.

"So, let me get this straight." Gigi stands up to face me, eyes blazing. "You were ready to take down a famous chef and his girlfriend, both of whom could probably have you black-listed from every major culinary school in the nation, but you won't even *consider* the possibility that Christian is the one responsible?"

I give an exasperated sigh. "I just think we aren't getting anywhere by accusing people."

"I can't believe you—you are a total hypocrite. Whatever happened to the great conspiracy, Nora?"

"I guess I was wrong," I say, shrugging. Gigi just shakes her head before walking to her door and opening it.

"I want you to go."

"Gigi . . ."

"Just. Go."

Her face is like stone, the skin near her eyes and mouth stretched taut. Blinking hard, I walk out of the room. The door slams behind me. I stand there for a minute, red faced and frustrated, wanting to bang on the door and give her a piece of my mind. Nothing seems good enough, important enough, to say. It's the first time Gigi and I have fought and I'm completely flummoxed as to how to fix it.

As I walk back to my room, I make an abrupt turn and head in the opposite direction. Maybe if I hear it from him—maybe if I can get him to talk to her . . .

When I get to Christian's room, I notice that the pictures of half-naked women and his taunting nameplate have been removed. When he answers, I raise one eyebrow and gesture to the door.

"You got rid of your ladies?"

"Huh?" He looks blankly at the pockmarked wood. "Oh, those. They were vandalized, if you recall."

"Oh. Right."

He leans against the doorjamb. "What do you want, Nora?"

"Jeez, everyone is so welcoming today."

I push past him. I figure that if he has something to hide, he'll hurry to move it. But he doesn't follow me—just watches me walk the perimeter of his room.

"Are you looking for something?"

I turn to look at him.

"Are you the one sabotaging *Taste Test*?"

It's his turn to raise his eyebrows at me. He leans back against the closet door. "Who said someone's sabotaging *Taste Test*?"

"Please—it's pretty obvious. The faucet, the equipment, now the outlets. Angela's accident, then Joy's. You can't tell me you just think all that stuff was a series of random accidents."

"And you think *I'm* behind all of that stuff?"

I shrug. "Can you prove that you aren't?"

"No. No, I probably can't prove it, not unless you're here to give me a polygraph."

"Are you sure?" I try to sound like I don't care. He doesn't need to know I'm on his side. He doesn't need to know that I *want* him to be innocent.

"I told you before—I had no idea that sink was going to explode. If I had, don't you think I would have requested a station switch rather than risk flying faucet shrapnel?"

It's a good point. I wish I'd thought to say that to Gigi earlier.

"Besides," Christian continues, "I know you don't want to hear this, but, if it *is* sabotage, I think they're probably investigating the right person."

"What do you mean?"

He sits down on his bed. "She was right there. They were arguing and then . . . well, and then you know what happened."

I shake my head. "Gigi didn't have anything to do with this."

"How do you know?"

"Because I know!"

Christian snorts. "Wow, what a well-supported argument. You *must* be right!"

"Gigi doesn't have any reason to hurt Joy, or anyone else for that matter."

"Are you kidding?" He stares at me like I'm crazy. "She's *losing,* Nora. She's *this close* to being voted off the show. The easiest way to remedy that is to get rid of someone before the judges can get rid of you."

I narrow my eyes. "Sounds like you've given this a lot of thought."

"No, but I'm willing to state the obvious. I know she's your friend, but that doesn't mean she's innocent."

"It also doesn't mean that she would be willing to risk

someone's *life* for a stupid TV show—only someone really self-ish, really *manipulative* would be able to do that."

Christian gets up and walks to the window. After a few seconds, he looks back at me and shrugs.

"I don't know what to tell you. It just seems shady—*she* seems shady. And if you can't see that, you're delusional. Or in denial."

Furious, I head for the door, then stop and look back at him. He's standing with both arms crossed like some sort of dictator.

"You know, I stuck up for you—and now you just want to throw other people under the bus. Guess I should have trusted my instincts—you really are as arrogant as you look. And here I was thinking *I* was the one who misjudged *you*. What a joke!"

I slam the door behind me and stomp back toward my room, feeling frustration rise like heat out of the neck of my sweater.

I want to be mad at Christian, but I'm really only angry at myself. Rather than support my friend, I chose to take his side—only to be reminded why first impressions are usually right. I knew Christian was a selfish jerk the moment I met him. Too bad it took me this long to remember why.

To: Billy Watkins **billythekid@westonhighschool.edu**
From: Nora Henderson **norahenderson@naca.edu**
Subject: I'm so done with this place

I don't even know what to say.

You remember that time I tried out for the school play? It

was stupid—I can't even remember why I did it. I'm sure it was to prove you wrong about something. Then, when I actually got a role, you convinced me not to quit. You said that it would look good on my college applications, that it made my interests seem more diverse or something like that.

Anyway, I stuck with it. I figured out that some of the drama kids were actually pretty cool. When we finally performed, you and Dad and Joanie came every night, hooting and hollering when I took a bow at the end.

I wish you were here to cheer me on. No one knows me like you do.

Can I come home yet?

Nora

We find out that Joy's been admitted to New Haven Medical Center for observation, but there's still no word about where Prescott went. My brain speeds through various scenarios— maybe he rigged the outlet before he left. Maybe it was his plan to "get rid" of Joy all along. It's almost impossible to concentrate in class while I'm imagining various Mafia-like scenarios.

Gigi's still not talking to me and now I'm avoiding Christian, so it makes for an uncomfortable day in classes, not looking in one direction or another. On top of that, we have tests at the end of the week in three of our five classes. I don't know how I can possibly prep, compete, and study while still keeping up with homework *and* trying to get some sleep.

Oh, and trying to figure out the truth behind the show's "accidents." Can't forget about that little detail.

The one good thing, if I'm looking on the very, very tiny slice of a bright side, is that I don't have much distracting me from my studies. Without Joy around or Gigi coming to visit, I'm able to focus on school and nothing else. Of course, that means that I hardly leave my room unless I'm going to class or forcing myself to eat something.

It's almost midnight and I'm in the dorm lounge, ready to snarf down a late-night grilled cheese, when I hear footsteps. Gigi stops in her tracks when she sees me sitting there. At first, I think she might just turn around and head back up the stairs. Instead, she shakes her hair back away from her face and strides over to the refrigerator. I watch her unwrap a slice of leftover pizza and take an enormous bite.

"You must be hungry if you're willing to eat it cold."

She shrugs and takes another bite. "I like it like this. No cheese burning the roof of my mouth."

I smile before looking back at my plate. She walks over to the table and picks up a napkin.

"Do you want to sit down?" I ask her quietly, not looking up.

It takes her a few seconds to pull out the chair across from me and flop down.

"Gigi," I begin. She holds up a hand.

"Let's just squash it," she says.

I frown. "No, you were right."

"No. I wasn't. I wanted someone else to blame. Christian was an easy target."

"But it could have been him," I argue.

She shakes her head.

"No, it couldn't have."

"Why not?"

"Because." She sighs, picking at her pizza crust. "You were right all along."

"Right about what?"

"About Prescott." She looks up, her eyes serious. "It was him the whole time, Nora. Prescott's the one who's been sabotaging the show."

WITNESS STATEMENT TRANSCRIPT
Connecticut State Sheriff's Office

LEAD DETECTIVE DOBBS: State your name and position
for the record.

KATHRYN SVINCEK: Kathryn Svincek, President of the
North American Culinary Academy

DOBBS: In your own words, please recall the details
of the events you witnessed.

SVINCEK: I was informed by Bernie Lightwood, one
of our set technicians, that last month Holden
Prescott arrived on set late at night, accompanied by one of the female contestants. Holden
told Bernie he was giving the girl private
coaching and that he wasn't to tell the other
judges. He gave him $500 and asked him to leave
the set.

DOBBS: And when did Mr. Lightwood bring this to your
attention?

SVINCEK: After the accident involving Angela
    Moore.

DOBBS: And this accident caused physical injury to
    a contestant?

SVINCEK: Yes.

DOBBS: Anything else?

SVINCEK: Two weeks ago, I was supervising the testing
    of the station outlets to make sure they were in
    proper working order, which we do before every
    challenge. The station at the farthest end of the
    set had an outlet that wasn't working, and I
    reported it to one of the electrical specialists.
    Holden walked over to me privately and said that
    he would take care of the outlet himself. When I
    protested, Holden said he was "experienced" with
    electrical work and that it was his "hobby."
    Holden and I were the last two people on set
    that night. When I left, he was still working
    on the outlet.

DOBBS: And this was the same outlet that caused
    the injury to Joy Kennedy-Swanson last
    week?

SVINCEK: Yes, it was.

DOBBS: Thank you, Ms. Svincek. I'll be in touch. Let
me know if you remember anything else.

SVINCEK: Of course. Thank you, Detective.

CHAPTER fourteen

I'll Take Douche Bags for $200, Alex.

"So, what do you think happens now?"

Gigi shrugs. "I don't know. Nothing would surprise me at this point."

"I still can't believe it." It's been two days since Gigi told me about Prescott's arrest, but I still find the whole thing baffling.

"Nora, what don't you believe? I mean, hell, *you* were the one who suspected him all along. I just feel bad that I never told you to talk to someone about it."

I shake my head.

"What was I going to say? 'Hey, I think a celebrity judge is sabotaging the show, please don't eliminate me now?' No one would have listened."

"Well, apparently Svincek wants the book thrown at him. She's pushing for jail time. I think she's good friends with the DA or something."

"That is one thing that doesn't surprise me," I say, opening the door to our classroom. "She seems like the kind of person who'll do everything she can to make Prescott pay for what he's done."

"I wonder what they're going to do about Joy, though. I mean, if she's the one who rigged the sink, maybe she'll get charged, too."

I pull out one of the stools at our lab table.

"Maybe. I don't know, though. It'll be hard to blame someone who ended up a victim herself."

Around the classroom, you can hear snatches of conversations just like ours—murmurings about Prescott's plotting and whispers of Joy's involvement. Someone says Svincek met with a detective last night. Others swear that Prescott's fled the state, maybe even the country.

I'm sorting through a utensil drawer for a candy thermometer when I see Christian standing next to me. His hair is catching some of the afternoon light and, for a second, I'm involuntarily dazzled. I blink hard and look down, sifting through a handful of silverware.

"Are you still not speaking to me?" he asks.

"Yes."

"Why not?" he presses. I give him a withering look.

"Seriously?"

He rolls his eyes. "You can't be mad at me for telling you what I think."

"I can when it's total crap. And when you tell me I'm in denial."

"I didn't say you *were* in denial—I said you *could* be. Besides, I had good reason to be suspicious."

"Christian." I turn to face him. "Is it that hard for you to admit you were wrong?"

"I wasn't wrong."

"Jeez, can't you let it go?" I glance over at Gigi, who is busy melting our sugar into caramel. "Everyone knows she's innocent. Svincek gave her a whole apology letter and everything."

"Just because they found one person guilty doesn't mean there aren't more people involved."

He walks away before I can respond. Then I notice Gigi standing a few feet from me.

"What was that all about?" she asks. I pat her shoulder.

"Nothing. Just reconfirming that he's a tool. Don't worry about him."

I guide her back to our lab table and proceed to ignore Christian for the rest of class. When Professor Black excuses us, I'm out the door and down the hall before Christian can say anything else to piss me off.

Back home, whenever I had a major test to study for, Billy and I would make flash cards or facts sheets or some other kind of study strategy. Here, though, our finals are looming and we've been overloaded with *far* too much information to possibly copy it on index cards or a sheet of looseleaf. Instead, Gigi and I gather all our notes and handouts into a big pile on my desk. For a minute, we just stare at the two-inch stack.

"There is no way we're going to get through all this stuff," I grumble, flicking the ripped spiral edge of the top sheet.

Gigi grabs half the pile and plops onto my bed.

"Well, we can complain or we can get started. I, for one, would like to attempt to pass these tests."

"That's the problem—it's *tests*, not test. Three of them at once."

"Well, we could join the study group downstairs," I suggest, watching for her reaction. Gigi's been super shy since she got on—and off—probation. "I think they've put together some sort of *Jeopardy!* review thing. Might actually be fun, you know?"

"I can't deal with people staring at me. I know everybody still thinks I did it."

"No, they don't. You got that apology—"

"Yeah, but the whole 'innocent until proven guilty' thing really only works in theory. Once you've been accused of something, everyone just assumes you did it."

I try to convince Gigi she's wrong, but she won't budge. In the end, she decides to go back to her room and study on her own. I think I pushed her too hard, but when I ask her to stick around, she shakes her head.

"I really study better on my own, anyway. But you should go downstairs. Do what you gotta do."

The way she says it, though, I can tell she doesn't want me to.

But an hour later, I give up. I slam my books shut, grab a soda, and head for the common room.

"Um . . . um . . . duck fat!"

I watch from the doorway as Kelsey jumps up and down at her seat. Pierce is standing at the front of the room holding a stack of cards. He nods and points at her.

"That is . . . CORRECT!"

To his left, Christian is marking a poster with points. I sit down next to Kelsey.

"Hey, Nora. Where's Gigi?"

"Upstairs. She—uh—she studies better on her own."

Kelsey just nods but doesn't say anything. I watch her turn around, wondering if Gigi is right—if people *are* believing the rumors over the truth.

For the next few rounds, I just watch. A couple of times, heated arguments break out. Are sweet potatoes and yams the same thing? Do you need to salt eggplant slices for flavor or just to remove moisture? In the end, though, I know that I've reviewed more down here than I ever could have alone.

"Okay, we're down to the last question," Pierce announces, looking at me. "And we're going to have Nora answer it."

"Me?" I balk. "Why me?"

"Because you haven't said a word since you got here and you're preventing us simple folk from benefiting from your endless knowledge."

"Right." I roll my eyes. "Fine. What's the category?"

"The category is . . . Tools of the Trade," he says in a mock-hushed voice.

"Okay, shoot."

"According to our lecture on deep frying, how often should you change the oil in a restaurant-grade fryer?"

That's an easy one. "Once a week," I say confidently, just as Christian calls out, "Every three days."

I glare at him. Pierce glances down at his cards, then back up at the rest of us.

"What do you think, Kels?"

Kelsey looks between me and Christian. "I'm not sure . . ."

I don't know if she really isn't sure or if she's just afraid to get her head bitten off.

"It's three days," Pierce says matter-of-factly. Christian slaps him a high five and I groan.

"That's such BS and you know it. Half the time you use the fryer, it's for French fries, and those practically *clean* the oil. If you strain it right, you don't need to replace it until it changes color. Or starts smoking."

"Sounds like you've got a whole lot of experience frying stuff," Christian remarks, sitting down and putting his feet up on the table. "You know, the rest of us—we actually *cook* things where we're from."

I clench my teeth and glare at him before standing up. I turn to Pierce.

"Thanks for the review."

Without another word, I walk back out into the wood-paneled hallway and toward the nearest elevator. My face is hot with humiliation and, to my absolute horror, I feel my eyes prick with tears. Why do I let him get to me? Why can't I realize he's just a complete—

"Nora, wait up."

When I hear his voice, I start pressing the up button frantically. I don't want him to see he got to me. I don't want to have to look him in the eye right now.

"Hey, wait a second."

Christian's standing next to me and tugs my sleeve, turning me around to face him. I refuse to look up.

"What do you want?"

"I wanted to apologize, all right? I know that was messed up—I, uh, I guess I'm just used to you dishing it right back out or something. Obviously I went too far."

"Wow, an apology from the one and only Christian Van Lorton. Am I supposed to swoon now?"

He shrugs. "If you must."

"Whatever." I shake my head. "It's fine. Don't worry about it."

"No, seriously."

I feel his hand travel up my arm to my shoulder. I want to move away from him but his touch feels magnetic, with a surge of warmth where his hand is resting.

"I'm sorry if I hurt you."

I look up. I remember saying almost the exact same thing to him a while back—and his reaction was very clear. As the elevator doors pull apart, I draw away from him and walk inside.

"You couldn't hurt me if you tried."

I try to sound breezy, but my voice comes out sort of strained. The doors begin to move inward and Christian's face is screwed up, like he's making a choice. For a second, it looks like he might throw an arm out, might stop the doors from closing between us. I think about the two of us alone in the small space of the elevator—him standing *this close* to me, his hands at my waist and pulling me toward him.

But the reality is different. The reality is the click of the doors meeting in the middle, the whir of the elevator as it moves us farther and farther apart.

I want to climb right into bed when I get to my room, but there's an e-mail from my dad and I feel too guilty not reading it. I'd hoped that Billy would e-mail me back; it's been a few days since he's written and I could really use someone to talk to—I mean, *really* talk to—who doesn't have anything to do with this stupid show.

With a sigh, I scan over Dad's e-mail.

To: Nora Henderson **norahenderson@naca.edu**
From: Judd Henderson **smokesignals@ncbbq.org**
Subject: Away

Nora,

Gonna be heading down to Atlanta for an equipment trade show for a few days. Just wanted to give you a heads-up in case you try to e-mail and I don't answer. Talk to you when I get back.

Love ya,
Dad

Weird.

In all the years my dad's owned Smoke Signals, and that's more years than I've been alive, I've never known him to go to any trade show, especially for equipment. He calls those things "vendor vacuums, only meant to waste a man's time and money."

I wonder if I should take this as a sign of something bigger—as in, change is happening everywhere—or if I'm just being paranoid. I can't help it; I take a lot of comfort in knowing my dad will always be who he is. In fact, I think I'd feel a lot better about things if he were here with me right now.

For the first time since I got here, I fall asleep feeling homesick, wondering what I'd be doing right now if I were in Weston. What I'd be doing if I hadn't come here at all.

CONTESTANT INTERVIEW

Nora Henderson

Producer (P): Well, Nora, we're getting down to it—there are only a handful of contestants left, giving you a greater chance of winning. How are you feeling at this point? Nervous?

NH: Sure. I'd be an idiot if I weren't.

P: There's definitely some competition you'll need to confront, mostly by the name of Christian Van Lorton. Do you see him as a worthy opponent?

NH: If you mean do I think he's talented, then yes, I do. He knows what he's doing.

P: In the kitchen and out?

NH: Huh?

P: Well, I mean, he's quite a good-looking guy, Nora. I would imagine he's had his fair share of girlfriends.

NH: I would imagine you're right.

P: So, you're saying he is good-looking?

NH: [loud exhale] Sure. Fine. He's good-looking.

P: Any other thoughts you'd like to share on that subject?

NH: [pause] On the subject of Christian? Only that his looks aren't doing him any favors in the kitchen.

P: Meaning?

NH: Meaning it doesn't matter how hot he is—looks can't cook.

P: You think Christian is hot?

NH: [flustered] You know what I mean.

P: Yes . . . I believe I do . . .

CHAPTER fifteen

Old Home Week

Every time we walk into the arena now, it looks completely different. I don't know if it's because of Joy's accident or because there are less people, but, once again, the stations are rearranged into a different setup from before. The judges, as per usual, are at the front of the room—but this time they're sitting on tall barstools next to high-hat tables. They smile as we walk in.

"For all intents and purposes," Ms. Svincek begins, "this is the beginning of the end. I know that we've had some very stressful moments in this room; in fact, because of recent events, we've decided to dissolve the partnerships in favor of one-on-one challenges. All of you have held yourselves together with poise, with grace. I hope you will show the same maturity with these new changes and as we get closer to the season finale.

"Tonight, however, we have a little surprise for you. We

know that you have been cooking to impress us as judges. We want to know more about how you cook outside of the arena—how you would cook for your family, your friends."

A door at one side of the arena opens and a woman in a cranberry-colored dress is standing there, blinking into the bright spotlight. I hear someone gasp behind me.

"Mom! Oh my gosh, what are you doing here?"

Kelsey runs past the rest of us and hugs the woman. Other people start coming into the room—a middle-aged couple, an older woman who must be someone's grandmother, a female version of Pierce who is obviously his sister. Contestants are embracing their family members. Some of them are crying. It's more emotion than I've ever seen in the arena—most of the time we try to hold it all together, to steel ourselves in the face of criticism. Apparently, all it takes is one hug from home to turn that facade into a mercury-like puddle on the floor.

A blond girl with huge sunglasses emerges from the door next. She's wearing a short black skirt and high-heeled boots. When the spotlight shifts away from her face, she shoves her shades into her platinum-blond curls. She isn't just nice looking, she's gorgeous. I wonder who she's related to, who could possibly be her brother or sister.

And that's when I notice Christian walking toward her. When he reaches her, she throws both arms around his neck and plants a kiss right on his lips.

I feel my heart stutter and sink, a tiny boat in a sudden storm.

"Christian," she drawls, her voice sort of gravelly like a smoker's. "Omigod, I've missed you SO much!"

"Mel," he says, squeezing her hard. "I've missed you, too."

Like it's the proverbial train wreck, I just can't stop watching. I hardly even feel the tap on my shoulder.

"Hey there, North Star."

Seeing my dad here makes me forget about Christian and his visitor. I throw myself at him and he wraps me in his trademark bear hug.

"I knew you weren't at a trade show!" I say, pulling back to look at him. He ducks his head.

"Yeah. I probably shoulda thought of a better lie, huh?"

I grin and hug him again.

"It's so good to see you, Daddy."

"Well now, honey, don't get all sappy on me. Besides, there's someone else who wants to say hello." He untangles himself from me and moves aside.

I watch Billy step forward, his smile both familiar and foreign. It's something I've known my whole life, but I feel like I haven't seen it in years. I blink over and over, as though to figure out if he's really here. Laughing, he pulls me into his arms and holds me tight.

"I'm real, Nor. No need to pinch yourself."

I bury my face into his shoulder. Somehow, he feels the same *and* different.

"God, you look good." Billy finally pulls away and holds me at arm's length. "I feel like it's been forever."

I nod, still having trouble speaking. He grins.

"I've been following the news—I can't *believe* what happened to that girl Joy. Wasn't she your roommate?"

"Yeah," I manage, finally finding my voice. "She's going to be okay. She went home to New York."

Ms. Svincek stands up and claps her hands to get everyone's attention. Out of the corner of my eye, I watch Christian and Blondie turn toward the judges. His arm is still around her waist. I look away and, without much thought, grab Billy's hand and squeeze. He smiles at me and squeezes back.

"I missed you so much," he whispers.

"Friends and family of our contestants!" Ms. Svincek calls out over the crowd. "Thank you so much for joining us for this very special night. I hope you are all as excited as we are about the challenge occurring this evening. Contestants— what you *don't* know is that these surprise guests are actually your critics tonight. You'll be cooking for your opponents' loved ones, as well as your own. Their opinions of your dishes will contribute to your chance of remaining in the competition. Four of you will go on to our coveted 'Final Four' pre-finale.

"So, honored guests, please bid the contestants good-bye— for now, that is. And, contestants, head to your stations."

I turn to my dad and Billy and give them a small smile.

"Off to work I go."

Dad slings an arm around my shoulder and squeezes. "We'll see you at judging, pumpkin. Knock 'em dead!"

He heads toward the door with the rest of the visitors. Billy pauses and puts both hands on my shoulders.

"You totally rock this show—you know that, kid?"

I can't help but grin. "Of course—I rock everything I do."

"That's the attitude you need to win this thing."

He reaches a hand up and moves a strand of hair from my face. Something flutters deep in my stomach.

"I'll see you," he says, bending down and pressing his lips to my forehead. Over his shoulder, I see Christian watching us. Billy gives me a wink before passing through the doors, and they shut loudly behind him.

I'm grinding spices when Christian wanders into my station and leans against the counter. I press the button and pretend I don't see him. The peppercorns spin and pulverize into tiny flecks of their former selves. Unfortunately, Christian decides to wait patiently until they've reached the right consistency.

"Can I help you?" I finally ask.

"That guy. Is he your boyfriend?"

I give him a sugary smile. "No, actually, that's my dad. I'm not really into older guys."

"Har-har."

"Why do you care, anyway? Blondie or Bambi or whatever her name is seemed *very* pleased to be back in your presence."

Christian raises his eyebrows. "Well, can you blame her?"

"Guess there's no accounting for taste," I grumble as he heads back to his station.

By the time our two hours are up, I've succeeded in burning my fish twice and curdling my first batch of mango butter. I don't know why I'm so off tonight, but it doesn't help knowing that Christian's girlfriend-person-thingy is going to be eating my dish and I haven't laced it with some sort of laxative or something.

I think I'm more bothered, though, about the fact that I care so much. I try to erase her, and him, from my mind as I plate my food.

Judging takes place in the usual room, but a long dining table has replaced the typical setup. The judges and all the guests are seated side by side, like a surreal, televised Thanksgiving dinner. All of the contestants line up parallel to the table. I rock back and forth on my heels, trying not to let my nerves show. Chef Mason stands to greet us as a dozen servers file in carrying trays of food.

"As you can see, we'll be trying your creations one by one. Each of you will hear the critiques of all the dishes, including your own."

A few people nod. I wonder if everyone else feels the same trepidation I do. Having a dozen people I don't know try my food in front of me is completely nerve-racking. There's a reason why chefs stay in the kitchen.

They start with Pierce's rib eye with asparagus risotto, then Kelsey's chipotle chicken. Aside from some minor complaints (the beef is too rare, the chicken's too dry), most of the guests are very complimentary. In some ways it's a relief—in others, it's a disappointment. This is the reason why you don't give things to your family to judge. They can't possibly be impartial critics of your work.

"And now we're on to Nora Henderson's blackened mahi-mahi with mango butter," Madame Bouchon announces, reading the description off a card in front of her.

"Blackened is right," Christian says, loud enough for the table to hear. "She burnt it the first two times she cooked it."

"Whatever—your pork looks like tree bark," I growl at him.

"Ahem." Chef Mason clears his throat. "Contestants, please withhold your commentary until Elimination Table."

"Besides, practice makes perfect," Madame Bouchon says breezily. She gives me an encouraging smile.

The servers walk around the table, presenting a plate to each person. For a moment, there is complete silence, aside from the clink of forks on porcelain.

"Nice and spicy," Ms. Svincek nods. "I like that the mango butter has a creamy texture. It really cuts through the heat of the pepper."

"I agree." Pierce's sister is nodding. "I like the combination of flavors."

"I don't know . . ."

I turn to see Blondie poking at her fish with a fork, frowning.

"I think it's a little dry. And the spices are too thick, more like a crust."

I can't help but glare at her. What the hell does she know, anyway? The last meal she probably had was a Tic Tac.

The rest of the table has their say. My dad, of course, loves it, calling it a "fish rub my granddaddy would be proud of." Billy grins at me when he says, "It's got true, Southern flavor with a sophisticated spin."

"Sophisticated. Please." Christian scoffs under his breath. I give him a beatific smile.

So by the time we get to his dish, I'm ready to walk out or punch something. When his peppercorn pork loin is presented, everyone admires the crusty roast resting on a bed of greens. Christian moves forward to the head of the table and begins to slice the meat.

"Carving is an important skill to have," he says, smiling at the table. Then he glances back at me. "That can be hard to understand if you've only ever cooked cheap cuts of meat—the kind you chop or shred. Or spit back out."

I watch my dad's face turn red, then purple, and his lips press into a hard line. Billy looks like he might jump up and grab the knife out of Christian's hand. I decide not to react, even though I'm fuming. Making fun of me is one thing, but going after my dad and his cooking is completely uncalled for. I remind myself that when the table actually gets to taste Christian's food, Dad and Billy will have a chance to stick it to him.

"This is probably the driest pork I've ever eaten," Billy complains a minute later, chewing as though it's leather. "I don't know how you cooked this, man, but it's tough as all get-out."

Only because we have to be silent during our own judging, Christian stands stock-still and doesn't respond. Actually, he doesn't even look at Billy; he's got his eyes trained on Blondie. I watch him wink at her and she giggles. I struggle with my gag reflex.

"You know, pork can be a pretty challenging meat to cook, especially when the cut has very little fat," my dad puts in, giving Christian a kind smile. "You could always wrap some bacon around the loin—like a little cushion to add some moisture to the meat."

Christian's expression is tight. He doesn't smile back.

When we're excused to wait for elimination, the contestants file out of the room. Once we're in the hall, though, I speed up and tap Christian's shoulder. He turns around and, upon seeing me, rolls his eyes.

"What is it, Henderson?"

"You want to explain why you found it necessary to insult my father *and* my best friend? They make their living working with—what did you call it? Cheap meat? That's crap, Christian, a low blow, and just plain mean."

Pierce walks over and moves between the two of us, as though to prevent a full-on attack. Christian leans against the wall and crosses his arms.

"Best friend, huh?"

"Yes," I snap, "Billy is my best friend. I've known him since middle school and we've been friends ever since. He works for my dad. Happy now?"

"It doesn't make a difference to me what he is to you—but, just so you know, that friendship is completely one-sided."

"What the hell are you talking about?"

"Willy, or whatever his name is, sure isn't thinking 'friendship' when he looks at you."

I shake my head, beyond done with this whole conversation.

"*Billy*," I say, emphasizing the *B*, "is none of your business. Clearly you have your hands full with your own visitor, so how about laying off mine?"

"Okay, okay," Christian says, holding up both hands. "Don't get your panties in a bunch."

"Trust me." I practically spit the words. "You have no effect on my panties."

"Well, for someone whose panties aren't affected, you sure seem upset."

"Why don't you go practice slicing something?" I yell as

Gigi pulls me away by the sleeve. "You let me know if you need some help figuring out how to cook pork correctly."

"When I need your advice, I'll ask for it," he shoots back.

"Come on, Nora. He's not worth it," Gigi says, tugging my arm again.

I don't say anything in response. Instead, I wrench my arm away from her and head toward wardrobe, feeling furious for being so furious and for caring at all.

GUEST JUDGE ONE-ON-ONE

Judd Henderson

Producer (P): Mr. Henderson, welcome. It's a pleasure to have you here.

Judd Henderson (JH): Please, call me Judd.

P: Well, Judd, you must be very proud of your daughter, Nora.

JH: [nods] Absolutely. She's doin' real good.

P: Yes, exceptionally well. She may even end up in Paris next fall!

JH: [crosses arms] Yeah, I guess that's a good possibility now.

P: And how do you feel about that? Having your daughter halfway across the world?

JH: Well, now, I know it'll be a challenge. Nora and me—we've always been real close. I know she'll be missed at home.

P: Yes, speaking of home—I know that the young man joining you today, Billy, is one of Nora's closest friends.

JH: Yes, indeedy. Billy 'n' Nora are like brother and sister. It's been that way for years.

P: Brother and sister . . . I was thinking there might be something more . . . *romantic* there.

JH: [removes hat, rubs head] I'm not really in the habit of discussing my daughter's love life.

P: Of course. I'm sure it's strange for you to discuss Nora's potential boyfriend. Or boy*friends*, as the case may be here.

JH: Meaning?

P: [smiles] Let's just say that Billy isn't the *only* one potentially harboring affections for your daughter. It seems like Christian Van Lorton has his own feelings to contend with.

JH: Oh lordy. [covers face] See, now—this is why some fathers don't let their daughters out of the house till they're twenty-one!

CHAPTER sixteen

You Always Hurt the Ones You Like(ish)

At the dim Italian restaurant, the table is being monitored by a stationary camera and a hanging microphone, just in case anything show worthy happens over our Bolognese. Dad immediately walks over to the bar, so Billy and I sit down across from each other and wait for him to come back.

"You did good tonight, Nors!" he says enthusiastically. "Another win under your belt—that's gotta feel good."

I nod. The win was definitely a plus, but Christian's loss is what really makes me feel victorious.

"So now that it's down to the final four—I mean, you've only got one more challenge until the finale. That's got to be nerve-racking."

"Yeah, thanks for the reminder." I kick him under the table and he winces.

"Sorry. I guess the last thing you need is more pressure right now, huh?"

"It's all right. It's just supertense here, that's all. Sometimes I don't want to have to talk about the competition—I just want to talk about regular stuff."

He reaches across the table and pats my hand. For a split second, his fingers curl around mine before letting go. I feel a little warm in my sweater.

"All righty." Dad plops down next to me, Budweiser in hand. "What are we talkin' about?"

"Anything but *Taste Test*," Billy says, leaning back in his chair. I notice he's gotten a fresh haircut—he looks more preppy than usual. He cocks his head a little, his smile unfolding into an outright grin. I look down at my hands, trying to figure out why I suddenly feel so shy, so awkward around my best friend.

But once the three of us start eating and talking, it is just like old times. I mean, I can't even attempt to count how many nights Dad, Billy, and I sat around a table at Smoke Signals, just talking about life. The awkwardness doesn't resurface, even after dinner when Billy and I take a long walk on campus.

"So school's the same?" I ask him. He shrugs.

"What do you think? Nothing ever changes around that place."

"Celia Franklin still asking you out every other day?"

He smirks, puffing out his chest a little. "Of course. What do you expect? The freshmen girls are completely infatuated with me."

"Ugh," I groan. "I leave for four months and already you've become a total man-whore."

"Oh, you think so?"

In a split second, he manages to get my arm pinned behind my back and uses his free hand to tickle my side, which is by far my most sensitive spot. I yelp and try to squirm away from him, but he just holds me tighter. We both struggle a little, out of breath and red faced.

"Say I'm the man," Billy demands.

"Never." I wriggle hard, but he's gotten hold of both my arms.

"Come on—say it."

I roll my eyes, knowing there is only one way out. "Fine, fine," I grumble. "You're the man."

"What?" Billy holds a hand up to his ear as though he can't hear me clearly. "What did you say?"

"I said, 'you're the man.'"

This time, though, I manage to get one arm free. I yank it from his grip and start pummeling him.

"Ouch—crap. Nora, quit it."

"Say I'm the coolest girl you've ever met," I demand. He laughs.

"Not a chance."

"Your loss." I continue to clobber his back and shoulders until he throws up both hands in surrender.

"Okay, okay!" He looks down at me, his green eyes sparkling. "Fine. You're the coolest girl I've ever met."

"Damn right," I say, crossing my arms smugly. "And don't you forget it."

"How could I, what with you reminding me via public humiliation?"

"Nah, no one's watching," I say, punching his arm lightly.

"Well, in that case . . ." He ducks down and sweeps me up over his shoulder like a potato sack.

"Stop it!" I yell, flailing my arms. "Let me down, you jerk."

"Gimme one good reason."

"Because I'll kick your butt . . . again!"

He guffaws. "Right. Keep telling yourself that."

"Dammit, Billy." I can feel the blood rushing up into my head and I'm starting to get a little nauseated.

Without a word, he heaves me back over and holds me bride-and-groom style before plopping down on a bench and taking me with him. I fall into his lap, both of us breathing hard.

"You are ridiculous," I say, pushing myself up to sitting.

He shakes his head.

"I'm just making up for lost time." He looks down at the ground, then back up at me. "I miss you, you know. A lot."

"I miss you, too," I say, giving him a small smile. He puts a hand on my shoulder and squeezes.

"Well, I guess I better get you back, right? You've probably got a big day tomorrow."

I nod reluctantly, scooting myself off the bench. "Every day is a big day around here."

The walk back to the dorm is far more composed than our earlier roughhousing. I watch the cold wisps of New England fog settle down near the grass on either side of the dorm.

"So." I turn to look at him when we reach the building's front steps. He has both hands shoved in his pockets and looks like he is probably freezing in his T-shirt and jeans.

"So," he repeats.

"I'll see you in the morning before you leave, right?" I feel a distinct sensation of déjà vu. That's the part that sucks about Billy and my dad coming up here—I have to say good-bye all over again.

"Of course."

He pulls me in for a long hug, the Billy hug I've come to rely on over the years. As he lets me go, I smile up at him.

"You have no idea how many times I've needed one of those hugs lately."

He grins. "Me too, kid."

"Ugh! You know I hate when you call me that!"

Pouting, I start to cross my arms, but he grabs my hand first. For a second, he looks in my eyes as though he is searching for something, as though the answer to an important question is there. Then carefully, he leans in and kisses me.

It is a short, sweet kiss—the kind that feels like a warm summer rain, a simmer rather than a boil or a sizzle. Not like the one with Christian: that was all bravado and tension and urgency. This is softer, like a quiet moment in a world drowning in sound. As he pulls back, I keep my eyes closed for a second. I know that when I open them, nothing will be the same.

"I'll see you tomorrow," he whispers, touching my face again. Giving me a final smile, he turns and walks toward the parking lot. Unable to move, all I can do is watch him leave.

"I." BANG. "Don't." BANG. "Know." BANG. "Why." BANG. "You." BANG. "Keep." BANG. "Doing this," Gigi accuses between the pounding rhythm of her rolling-pin-turned-weapon.

"Doing what?" I demand.

She gives one last whack to the plastic bag of cornflakes before adding the melted butter and cayenne. We're trying different types of breading for oven-fried chicken, but I'm really just using it as an excuse to hit something.

"Fighting with Christian. It's pointless and time consuming. And, if it's making me tired, I can only imagine how exhausted *you* must be."

"Oh. Right." I'd almost forgotten about my knock-down-drag-out with Christian last night. All I've really been doing is thinking about my unexpected kiss last night.

"I think I just let Christian get under my skin," I mutter.

"Uh, *yeah*. Clearly."

"I'm just . . . I'm just *done* with the whole thing. I want Christian to stay away from me. I'm starting to think that life would have been easier if I'd never applied to this program in the first place."

Gigi puts a hand on my shoulder. "Come on, you know that's BS. You're an amazing chef and you're giving that self-obsessed jerk a run for his mashed potatoes. Just hang in there. We really don't have that much further to go."

Despite Christian's crap about Gigi and her lack of talent, she, too, made it through Elimination to the Final Four—and because we spend all our time together, she moved into my room a few nights ago. It's great to stay up really late talking, giggling in the dark. She's the closest thing I've ever had to a sister. It's what I hoped sharing a room would be like when I got here in the first place. Of course, that was before I met Joy.

"So what about Billy?" Gigi asks, wiping away a smattering of buttery crumbs.

I take a deep breath, then exhale hard. "I don't know. I mean, I love Billy—he's my best friend."

"But I bet that kiss was a long time coming."

"Maybe," I concede, covering the butter with its waxy wrapper. I'd be lying if I said I hadn't thought about kissing Billy. Especially in the last year—it was like he turned from a boy wonder to a superhero overnight.

"So . . ." Gigi waggles her eyebrows.

"So what?"

"So, what was the kiss like?" she says, bumping her hip against mine. I smile in spite of myself.

"It was . . . nice."

"Nice?"

"Yeah," I say, nodding. I look down at my hands, thinking about Billy's mouth against mine. It was warm and soft and comfortable, like something you need to keep you safe.

"But . . ." Gigi looks at me, clearly skeptical. "I know there's a 'but' in there somewhere."

I shake my head hard. "But he's my best friend! He's my rock—my sure thing. I mean, without Billy, I'd have—I'd have no one, really. No one to count on. No one to talk to."

"You'd have your dad. You'd have me."

"I know—it's just . . . it's not the same. Up until now—or at least until recently, Billy's been my purely platonic anchor. He's the one thing that keeps me grounded when I lose my focus or forget my way."

"He sounds like a road map," Gigi says, less than enthusiastic about the decidedly unsexy turn the conversation has taken. I grip my head in both hands and rest my elbows on the counter.

"But what if that was it, Gigi? What if that was the end of our friendship?" Already, I can feel my thoughts spinning out of control. "The kiss could ruin everything. Now when Billy and I talk, it'll be awkward and uncomfortable. We'll stop writing or calling or seeing each other. He'll quit the restaurant. He'll date a Bonne Bell devotee. He'll forget all about who we used to be for each other. What we used to be together."

I don't realize how hard I'm breathing until Gigi's hand is on my back.

"Nora, calm down." She gives my shoulder a squeeze. "You don't know anything for sure—and you won't know anything for sure—until you talk to Billy face-to-face."

I inhale slowly, watching her rinse her sponge and squeeze it out before taking one last swipe of the countertop. I know she's right. Billy and I have to talk. Those words become my mantra as I head upstairs and change my clothes, both anxious and terrified of what will happen next.

I'm still trying to figure it out when I head toward Cyber Cup, where Dad and Billy agreed to meet me before flying back home. Even after a brisk walk, I'm no closer to figuring out what I'm going to say.

When I come around the side of the building, I spot my father leaning against the plate glass, a steaming paper cup in his hand. Through the window, I see Billy inside ordering at the counter. I reach Dad, smiling up at him as we hug.

"I'm gonna miss you so much!" I say, my words slightly muffled against his coat.

"Nah." Dad shakes his head, gently moving me away and looking into my eyes. "You've got a contest to win, kiddo. You won't have time to miss anyone. Although it won't stop us from missing you."

"You got that right," a voice says behind me.

I turn to see Billy a few feet away, holding a coffee in one hand and a muffin in the other. I'm grateful that his full hands make leaning in for a hug too hard to attempt.

"Do you have time to sit down?" I ask a little too brightly, gesturing to a bench nearby. "Or we could go inside instead?"

Dad's shaking his head. "We actually need to head out a little early—you know how airport security is these days."

I nod, watching Billy scarf down his muffin. He wipes a few stray crumbs from above his lip.

"Hey, Dad," I begin tentatively, "would you mind if I talked to Billy alone for a minute?"

Dad looks from me to Billy, then shrugs. "Sure. I'll head inside and see if I can snag someone's sports section."

Billy and I both watch him head through the glass door. As it shuts silently behind him, I slowly turn to face my best friend.

"So . . ."

"So." Billy gives me a tentative smile.

"About last night . . ."

"Yeah."

I shuffle my feet, wishing we'd decided to talk inside. My toes are beginning to get numb with the cold, reminding me of the day I arrived here—the first day I spent away from Billy. Silently, he moves a little closer to me.

"Nora," he says, his voice already asking the question. I take a deep breath.

"I don't know what that was last night." My voice is breathy and almost impossible to hear.

"I think it was kissing." Billy gives a lopsided grin and I roll my eyes.

"Yeah, obviously—but, you know . . . I mean . . . I don't know . . ."

"Wow, you are superarticulate this morning."

I swat at his shoulder. "Stop trying to make me laugh. This is serious."

It's Billy's turn to roll his eyes. "Why?"

"Why what?"

"Why does it have to be serious?"

I squint up at the bright sky, wondering if maybe I was wrong. If what I felt wasn't nearly as life changing for Billy as it was for me.

"Look, Nors," Billy says, taking one of my gloved hands, "you're my best friend. I care about you more than anyone. Having you gone—well, it made me realize how much I love having you around every day."

I nod. "I know what you mean."

Billy runs a hand through his hair. "I guess feeling that way—missing you so much—made me sort of think that this friendship thing we've always had is something more . . . romantic."

I swallow hard. So does Billy. He reaches for my hand again.

"I didn't realize how hard it would be to let you go. When I suggested you apply, maybe a part of me didn't think you'd get in, either. But you did and you're here and . . . well, I miss you. I think that's the point I'm trying to make.

"Look," he continues, shaking his head, "you've got enough on your plate, what with winning this contest and going off to Paris. I think it just took me coming here and seeing you to understand that you're never coming back to Weston."

I can't help but smile. He's right; my goals haven't changed. It's Paris or bust for me, even though it requires more time away from everyone I care about.

"So . . . now what?" I ask, looking up at him.

"Now," Billy says with a sigh, "I go back. You win the contest. I'll be home when you get there. We'll hang for the summer before you go to France with your scholarship."

"Sounds like normal," I say slowly, watching Billy's expression. "Like nothing's changed."

"Nothing *has* changed," Billy says firmly, pulling me in for a hug. "We're the best of the best of friends. The closest you get."

I smile over his shoulder, then pull away.

"Besides," he says, eyeing me intently, "you've got some major fish to fry up here before you make it to the top of the heap."

"What do you mean?" I ask, confused.

"I mean, it looks like that Van Lorton kid is out for blood. That, or he's head over heels in love with you."

"Please," I scoff. "Christian wants to win as bad as I do."

"Maybe," Billy says thoughtfully. "I'm just not sure what he wants to win more—this contest or you."

I don't know what to say to that. Billy tweaks my hair and grins.

"We're best friends, Nors, kiss or no kiss. Don't waste

your time trying to analyze it. Get back in the game and kick some ass."

It isn't easy to get my head back in the game after Dad and Billy leave. After an afternoon of recipe drafts and ingredient lists, I decide to practice a couple of potential dishes in the dorm kitchen. Christian walks in about twenty minutes after I start my polenta. I stiffen, remembering the volatile exchange not twenty-four hours before.

"Grits?" he asks, approaching me with something like caution. I shake my head.

"No. Polenta."

We stand there for a second, not speaking. I stir the cornmeal vigorously and drop in a generous scoop of butter. Christian gestures to the zucchini and yellow squash I have lying next to a cutting board.

"You want me to dice them up?"

I glance at him sideways. "Why, so you can throw them at me?"

He sighs and sort of throws up his hands in mock defeat. "Look, about last night—I'm really sorry if I offended you or your family. I—I guess I was just . . . caught up. In the competition."

I shake my head and turn to face him. "It's fine. It's done. We both said things we didn't mean. Let's just move on."

"Okay . . . great." Christian sounds surprised and a little relieved.

We work silently, side by side, for several minutes. Finally, my heart gets the better of my head and I can't help but ask the question that's been plaguing me.

"So . . . how long have you been with your girlfriend?"

When I glance up, Christian looks confused.

"What do you mean?"

"Your 'guest' at the reunion challenge?"

Christian shakes his head and laughs a little. "She's not my girlfriend."

"Oh, I'm sorry—are you afraid of labels? Don't want to be committed?" I try to sound like I'm teasing, but it comes out a little like an accusation. But Christian's shaking his head.

"No, no. She isn't my girlfriend or my friend with benefits or my hookup buddy or anything." He takes a deep breath. "She's my dad's fiancée."

I raise an eyebrow. "And you're telling me you kiss your dad's fiancée on the lips?"

He shrugs. "She kisses everyone on the lips. She kisses her dog on the lips."

"Doesn't say much for you, then, does it?"

"Or my dad, actually, if you think about it."

I let out a snort of laughter.

"You know," I say slowly, "she seemed a little . . . young . . . to be engaged to your dad."

He rolls his eyes. "You're telling me. She's twenty-three—I know, I know," he says when my mouth falls open. "It's gross and weird. Imagine how I feel."

"I don't think I can." I try to picture my dad with someone just a few years older than me. It's pretty nauseating.

"So, anyway," Christian leans back against the counter,

"my mom was supposed to come but couldn't and my dad was on a book tour, so Mel came instead."

"Oh. Right."

I'm floored. I don't know what to say. I'd been sure of what Christian was and who he was with. It seems that the guy I was convinced Christian was is actually someone completely different—someone complex and troubled. Someone I don't know everything about.

I put down my spoon, trying to decide what to say next, just as he scoops the diced squash into a sauté pan and wipes his hands on a dish towel.

"Well, good luck with your recipe," he says, smiling his lopsided grin at me.

"Oh—okay, thanks. You too," I manage to stammer, wanting him to stay but unable to ask him to. Instead, my heart kind of hiccups as I watch him walk away. It takes a sudden smoky haze and horrible smell to remember my polenta, now burned to the bottom of the pan. I cough and my eyes fill with involuntary tears.

Here you go again, Nora, wasting something with great potential.

CONTESTANT INTERVIEW

Christian Van Lorton

Producer (P): So, tonight's the night—the judges will be choosing the top three contestants for the finale. How are you feeling?

Christian Van Lorton (CVL): Pretty good.

P: Confident?

CVL: Of course. You know me.

P: [smiles] So, who do you think is your greatest competition? Or do we even need to ask? It's been Christian vs. Nora for weeks now.

CVL: Don't discount Pierce immediately—he's talented and can cook one hell of a steak. I'll bet he blows 'em away tonight with some red-meat wonder.

P: So, you're saying that Gigi isn't a threat at all.

CVL: [shrugs] I didn't say that.

P: Right, but you made it sound like Nora and Pierce were the only competition you'd need to be concerned about.

CVL: A) I didn't say anything about Nora, you did, and B) no one is competition for me. I'm a head above the rest.

P: What do you think the others would say about that?

CVL: Who knows? I'm sure they'd come up with some elaborate game plan to dethrone me. And I'd remind them that I'm the one with the most challenge wins.

P: Actually, Nora won the last challenge, which makes you tied.

CVL: Well, as of tonight, we won't be.

P: Do you mind if I tell Nora you said that?

CVL: Knock yourself out. I'd love to see her face when you do.

CONTESTANT INTERVIEW

Nora Henderson

Nora Henderson (NH): He said WHAT?

Producer (P): That he had the most wins and that you were no competition for him.

NH: [laughs] Right. He's so full of it.

P: So do you see *him* as competition?

NH: Um, DUH. Of course he's competition. I'm not arrogant enough to think I'm going to win, or win easily, when I'm up against cooks like Christian, Pierce, and Gigi.

P: So you see Gigi as a fierce competitor? A talented chef?

NH: [brows furrowed] Sure, of course. She's still here, isn't she?

P: That's true. But Christian may have hinted that he didn't see her as much of a threat.

NH: Yeah, well, he doesn't see *anyone* as a threat, apparently.

P: Something about the way he referred to Gigi though was different. Like he didn't think she deserved to even be here.

NH: [shakes head] He's a piece of work, isn't he? Who knows what he means—I sure don't.

P: You sound more amused than annoyed.

NH: At some point, you gotta just laugh at the guy. Someone that delusional is clearly not worth arguing with.

CHAPTER *seventeen*

Keeping an Eye Out

"I totally blew it," Gigi groans. Pierce and Christian don't say anything. I give her a sympathetic smile.

"You don't know that, Gigi. There's a lot to be said for committing to a vision. You looked at the challenge like a . . . a literal interpretation. There's nothing wrong with that."

But she shakes her head and starts gnawing at her thumbnail. "I was really hoping you and I would make it all the way to the end," she whispers sadly.

I reach out and grab her hand, giving it a squeeze.

The Final Four challenge was unlike any we'd experienced so far. You'd think that, with fewer competitors, the challenges would be even more complex—creating a flight of soufflés, maybe, or experimenting with obscure ingredients. So when Ms. Svincek stood in front of us, explaining our directions, we just stared at her in disbelief.

"Fast food?"

Gigi and I looked at each other. When I glanced at Christian and Pierce, they looked equally baffled.

"Yes," Ms. Svincek said. "You need to put together a fast-food meal with an entrée, side dish, and drink in thirty minutes."

"Ms. Svincek," I began, "it's not that we don't *want* to do the challenge, it's just that . . . well, most fast food is prepackaged frozen junk that they just fry up before serving. We don't have food like that here."

"Yeah, and who wants to eat that stuff, anyway?" Pierce added, cringing. "You couldn't pay me enough!"

"Exactly," she said, smiling, "which means you need to use the ingredients at your disposal to come up with a fast food–*style* meal."

Visions of deep-fried sweetbreads and mascarpone milkshakes danced in my head. I was starting to understand— it's like a gourmet drive-thru challenge. When the clock was set and the button was pressed, I was off like a shot to the refrigerators, yanking out every expensive ingredient I could find.

In the end, the four of us came up with distinctly different takes on what fast food, *Taste Test*–style, should actually look like. The judges loved my truffle-salted French fries and Pierce's Verona chocolate malt. Christian did a New England lobster roll that Ms. Svincek called "a creamy kiss from the sea," which, I think is, unfortunately, a good thing.

But Chef Mason and Madame Bouchon were less than impressed by Gigi's cheddar cheeseburger with shoestring potatoes—they both complained about overcooked meat and soggy fries. Ms. Svincek complimented her aioli dipping sauce, but she looked pretty disappointed overall. When we line up for Elimination, I have a sinking feeling that this will be the last time Gigi and I will be standing next to each other for a while.

"As I'm sure you can imagine," Ms. Svincek begins, "this was the most challenging Elimination Table we've had thus far. All four of you are tremendously talented chefs and we see nothing but bright things in your future.

"But," she continues with a sigh, "as you know, one of you has to go. One of you will not be joining us for the finale. And I'm very sorry to have to send that person home."

I bite my lip hard and look at Gigi. Her eyes, full of tears, are trained on Ms. Svincek. I can't bear the thought of saying good-bye to her.

"Christian Van Lorton."

I snap my head forward as Christian takes a step toward the judges.

"Your lobster roll and sweet-potato hush puppies showed a mastery of both fast food and regional cuisine. Bravo—you are the challenge winner."

Well, there it is, I guess. God knows, I'm never going to hear the end of that.

"Nora Henderson."

I give Gigi a small smile and walk forward.

"Nora, we thoroughly enjoyed your Cajun crab cake sandwich and those delicious truffle French fries. Congratulations, you're still in the running to win the *Taste Test* competition."

I exhale hard. I did it—I'm going to be in the finale. Half

the weight pressing on my shoulders lifts—and the other half bears down as the judges look from Pierce to Gigi.

"Pierce Johnson."

My heart sinks.

"You put forth a valiant effort today, Pierce."

I wait for Svincek to say that he's the last of the three finalists. I wait for Gigi to choke out a sob.

"I'm sorry. You've been eighty-sixed from *Taste Test*."

It's as though all the air is sucked from the room. I look at Pierce, then at Gigi. Both of them look equally shell-shocked.

"Okay . . . well, thank you for—for this opportunity."

Pierce gulps back whatever he's feeling and walks forward to shake the judges' hands. Christian, on the other hand, is glaring at the Elimination Table with his arms crossed over his chest.

"This is complete crap," he says, practically spitting the words.

Ms. Svincek's expression turns icy.

"I'm sorry, Christian. If you're unhappy with the outcome, you're more than welcome to sacrifice your spot in the finals to Pierce. I'm sure he'd jump at the opportunity."

"Whatever. This place is totally corrupt."

He rips off his apron and tosses it on the floor before stomping out of the room and slamming the door behind him. I look over at Gigi, who's staring down at her shoes.

"You've got nothing to feel bad about," I tell her quietly. "The judges made their decision—and see, you were worried for nothing."

"I guess so . . ."

She trails off, watching Svincek chatting with the other

judges. Seeing us still standing there, she turns and claps her hands.

"Congratulations, ladies. And welcome to the final three!"

With every step we take up to the second floor, I feel my anger growing. How could Christian have reacted like that, and right in front of Gigi? I mean, sure, her food wasn't elaborate or anything—but maybe it was perfect just as it was! Things don't always have to be complicated to be delicious.

I'm about to say as much to Gigi when we notice Benny and a couple of burly guys hovering outside our dorm door. When we get closer, I can see they're security guards. Gigi sucks in a breath.

"What's going on?" I ask, bewildered.

"Standard operating procedure. Finalists can't live together in the same room. Gigi, you're gonna need to move your stuff back to your old room, or we can move Nora to another one."

"No, that's okay, I'll go back." She exhales, looking a little relieved. "What's with the bouncers? Did you think I was going to throw a fit and have to be restrained or something?"

Benny laughs.

"Nah, we just needed their muscle to disconnect the computers and TVs in your rooms."

"You can't be serious," I groan.

"No Internet or television access allowed while you're prepping for the finale."

"I'm assuming a petition against this signed by the two of us isn't going to sway you?"

"Nope. Step aside, ladies, so we can let these guys do their jobs."

An hour later, I'm sitting in a deserted room. No computer, no TV, and no Gigi. And all of it happened so fast, I didn't even get a chance to talk to her again. She walked away from the room with an eggcrate of her stuff and a depressed look on her face. I could throttle Christian for making her feel so guilty.

Before he left, Benny handed me a packet of information about the hours leading up to the final challenge. There's the Tools of the Trade final exam at 8 a.m., then a TV appearance as well as photo shoots and interviews. The remainder of my exams are back-to-back throughout the afternoon. I want to groan. The only good thing about getting eliminated is that you get to skip the finals entirely.

I scan over the rest of the packet. Other than tomorrow's interview, the three contestants can't see each other at all, at least not without being monitored. Starting at midnight, if we want to talk to a fellow contestant, it needs to go through production and be approved first. And we'll have to have a chaperone.

I glance at the clock. I've still got a few more minutes of freedom.

I pull on my slippers and a hoodie before padding down the hall. When he answers the door, Christian's wearing nothing but boxers and a sleepy smile.

"Well, well. To what do I owe the pleasure?"

His smile falters a little bit, though, when he sees my expression. He rolls his eyes as I shade my eyes and he steps aside to let me in.

"Lemme guess—I have something to apologize for. Again."

"You know, you really made Gigi feel awful at Elimination Table," I say, still covering my eyes.

"She *should* feel awful. Her food had nothing, NOTHING on Pierce's. It's totally ridiculous that she gets to stay over him."

"And who are you to second-guess the judges? How hypocritical can you get? I don't see you questioning their opinions when you *win* a challenge."

"Nora, can you honestly say that you think Gigi's dish was better than Pierce's?"

"I didn't taste either of them. Neither did you—you can't make that assumption based solely on looks."

"I'm not basing it on looks—I'm basing it on sophistication, on level of difficulty."

"It's not easy to cook a great burger."

"Seriously?"

"Yes, seriously. And can you please put some clothes on?!"

Christian sits down on his bed and yanks a T-shirt over his head.

"Look, I *am* sorry if Gigi's feelings are hurt. But, that doesn't mean she deserves to be here."

"Oh, how big of you. I'm sure that will make her feel *so* much better."

"Why are you defending her, anyway?" he asks. "She's your competition, just like I am."

"Yeah, but she's also my friend, which *you* are *not*."

He gives a smug smile. "Finally admitting we're more than friends, I see."

"You're unbelievable. I'm leaving."

He flops back on his bed. "I know it's going to be hard for you not to just drop in on me anymore—I'm glad you managed to get your fix tonight."

I snort. "Right. See you whenever—emphasis on 'never.'"

But "never" ends up being at our *Good Day Today* interview the next morning. Deanna Fisher, one of the hosts, drove up from the city to talk to us, and the crew has transformed the conference room into a lounge where all of us sit, sipping sparkling water in fancy glasses and trying to look relaxed.

"Nora and Gigi."

Deanna Fisher gives us a gleaming smile. I try not to squint. I think her teeth might actually be their own light source. She'd be good to have around during an emergency.

"You two seem as though you're the best of friends on the show. Is that friendship real?"

I nod. "Of course it's real."

I look over at Gigi. She's staring down at her hands.

Deanna pounces, giving an encouraging, if not eager, smile.

"Gigi, you seem particularly quiet this morning. Is something bothering you?"

Gigi finally looks up, glancing around as though she just realized where she was.

"What? I mean, no. I mean, yes, everything's fine."

Deanna raises an eyebrow before turning to Christian.

"And Christian, you made it clear at last night's Elimination that you don't think Gigi deserves to be in the competition—at least not when compared to Pierce Johnson. Can you tell us why?"

Christian leans back in his chair. "You know, Deanna, I don't want to dwell on the past. Let's just move on to the future—and that's the finale."

"Of course," she responds smoothly, giving the three of us a saccharine smile. "Speaking of which, I spoke with some of the producers of the show this morning and they have a little surprise they'd like me to share with you."

Oh, God. What now?

From behind a curtained-off area, Holden Prescott walks out in front of us, smiling like he's won the competition himself. I freeze. I see Gigi tense up in her chair. Even Christian looks shocked. Prescott holds out a hand to Deanna and she takes it.

"Chef Prescott," she sort of purrs, "the finalists are clearly surprised by your appearance this morning."

Wow, nothing gets past you, Deanna. What tipped you off?

"After all the rumors, the accusations," she continues, lowering her voice for dramatic effect, "can you explain to us exactly what happened on the set of *Taste Test*? How *did* those contestants get hurt, anyway?"

Prescott smiles at her.

"Well, unfortunately, no, I can't explain that to you. That's because, as I've maintained since the accidents occurred, I'm completely innocent. And I'm here today because, after an extensive investigation by the network and the police, I've been cleared of all charges."

I almost choke on the water I'm sipping.

"So," Prescott continues, "the producers wanted me to come here this morning to let everyone know, including the contestants, that I will be returning to judge the season five finale.

And, let me just say, Deanna, I can't wait to be part of the show again!"

I cross my arms and try to stay calm while I watch Prescott flirt with Deanna. But I can't help it—I'm fuming. I think of Angela, at home, missing out on the chance to be here. I think of Joy, still lying in a hospital bed. Christian was right about one thing—this place *is* completely corrupt.

I don't know what strings he pulled or what he has to gain from all this, but one thing is absolutely certain—Holden Prescott is the furthest thing from innocent. And I'm going to have to be the one to prove it, once and for all. Just as soon as this finale is over, Prescott's going down.

CONTESTANT INTERVIEW

Giada "Gigi" Orsoni

Producer (P): You seem a little tense. A little off-balance. Is that a fair assessment?

Giada "Gigi" Orsoni (GO): Probably.

P: You're nervous about this whole thing?

GO: [glaring] Are you kidding? Of course I'm nervous. I'm terrified.

P: There's no need for you to be this unraveled, Gigi. You made it into the finals! You are just as good as Nora or Christian—the judges believe you're a competitor to be reckoned with!

GO: [shrugging] Whatever.

P: Gigi, one would expect that, in your position, you might be a little less hostile.

GO: My position? MY position? Trust me—you know absolutely nothing about *my* position.

P: I've been producing this show since the beginning. I think I have a pretty good idea.

GO: [shakes her head] That's not what I mean.

P: Most people seem at least a *little* excited about competing in the finale—not so sullen and moody.

GO: [snaps] Well, I'm so sorry to disappoint you. [gets up] I guess I'm not "most people."

CHAPTER *eighteen*

Fool Me Once? Shame On You.

Kathryn Svincek beams as Christian, Gigi, and I take the floor.

"Welcome, competitors! And congratulations on making it to the season five finale of *Taste Test*!"

I think I might pee my pants. Next to me, I can see Gigi's hands trembling. Of course, Christian looks as relaxed as ever. I really think he might be taking sedatives.

"We'll begin filming in just a few minutes. Before then, please look over your station and make sure that you have everything you need. If anything is missing, let one of the production assistants know immediately."

I guess they've decided now, for liability's sake, that we need to inspect our own kitchens. That way, when one of us catapults across the room from a pressure cooker malfunction, we have no one to blame but ourselves.

Just a little sabotage humor—I've got to do *something* to keep from attacking Prescott with an oyster shucker.

"All right, we're on in sixty seconds," someone calls out. The three of us move behind our counters. I stare at the *X* of tape on the floor. This is the last time I'll need to stand here, the last time I'll be competing in this arena. It's weird how quickly things become so familiar, you can't imagine life without them.

The rest of the judges, including Prescott, come out onto the set and stand in their assigned positions. I hold back the animal-like growl I feel in my throat. A director's assistant runs forward with the black-and-white marker board and, moments later, Marcus calls "action." Chef Mason moves to stand next to a covered cart.

"Tonight, one of you will receive the gift of a lifetime—a chance to study cooking in one of the food capitals of the world. In Paris, there is a section on every menu in every restaurant—*'le fruit de la mer'*: the fruit of the ocean. Tonight, you will be creating a dish that highlights the best these gifts from the sea have to offer."

He removes the sheet to reveal dozens of oysters, scallops, crab, clams, and shrimp, all chilling on a bed of chipped ice. He gestures to the mountain and smiles.

"These are your ingredients. You will have five minutes to map out your recipes and ninety minutes to prepare two dishes—one entrée and an accompanying side."

At the sound of the buzzer, I practically fly to the cart. I reach for the scallops just as Christian starts putting some on his platter. I hurry to grab a dozen before he's claimed them all. When I pass by Gigi picking through the clams, I give her arm a squeeze.

I decide on cranberry-glazed scallops with a sweet-potato

puree, an adaptation of a dish we do at Smoke Signals around the holidays. Once I've got the potatoes diced, I drop them in a pot of salted water and reach for the dial for my front burner.

I click it to the right, waiting for it to flare—nothing happens.

I try a few more times, but there's nothing—no spark, no flame. I try one of the other burners. Turning the dial further, I lean down and sniff.

Nothing.

Crap. Of all the days not to check my burners first thing . . .

"Excuse me!" I call out to a group of techs loitering on one side of the set. "There's something wrong with the stove—it's not lighting."

"Really?" One of them comes over and tinkers with the knobs. A minute passes as he continues to turn them again and again.

"I've already tried that. A lot."

More technicians, and then Chef Mason, come to look at the broken range. After a few minutes, I can't help but get a little impatient. There's never been a more important night—the last thing I need is a nonworking stove.

"Nora." Chef Mason pulls me aside. "Listen, I know this isn't exactly the most appealing solution, but we're going to have to have you buddy up with Christian—use his stove while we try to fix yours."

Reluctantly, I look over at Christian. He shrugs.

"It's fine—come on over. I have two open burners."

I grimace.

"Just use mine, Nora," Gigi calls over to me. "I'll help you carry your stuff over."

But Chef Mason has already moved my sauté pan to Christian's station. I shrug, grabbing my tray of scallops.

"I'll just stay here, Gigi."

"But—"

"Contestants, please!" Ms. Svincek calls out, clapping her hands. "We're *filming*!"

Gigi is shaking her head, her eyes troubled.

It's fine, I mouth at her.

I set myself up on the farthest end of Christian's station and start prepping my pan for the scallops. A good sear is the most important element of the whole dish. Too wet and the scallops boil, not brown. Too dry and they burn. You need a smoking-hot pan to do it right. People rely way too much on nonstick surfaces and, like Dad says, the only thing they're good for is gray food.

I hear the hissing before I see—or smell—anything.

"What the hell is that sound?"

I look at Christian. He turns the knob for his front burner, but nothing happens. He shakes his head, tries again.

"You have *got* to be kidding me!" He kicks at a rubber tube that's sticking out from the bottom of the range.

I freeze.

And then, the pungent odor of gas burns my nostrils.

When you're terrified, it's as if all your senses are on high alert. I can see everything so sharply, so clearly, that it's somehow more real, more urgent. My ears capture even the tiniest, most insignificant sounds. Sounds that, under normal circumstances, are nothing more than mundane.

Sounds like the flint of a seemingly broken burner finally sparking to life.

I'm not fast enough. I can't cry out. I watch in horror as Christian looks at me, his triumph melting to confusion at the expression on my face.

A split second later, the world around me explodes. I'm blinded by fire so pale, it's almost white under the fluorescent lighting. The piercing burn of my skin forces me backward, in the opposite direction of where I want to be going.

All that clarity from moments ago is gone.

The only thing I'm aware of is what's in front of me: Christian, paralyzed in the middle of the room, his helpless body engulfed in flames.

"Nora, get back!"

I hear Gigi's voice, feel her arms around my waist, dragging me away from the fire. I watch as someone tackles Christian to the ground, smothering his body with something—a blanket, maybe? As though a dam breaks inside me, a scream rises up and out of my throat.

Before I can attempt to stop them, Benny and Gigi pull me out of the arena and into the hallway. I beat my fists against the painted cinder-block walls, clawing my way toward the door, my mouth unable to close—unable to utter anything but a howl of terror. Gigi's still holding me, trying to grab my hands, to force me not to break them as I punch anything I can reach.

"Shh. Nora, please. He's gonna be okay."

I don't believe her. I don't believe anyone anymore. I think about Angela—the blood leeching into her clothing. I think about Joy—unconscious on the arena floor. It's only fair that now, today, would be the worst one. The last one. Christian is Holden Prescott's next victim.

No.

Christian is Prescott's *last* victim.

I push Gigi off me, force myself up to standing, and head for the arena doors.

"Nora, what are you doing? There's nothing you can do for him right now."

"I'm not going in there for Christian. I'm going in there for Prescott."

"Nora . . ." Gigi trails off, her expression pale. "I really don't—I mean, you need to wait for the paramedics. They might want to check you out, too."

I ignore her. Moments later, I burst into the almost-empty arena. A haze of smoke and the smell of burnt fabric hangs heavy in the air. I want to cough, but I don't. Coughing is weak. I need to look strong. I walk toward where the judges are standing, talking to several of the show's producers.

"You."

Heads spin around to look at me. There's no sign of Christian, which I can only hope means he's somewhere safe, getting help. Good. That will make this easier.

"You." I say it again, wishing my eyes could pierce Prescott's skin. I take a step toward him, but there's no panic, no worry in his face. He seems completely unaffected by my presence. Then, he crosses his arms over his chest. A protective pose. A shield.

"Nora . . ." Benny is walking toward me, his face full of concern. "Honey, we really need you to get checked out by emergency personnel. Please, whatever this is, it can wait."

"NO!" I brush his hand away, never taking my eyes off of Prescott.

"Nora." Ms. Svincek steps forward. "Why don't you sit down? We'll get you a glass of water."

She, like Gigi and Benny, looks a little nervous, as though she expects me to grab a butcher knife and go for the jugular.

I shake my head again, still moving toward Prescott.

"So, how did you do it?"

"How did I do what?" His voice is chilled and slick, leaving nothing for me to cling on to except what I know is true.

"Let's start with the sink," I hiss. "Was it some kind of minibomb? Liquid gunpowder you can slip inside a faucet?"

His eyes narrow. "I don't know what you're talking about."

"Right. Fine—then what about the food processors. And the microwaves? They malfunctioned on their own? And, let me guess, the meat cleavers just up and walked away?"

He opens his mouth again, but I interrupt him.

"How exactly did it feel to electrocute your girlfriend, huh?"

"Nora . . . ," Gigi says weakly, looking at me with a pained expression. "Don't."

I ignore her. Instead, I start walking closer to Prescott, glaring at him as though my gaze alone could set him on fire.

"You didn't get to see her on the ground, motionless," I say in almost a whisper, "but the rest of us did. Why—why did it matter to you if she won or lost? Why did you need to hurt her—or Angela?"

"Look"—he leans toward me, eyes flashing—"I don't know what you *think* you know—but what you're accusing me of is both impossible and ridiculous."

"Oh, really? Why is that?" I shoot back.

"Because the judges don't have access to the arena unless

the contestants are in here. What do you think the guards are for, genius?"

I stop for a second, a stutter in my rant. Then I shake my head.

"Ms. Svincek saw you—she told the cops."

Prescott looks from me to Ms. Svincek, his eyes wide. I guess he didn't know she'd been the one to turn him in.

"Nora, listen—" Gigi starts toward me, but Ms. Svincek grabs her arm. Gigi shakes her off. "Look, I need to tell you something."

Ms. Svincek stands up quickly, her expression strained.

"You know, we've had an awfully long day, ladies and gentlemen! How about we go cool off? All of this will take care of itself."

"No," I snap. I refuse to let this go on one minute longer. I turn to Gigi and shake my head.

"Look, nothing you say could possibly be half as important as this right now." I glare at Prescott. "He's going down and he knows it."

"No," Gigi says quietly. "He isn't."

I hardly hear her, refusing to take my eyes off my target. To make me focus, to make me see her, Gigi moves into my line of vision, blocking my view of Prescott.

"He isn't going down, Nora, because he didn't do it. Any of it."

"What?" I straighten up, staring at her. "What are you talking about?"

"The explosions. The accidents. They weren't Prescott's fault."

"Well, then whose fault were they?" I ask, trying to look over her shoulder.

She grabs my face, forcing me to meet her eyes.

"Mine."

The world stops turning. I can't move.

"What—what do you mean?" I manage.

She looks incredibly sad as she focuses on the ground then back up at me.

"I'm the one who did it. The sink. The outlet." She pauses for another second. "The gas connection to the stoves. I'm the one who's been sabotaging *Taste Test*."

I stare at her dumbly. Her eyes are big and full of tears. I want to hug her. I want to slap her. I don't know what I want.

"Please," she pleads, reaching out to grab my arm. I pull away, shaking my head.

"How did you—why did—" I stumble over the questions I want to ask and, somehow, just can't get any out.

Chef Mason and Madame Bouchon are looking at Gigi in shock. Benny and several executives stand just a few yards back, whispering urgently. I can almost hear their conversation— what should we do? How should we proceed? Should we be filming this?

"But Gigi," Madame Bouchon says quietly, "why? Why would you do those horrible things?"

I expect Gigi to falter at any moment, to bend and break under the scrutiny. I know I would. Instead, she takes a deep breath and straightens up. She turns and looks at Ms. Svincek.

"Because my mother told me to."

Police Report
SERGEANT PHILIP JENKINS

Arrived at the North American Culinary Academy campus at approximately 8:00 p.m. upon receiving radio transmission about suspected criminal activity. Ambulance already on the scene at time of arrival. Male, 17 years old, treated for second-degree burns, taken to Lake Haven General for further treatment.

Arrested Kathryn Helen Svincek, age 47. Accused of assault with a deadly weapon, tampering with evidence, corruption—possible further charges pending.

IN CUSTODY—Georgina "Gigi" Svincek, daughter of the accused. Apparently infiltrated *Taste Test* competition per mother's instructions, responsible for two recent injuries to contestants Angela Moore and Joy Kennedy-Swanson, both of whom have been contacted for further interviews.

TO BE DETERMINED:

- Devices implemented or rigged to create seemingly accidental injuries
- Possible access to chemicals (waterline explosion)
- Assistance from crew members possible

CHAPTER nineteen

Fool Me Twice? Not a Chance.

When you're trying a new recipe, sometimes it's hard to see what it's missing. There are the obvious things—salt, pepper, sugar, things that balance the elements. Then there are the ones you've never thought of: a pinch of allspice in beef stew, a dusting of curry powder in chicken salad.

But, in any recipe, the missing ingredient is clear once you've put your finger on it.

"Your mother?" Mason asks, looking around the arena. A hundred questions hang in the space around us. Svincek pulls a cheerful mask on over the shell-shocked expression she's been wearing.

"Please, let me explain." She walks forward, shooting Gigi a murderous glance. "It's not what you think it is."

"It's *exactly* what you think it is," Gigi interjects. She looks at Ms. Svincek—her mother—and shakes her head. "I'm not going to do it, Mom. I'm not going to lie anymore."

Ms. Svincek moves in quickly, grabbing Gigi's arm hard enough that she winces. "And you're comfortable being responsible for ruining my career, Georgina?"

Gigi yanks her arm away.

"If that's what happens, it happens. All I know is that I can't do this anymore."

"You ungrateful brat, you're going to destroy what we've worked so hard for!"

Gigi shakes her head. "No, Mom. I've already destroyed enough. It's time for me to make things right."

She turns to face the judges, but her eyes are trained on me.

"My dad was the one who taught me to cook," she begins, "and I grew to love it as much as he did. My mom, however— well, she's always said that a talent is only good when it has a direct use. She insisted I work behind the scenes, helping to cater all the academic functions. I was ten when I made my first soufflé; at twelve, I orchestrated my first ten-course dinner. I loved to cook because my dad and I did it together.

"But once *Taste Test* moved to the NACA campus and Dad was put in charge, he didn't have time for anything else. In fact, I can't remember the last time I saw him cook anything just for fun."

"This is no one's business," Ms. Svincek snaps, but you can see her shoulders have slumped under the weight of her daughter's confession. Gigi ignores her.

"Last summer, my dad died while on set after hours. He had a heart attack, but no one was there to help him. My mom and I didn't even know until the next morning; they didn't find him until the crew came in for the day shift."

I look down at my hands. I remember Ms. Svincek lamenting the unfortunate loss of her husband at orientation. I could never imagine that her grief was Gigi's to share.

Reliving the tragedy has seemingly given new life to Ms. Svincek, who has straightened up and is walking toward the other judges with a sneer across her face.

"My husband devoted his life to this show. *And it killed him.*"

The room is completely silent. Everyone is staring at Ms. Svincek and Gigi.

"Mom . . . ," Gigi begins. Ms. Svincek shakes her head.

"Did you know that he left us nothing? No savings? No retirement? He sunk everything he had into *Taste Test*, so sure that it would pay him back in the end." She barks an angry, almost maniacal laugh. "Well, it did that all right!"

Unable to continue, Ms. Svincek collapses into a folding chair. Gigi moves to stand next to her mother, her eyes filled with tears.

"When they offered Mom the NACA presidency, she wasn't going to accept it. We talked about moving away, about starting over. And then, she came up with the *Taste Test* audition idea. Fifty thousand dollars is a lot of money and could really help us. It wasn't until later that I found out she had changed my name—since my parents never let me on the set, no one on the show knew who I was or what I looked like. Mom said I had to be Gigi Orsoni to get a fair shot with the judges. I didn't know what she was planning to do.

"She had me rig the sink first. After Angela got hurt, which she swore was an accident, she moved on to smaller things. She told me that shorting the microwaves and stealing the cleavers were actually strategies the judges approved of, ways to make the contestants think of alternatives on the fly."

Gigi swallows hard and looks frantically at the people surrounding her.

"I swear to you, I never thought someone could get hurt. Once Angela was gone, I told her I wouldn't do it anymore, but Mom made me continue. She said that enough accidents would force the production company to settle their losses. That we'd get back the money we'd lost when Dad invested in the show. That I only needed to help for a little bit longer."

She looked at me imploringly, shaking her head from side to side.

"Nora, I swear to you—I never meant to hurt Christian. The tubing was supposed to leak right away—as soon as someone smelled gas, we'd all get out of there—the finale would be canceled and I'd have more time to prepare. But instead, he lit the burner and then . . ." She trails off.

"And then Christian burst into flames," I finish for her.

"Gigi," Benny says, sitting down next to her, "we're going to need you to talk to the authorities about all of this."

He looks back at Ms. Svincek, who is now flanked by two of the show's security guards. "I'm going to need to know everything your mother told you to do, everything you planned together."

He motions to the guards to remove Ms. Svincek, but she struggles, narrowing her eyes at Benny.

"You should be ashamed of yourself, Benny Friedman. This network, this show, is the worst thing to ever happen to the North American Culinary Academy, and my husband would be disgusted to see what *Taste Test* has become."

She glares at her colleagues, then points at Prescott.

"You allowed that disgusting womanizer to stay on staff here, despite repeated violations of his contract. For Christ's sake, this isn't a dating show!"

"Kathryn," Chef Mason begins, clearing his throat, "it was the network that brought him back."

"Exactly."

She pulls free of the guards' grip and rushes forward until she is hardly three inches from Benny's face.

"You and your disgusting colleagues have no shame. No morals. It's *your fault* I had to resort to such methods to save my family."

To everyone's surprise, Benny laughs.

"Morals? Lady, you've lost your mind. What kind of morals does someone have when they force their own daughter to sabotage other kids' dreams? To hurt people? You have a lot to answer for and, fortunately, it has nothing to do with the network.

"Get her out of here," he orders, a look of disgust on his face. He turns to Gigi, his face a bit softer. "You better follow her. The police are going to want to talk to you, too."

Gigi gives me a final glance. I know she is looking for something—sympathy, understanding maybe? I can't give her that. I turn away and face the wall, refusing to meet her eyes as she's led from the room.

The burn unit at Lake Haven General is having a slow night. Benny and I are the only people in the waiting area and I'm disproportionately grateful. We have to give our names and IDs to the nurses' station for security purposes before we're allowed inside the "clean room." There, we each wash our hands and put on scrubs and hairnets, as though we were going to be performing surgery. I'd laugh at our appearance if I had the energy. Or if anything about this situation was even remotely funny.

"One at a time," a nurse instructs. I look at Benny and he motions me forward.

"Go ahead. I guarantee he'll want to see you more than he wants to see me."

"Thanks."

Christian has his own room with a large window. The blinds are closed and the lights are off, but it's easy to see my way around surrounded by brightly lit machines. At first, I think he's sleeping. Then, in the pale glow of the monitors, I see his eyelids flutter open.

"Hey."

His voice is dry, like walking through fallen leaves. I look at the thick white bandages wrapped around both his arms from his shoulders to his hands. The lump in my throat is back. I haven't felt it since I left Weston.

"Come here, Nora."

I can't say, *No, I'm scared. I don't want to see you this way.* I can't really say anything at all. Carefully, as though sneaking through enemy territory, I move up to the side of the bed until I can finally see his face, still half-shrouded in shadow.

Thankfully, it's the same. The face that's made me angry, made me crazy, and made me fall for him. Aside from a large bandage covering part of one cheek and half his neck, it's the face I've come to care so much about. A face is how you know someone best, and the fact that his is intact makes me feel incredibly thankful.

Seeing him like this makes me realize that I've got no fight left—especially about how I feel. I may have denied it, I may have tried to ignore it, but the truth is too hard to dispute anymore: I feel something for Christian that is pure and true and real. Something that feels a lot like love.

I go to reach for his hand, but remember the bandages just before I touch him. He gives me a rueful smile.

"You can hold it—it just might feel like you're hanging on to a roll of Charmin."

"I think I can handle that," I say, smiling.

"How are you doing?" he asks, a concerned expression on his face. I can't help but laugh.

"How am *I* doing? I'm fine. More importantly, how are *you* doing?"

Christian gives a sort of shrug.

"Okay. It hurts."

I look down at the bed. He's covered with a sheet, so I can't tell where the burns begin and end. He watches my eyes scan the length of the bed.

"The doctor said that my pants had some flame-retardant material in them or something. He says track pants—you know, the swishy ones—are the worst. They're like plastic—melt right onto your legs."

I can't help but shudder.

"Anyway," he continues, "my hair's a little singed and my ears and nose are going to blister in a few days, but other than that—what you see is what you get."

"Do you know how bad they are? The burns, I mean?"

He shakes his head and shifts his body weight to one side, wincing as he resettles himself.

"I haven't seen them—I was out cold when they cleaned me up. The doctor said that the worst ones are on my neck, but none of them are bad enough for skin grafts or anything."

"Did he say how long you'll be here?"

"A week, maybe two. It depends on these." He raises and lowers his wrapped arms like two baseball bats.

"Right. Of course."

"So," he shifts again, "what happened after I left. I haven't heard anything yet. Was everyone else okay?"

I shake my head. "I don't know how well I can explain this . . ."

"Give it a shot."

Silently, I close my eyes, wishing I didn't know the story. Wishing that none of it were even true. As I tell Christian everything I know, I can't help but remember how he was the only one who saw Gigi—Georgina—for who she really was.

"So, you were right," I say as I finish. "You were right all along."

Christian shakes his head slowly from side to side.

"This isn't about that. Jeez, Nora, her *mom*? How is that even possible? How in the world did Svincek manage to get her daughter on the show?"

"I don't know. I just can't believe it was Gigi the whole time. And I'm the idiot who *defended* her."

"You aren't an idiot, Nora. She's your best friend here."

"*Was.* Was my best friend here."

He shakes his head again.

"I know I'm probably the last person you'd expect to hear this from, considering the fact that I'm laid up here looking like the guy on the Boo Berry box, but I think you need to cut her some slack."

"I think *you've* had a few too many pain pills."

"All I'm saying is that maybe it's hard to understand Gigi's side. Sounds like her mom was some kind of culinary Nazi. And losing her dad, well, who knows how much that hurts."

"I don't know. Maybe." I look back at him and give a half smile. "What I do know, however, is that I owe you an apology."

"Really? Damn, it's about time!" He grins.

"I'm serious," I say. "You said it was her and I ignored you. I said a lot of things . . ." I trail off, looking down at my hands. "Anyway, I just want to say that I'm sorry."

"Apology accepted."

We sit there for a second, smiling at each other. I look away, feeling my cheeks coloring.

"How did you know, anyway?" I ask him, playing with the edge of the blanket.

"Know what?" He frowns.

"That it was Gigi."

He shrugs. "I didn't really. I mean, the whole thing with Joy was definitely suspicious."

"Well, I owe you for being such a pain."

"Hmmm." He smiles, narrowing his eyes a bit. "I like the idea of you owing me. Maybe backrubs for a year? Or, no, I got it—how about sponge baths?"

"Don't push your luck."

"What about a date, then," he suggests, a twinkle in his eye. "One night that *isn't* in a kitchen or a classroom—where someone cooks for *us*, for once."

"I don't know." I twist my hair around my finger. "I have an awful lot on my plate right now, what with preparing for the rescheduled finale and all."

Christian cocks an eyebrow. "What rescheduled finale?"

"I'll let Benny give you all the details. Basically, it's you and me, a one-shot deal. After you've healed and the doctor's given the go-ahead, they'll film a one-on-one battle. Winner takes all."

His face slides up into a smile. "Are you serious?"

"Hell yes!"

"Oh, man—I'm going to give you the fight of your life, Henderson."

"We'll see about that." I grin. "Don't expect me to go easy on you."

He grins, leaning forward a bit. "When it comes to you, Nora, I've learned to expect the unexpected."

This time when Christian kisses me, his lips taste sweet and warm, like Christmas morning. I guess that's appropriate, since sitting here feels like a gift. Losing him, even briefly, made me realize how much I want to be with him, how attached I already am.

Love is a funny thing. It makes you believe in things—like maybe there's a reason for this, for all of what's happened. Maybe this moment, this place—even this guy—is more than just a moment in time. More than that proverbial flash in the pan.

NACA

North American Culinary Academy
2929 Lakehurst Mountain Road
North Sullivan, CT 21842

FINALE LIABILITY SHEET

I have read and understand the following:

Initial here

____ You will be choosing your own dishes in advance. Please get a comprehensive, typed request for ingredients and equipment to Benny Friedman at least 24 hours before the competition.

____ Up until the finale taping, you will be sequestered from your opponent.

____ You will be required to come to the arena one hour before wardrobe to walk through your station with a set technician and approve all appliances and other essential items.

I, _____ (fill in name), certify that
I am of sound mind and body and able to participate in
the *Taste Test* finale. I have no knowledge of any accidental or intentional tampering with *Taste Test* sets, equipment, or ingredients.

CHAPTER *twenty*

Second (or Third or Fourth or Fifth) Chances

Knock-knock.

I can't help but groan. I thought one of the nice things about staying in a hotel would be the privacy, the silence. I squint at the clock.

7:34 a.m.

Oh yeah, this better be good.

I figure it's Benny with some last-minute changes to tonight's filming, or Bryce to start what will inevitably be the day-long process to tame my bedhead. The last person I expect to see standing there is Angela.

"Wow, that's some look you got going on. Are all TV stars as unglamorous as you?"

"Angela!" I yank her inside the door and give her a hug. "I can't believe it—what are you doing here?"

She grins. "Are you kidding? Miss your night of glory? I had to come!"

I motion her to sit down, tossing towels and clothes off the desk chair. She looks around skeptically.

"How long have you been staying here, Nora?"

"In the hotel? For a couple weeks—why?"

"No reason. It just looks very . . . lived-in."

I glance around at the wrappers on the floor and empty soda bottles lining the side table and shrug.

"What can I say? It's been a pretty crazy time."

"I'll bet."

The day after the finale—the *first* finale—*Taste Test* moved from the NACA campus to a downtown Lake Haven hotel. The crew spent day and night prepping a new arena kitchen for the re-finale while, blocks away, Christian lay in a hospital bed waiting to get word of when he'd be clear to compete again. It took ten days for the doctors to decide that he could endure an hour-long challenge shoot.

It's taken all that time and more for me to wrap my brain around everything that's happened.

Angela is watching my face and I shake my head, as though to clear it via the Etch A Sketch method.

"So, are you going to be in the audience tonight?" I ask her.

She nods. "Of course. I can't wait! And what about you? How are *you* feeling about tonight?"

I blow a gust of air out between my lips.

"Okay. Nervous. I think I'm just ready for this to be over—I want to figure out what I'm doing with my life and I sort of need to know whether that decision is or is not going to involve a passport."

"And how about Christian? How is he doing?"

"Good, I think. I haven't been allowed to see him much. We were sequestered at first because of the investigation; then, when the doctors agreed to release him, Benny wouldn't let me within ten feet of him. No communication with fellow contestants, no television, no connection to the outside world. Finale regulations." I look mournfully at the wall where my plasma-screen TV once hung.

"Right . . ." Angela looks down at her feet, then back at me, cocking her head. "And how about the investigation? What's the latest with Ms. Svincek?"

I sigh. "She's been charged with a felony for the sink—but you had to know that part." Angela was one of the witnesses for the original arraignment.

"Right. And Gigi?"

I shrug. "Nothing. Haven't heard from her."

Angela bites her lip. "I have."

I blink hard. "You're kidding. She called you?"

"No." She looks down. "I went to see her."

"In *prison*?"

"It's a detention center, Nora. But, yes, I went to see her last night when I got here."

I don't know what to say—of all people, Angela should be the most furious with Gigi. Her selfishness cost Angela the chance to be here competing tonight instead of watching from the sidelines.

"What did she say?"

"She wanted me to wish you luck. And she wanted me to give you this."

Angela reaches into her pocket and brings out a folded piece of paper. I shake my head.

"Ang, whatever it says, I'm not interes—"

"Nora." Her eyes are sad. "I know you're angry—trust me, I, of all people, understand why. And I'm not saying you need to read this now. Tonight's important and you need to focus. But you *should* read it at some point. Seriously."

"Why? What can she possibly say to make things better?"

"Nothing. She can't make anything better. She knows that."

"I just don't understand why you even went there, Angela. I mean, after what she did—after what she caused—"

Angela stands up and gives me a small smile.

"The right people are competing tonight—I have no delusions of grandeur here. It was always about you and Christian from the moment you both got on that shuttle."

I remember that day like it was yesterday—his blue eyes, that infuriating smirk. I feel a tug of residual jealousy remembering his arm casually slung around Joy's shoulders.

"Anyway"—Angela leans forward to hug me—"I wanted to wish you luck, but I will *not* say break a leg. The last thing you need is another accident."

"Yeah, thanks for that."

I watch as she sets the note on the corner of the desk. She gives me another smile.

"Next time I see you, you'll be the season five champion!"

She's out the door before I can respond. I'm too busy eyeing that letter like it might implode or burst into flames.

Hey, with Gigi's history, you never know.

And Angela was right—I could have ignored the note and

spent my time strategizing for tonight, trying to get myself psyched for the finale. But instead, I sit for twenty minutes staring at a folded piece of paper, attempting to convince myself that I don't care what it says.

At minute twenty-one, I snatch it off the desk.

At minute twenty-two, I unfold it.

Dear Nora,

I don't know what to write because nothing I say changes anything—I lied to you and I hurt people. That's something I have to live with every second of every day. I don't want to make excuses and tell you that I had to do what I did. I didn't—I could have said no. I just didn't.

Everything I said that night in the arena was the truth—I never, ever would have done the things I did if I thought people would get hurt. My mother is a very persuasive person—she made me believe that my actions were in honor of my dad, that we were finding a way to make up for what we lost. I've always done what my mother's told me to do, but I know that telling the truth was the best decision. Even if she ends up in jail for good—even if I do too—I know I did the right thing.

Angela told me they're doing another finale—I'm glad that you will get your fair chance to win this thing. I can't think of anyone who deserves it more. I only wish I'd had the courage to tell the truth sooner; maybe then, more people would have gotten a fair shot at the finals. Regardless, I know you would have made it to the end.

You are an amazing chef, Nora, and I admire your talent and your strength.

I hope, one day, you will read this and know how much I regret what I've done. Maybe a part of you will understand why I did it in the first place. As someone who loves her father more than anything, I'm hoping you can see how much it hurt to lose my own. I haven't felt whole since he died, but becoming your friend—well, it took away that ache in my chest. I'll always be grateful for that.

Love,

Gigi

So rather than looking over my recipe for peach-basted pork chops with Vidalia onions, rather than reconsidering glazed carrots in favor of a starchier side, I stare at Gigi's letter all afternoon.

Now, standing in the new arena, I'm still preoccupied with her words. I think about how it feels to disappoint a parent—how guilty I'd felt taking off for Connecticut in January, leaving my dad short staffed.

What if I actually *win* this thing? What if Paris isn't just a pipe dream, but a big, fat furnace reality?

I'd leave at the end of August, the middle of the peak season at the restaurant, right when business booms every year. It's not like I'm indispensible at the register, but not everyone knows the recipes by heart, not everyone can work the smoker when Dad has to deal with a late delivery or malfunctioning fridge. I'll be abandoning him at the worst possible time.

So, can I understand Gigi's predicament? Do I sympathize?

I don't know. I don't think I can—if I do, I'm saying it's okay that she hurt Angela and Joy. That she almost killed Christian. But I *do* understand what it feels like to want to make your widowed parent feel a little less lost—like you're really partners in this whole mess of life.

And that's what's keeping me from concentrating on basting and grilling and the dozen other things I should be doing right at this moment, in this new arena, cooking for my future.

"That's right, viewers, we are thirty minutes into the *Taste Test* season five finale—and what a finale it is! On one side we have Nora Henderson—small-town girl with a barbecue background! On the other, we've got culinary prince Christian Van Lorton, out of the hospital and in the zone! Folks, I'm telling you—I haven't seen a battle like this since . . ."

I try to block out the announcer's voice. Leave it to the network to make the "Re-Finale" as dramatic as possible by hiring an obnoxious sports commentator to detail the play-by-play—as though hospital stays and felony charges weren't enough to raise the already skyrocketing ratings.

"Again, folks, we're just twenty-nine minutes away from finding out whose dish is the most de-lish, whose food will set the mood . . ."

You know, you'd think if they were going to hire a moderator, or whatever this guy is, they'd shell out a few extra bucks for someone better than a Dr. Seuss wannabe.

I check on my stove-top smoker. I really hope the apple wood chips were the right choice. I've only got a few more minutes until I need to move my chops from the smoker to the grill. I pretend to check the clock while I watch Christian work. His shirt sleeves are rolled up to his elbows and you can see the bottom of what's left of the bandages. I swallow hard.

Competing against Christian was a lot easier when I wasn't focused on how he was feeling. Or how good he looks in his button-down shirt, his blond hair disheveled, his eyes narrowed in concentration. A bead of sweat trickles down his temple. Apparently, he's feeling as hot as he's looking.

Stop it. Find your zone.

But with so little time left in the challenge, I still haven't gotten to that point—the point where everything falls into place. And as I watch Christian's back hunched over his saucepan, his hands flying over his cutting board with lightning speed, I'm starting to think that maybe I'm not the person who's going to take this thing tonight.

Sometimes, it's hard to remember what you're fighting for. I squeeze my eyes shut and think about home. There are Dad, Joanie, and Billy watching the finale in the Smoke Signals dining room. There is the whole town of Weston crowded around their TVs, rooting for me to win. Then, I open my eyes and look at Christian again. He's wiping his face on the front of his apron, one hand dipping a metal spoon into a shallow pan. He looks intent and determined. I can't help but think about what he has to move back to after the show—a home, a school, a world where his father runs the show. Paris would be a chance for him to get out from under all of that.

So, when I pull my pork chops off the grill, painting them a final time with the apricot-colored sauce I've reduced a dozen times over, I really don't know what I'd rather have happen here—I could lose, go home, and live my life. The only life that, up until recently, I've ever known.

Or I could win.

And everything would change forever.

"FIVE."

"FOUR."

"THREE."

"TWO."

"ONE."

And like it's Times Square on New Year's Eve. The crowd is on their feet. Christian and I step back from our stations as tuxedoed servers whisk our platters away.

"That's it, ladies and gentlemen—the cooking is complete!" The announcer is yelling into his handheld microphone. "Stay tuned for our live Elimination Table, just after this break!"

"Bryce, seriously!" I swat his hand away. "If you put any more of that stuff on my face, my skin's going to stage a rebellion and create a makeup landslide."

Bryce swipes the big blush brush over my forehead one more time and looks at me critically.

"You're a little shiny, love. I just want you to look flawless when you win this thing."

"Don't jinx it," I mutter.

But when he walks away, I peer into the mirror and run a hand through my thick, loose curls. For the final elimination, I'm out of my apron and in a strapless cocktail dress. It's the color of red wine, and the satiny fabric skims my hips and pools around my ankles. Strappy gold sandals peek out from beneath the burgundy hemline. I feel glamorous, almost like I'm going to an awards show or something. Too bad I'm date-less for the main event.

"Psst."

I look up and my eyes widen. In the mirror, I see Christian partially concealed behind the dark-purple curtain of a nearby dressing room. I swivel around in my chair, checking to see if anyone is close enough to see or hear us.

"What are you doing here?" I whisper, struggling to stand up without tripping on my train. "We aren't supposed to 'frat-ernize' or whatever."

"Come here," he whispers, motioning for me to come closer. I hike up the skirt of my dress, trying not to let it drag on the cement floor. Once I've made it within a few feet of the curtain, Christian reaches out and pulls me inside the lit-tle cubicle. Like me, he's dressed up for the occasion; his dark wool suit looks expensive, especially with the pearl-gray shirt and matching tie underneath. He looks like he was born to dress this way. My breath catches in my throat as he looks down at me and smiles.

"I had to see you," he says softly, reaching a hand up to tweak one of my curls. I can feel myself blushing. I gesture at my dress self-consciously.

"I feel ridiculous. You'd think we were on the red carpet, not the chopping block."

Christian touches my shoulder, letting his palm slide down my arm. When his hand reaches mine, he gives it a squeeze.

"You look gorgeous," he murmurs. A warm sensation

fills my belly and sinks into my legs. I feel myself leaning into him.

"You don't look too bad yourself."

Curling a finger under my chin, he lifts my mouth up to meet his. I feel myself sinking into the kiss. What begins as sweet and innocent quickly turns more intense. I run my hands up his back; he has one arm around my waist and pulls me into him. I give a little sigh as his mouth moves to my neck, my collarbone.

"Christian . . ."

"Hmm?" I feel the slight vibration of his mouth along the hollow of my neck. The last thing I want to do is stop him.

"You'd better go."

He moves to look me in the eye. "And why would I want to do that?"

I smile, moving my hand from his shoulder to his hair. The silky, spiky strands are both sharp and soft—an appropriate analogy that isn't lost on me.

"Because we've got about five minutes before the cameras start rolling, and now I'm going to need to get my makeup touched up again."

"Too bad . . ." He brushes his lips against mine again, but before the kiss can deepen, I put my hand on his chest and push him back lightly.

"I'll see you at Elimination Table."

"Should I bring you a box of tissues?" he asks, raising an eyebrow. I narrow my eyes.

"Sure, if you think you'll need them. I know you'll be devastated when I win."

"Nah, I'll be far too distracted thinking about our date tonight."

He gives me a final wink before slipping out into the hall-way. I watch from behind the curtain as he saunters back toward his side of the room. I take a deep breath. Christian's bravado always brings out the sarcastic side of me—but now that he's gone, I have to face my nerves.

I'll tell you one thing—I won't miss this part. I hope this is the last time I'll *ever* have to wait while someone decides my fate.

There isn't really an Elimination *Table* anymore, per se. I guess that was left back at NACA in the old arena. Now it's just more of an Elimination Counter, which isn't quite as imposing.

The judges are the same though—sans Svincek, obviously. Prescott, who's really enjoyed his exoneration via the late night talk show circuit, is wearing a Cheshire cat smile—the kind that appears harmless . . . at first. I'm sure he'll have lots of *lovely* things to say about me since I accused him of electrocuting people and blowing up sinks. Chef Mason and Madame Bouchon, however, are almost stony faced. It makes me wish I could just fast forward through this part, or DVR it and watch the details later on when I'm not so nauseated.

Christian and I enter from opposite sides of the dark-ened room, equal distance from the spotlighted stools, which stand five feet apart from each other. As we walk toward them, our eyes lock. He gives me a wink and I can't help but smile.

"Nora Henderson and Christian Van Lorton," Madame Bouchon calls out.

We stop in front of our stools and turn to face the panel.

"We've had an opportunity to watch you work and to taste your dishes. We'd like to ask you both a question before we make our final decision."

Prescott stands up to face us. He cocks his head, the hint of a smile playing his lips.

"Nora, tell me, why do you think you should win *Taste Test*?"

I pause, thinking. I look at each of the judges.

"I don't know if I can answer that."

"This isn't optional, Nora. Unless, of course, you're forfeiting your chance of winning."

Prescott may not be a felon, but he's still a complete jerk. I shake my head.

"Here's what I *do* know—I know that I've never worked harder in my life than I have here. I know that I love to cook and that I'd love the opportunity to go to Paris and study."

I glance over at Christian, then back at the judges.

"But this place—this show—hasn't changed me. I came here thinking it was my big break. What I've realized is that I'm the same person here as I am in Weston, North Carolina. And I'll be the same person in Paris, too. I've learned so much here. I don't know if that makes me a winner or not. For me, this is a greater graduation ceremony than I could have imagined. I get to leave here and do what I love, whether I win or lose. And that seems to matter more than anything else."

Prescott's face is a little pinched.

"How touching," he says, his voice dripping with sarcasm. "And how about you, Mr. Van Lorton? More *Chicken Soup for the Taste Test Soul*?"

From the corner of my eye, I see Christian fidget just a little. It's the first hint of nervousness he's shown all season.

"Christian," Madam Bouchon speaks quietly, shooting Prescott a disapproving look, "why do you think you should win *Taste Test*?"

I watch him take a breath and, for a second, I think he might say something funny—he's got that smirk on his face, the same one he was wearing the night we met.

"Listen," Christian says, rocking back on his heels, "Nora Henderson has been nothing if not a valiant competitor, and there's nothing I'd rather do than come out on top. But you already know who you're voting for—what I say to you right now isn't really going to change that."

He folds his arms across his chest.

"So *I'm* not going to tell you why I should win. Maybe *you* should tell me that."

My eyes grow wide. I can't *believe* he just said that to the judges. Madame Bouchon purses her lips, looking nonplussed. Chef Mason gives Christian a long look.

"Thank you both for your, uh, candid responses," Mason says. "We'll need just a moment to discuss."

As the judges huddle into a human tripod, I stare at Christian. He glances back at me and shrugs.

"What?"

"Have you lost your mind?" I whisper.

"Maybe. Why?"

"Because you may have just sacrificed your win—and I swear, if you did that because of some misguided sense of chivalry or something . . ."

"Are you kidding?" he whispers, hiding his mouth behind one hand. "What better way to *get* the win than by pretending I couldn't care less? It's a foolproof plan!"

I roll my eyes. A strategy. Why am I not surprised?

"Nora and Christian?"

All of a sudden, I can feel my heart in my throat, as though it's nervous enough to jump ship and swim for shore. Chef Mason looks from Christian to me and back again.

"This season of *Taste Test* has been filled with more trouble, more drama, more disruption than any before it—but it's also never had more talent."

His face, always so serious, melts a bit. He smiles at the two of us.

"Both of you are going to do great things with your culinary careers—but one of you has fought the hardest to create the most delicious, inventive dishes. One of you wants this opportunity the most. But understand, regardless of who walks away from here a champion, both of your lives will never be the same. Talk to the other former contestants. Life after *Taste Test* is a whole new life indeed."

His words hang in the air, as though somehow made buoyant by how true they already are. Our lives will never be the same—I guess that's what I need to come to terms with. There is no going back. In the end, what made coming here possible was that I loved to cook and wanted to try—and those things haven't changed. Wherever I end up, it'll be because I chose to be there, not because a contest paid my way or a panel of chefs voted for me.

Christian reaches over and takes my hand. Chef Mason clears his throat.

"And the season five champion of *Taste Test* is . . ."

CONTESTANT INTERVIEW

Nora Henderson

Producer (P): Nora Henderson—congratulations! You must be ecstatic!

Nora Henderson (NH): Thanks—yes. I'm . . . God, I'm blown away, really. I never actually thought I'd win.

P: And now you're the season five champion! What are you thinking? What are you *feeling*?

NH: I'm . . . excited. Scared. A little overwhelmed.

P: Scared? Why is that?

NH: [shrugs] I guess it's fear of the unknown? I mean, coming here was a big step. I'd never been further north than Virginia. And now France? It's all really . . . surreal.

P: How do you think your father is going to react to the news of your win?

NH: I'm not sure. I hope—I hope my dad is proud. I hope he understands that I'm trying to do the best thing for myself and my future.

P: So, tell me—you're now fifty thousand dollars richer and heading to Europe. Your life has become something you never imagined. What are you going to do now?

NH: Well, I'll probably use a spackling knife to scrape off this pancake makeup and change out of this dress before I manage to stain or rip it.

P: And after that?

NH: [looks down, smiles] And after that, I have a date.

Contestant Interview

Christian Van Lorton

Producer (P): Well, Christian, it's been one hell of a season.

Christian Van Lorton (CVL): It's been real, man. I'll give you that much.

P: So, what's next for Christian Van Lorton? Are the rumors true?

CVL: Which rumors are those?

P: The ones about you opening up a place with your old man.

CVL: It could happen. Diamonds and Spades is doing really well in Manhattan—Dad's been wanting to open a sister restaurant, Hearts and Clubs, for years.

P: Right. And working for your father . . . you think that's—wise? It seems as though you two don't exactly get along.

CVL: Hey, I could just strike out on my own, try to do my own thing—but if I can use my dad's connections and cash and still do what I love? It sounds like a no-brainer to me.

P: So anywhere specific you're thinking of opening the new digs?

CVL: Well, now that you mention it, I hear all the best chefs are going to Paris this fall.

P: I see. Well, Paris is a culinary capital.

CVL: So I've heard. But, between you and me, it has a far more important reputation—one I plan on taking full advantage of.

P: And what reputation is that?

CVL: [raises eyebrows] The city of love, of course.

TASTE TEST *season five*

Contestant Recipes

Nora Henderson's Coffee-Cocoa-Cayenne Dry Rub and Three-Chili Macaroni and Cheese

Coffee-Cocoa-Cayenne Dry Rub

½ cup coffee, finely ground

¼ cup pepper, freshly ground

3 tablespoons kosher salt

3 tablespoons unsweetened cocoa

2 tablespoons raw sugar or brown sugar, finely ground

2 tablespoons cayenne pepper

1 tablespoon chili powder

1 teaspoon cumin

1 teaspoon garlic powder

1 teaspoon celery salt

1 teaspoon onion powder

Directions:

Mix all ingredients together in a small bowl. Measure out 2 tablespoons of the rub. Using your hands, rub it evenly onto the meat of your choice just before grilling. Chicken and fish need a lighter coating than a more substantial protein, like ribs or steak.

Three-Chili Macaroni and Cheese

1½ cups elbow macaroni

2 tablespoons butter

1 tablespoon flour

2 cups milk

⅛ teaspoon chili powder

⅛ teaspoon cayenne pepper

¾ teaspoon salt

1 teaspoon dry onion, minced

pinch of red chili flakes

2 cups cheddar cheese, grated

Directions:

Cook macaroni according to package directions. Melt the butter in a saucepan. Blend in flour. Cook until bubbly. Stir in milk. Heat to boiling. Boil and stir 1 minute. Add both chili powders. Combine macaroni, salt, onion, chili flakes, and cheddar cheese. Mix thoroughly in 2-quart casserole. Pour sauce over macaroni. Sprinkle chili flakes over the top, if desired. Bake at 350 degrees, covered, for 30 minutes. Uncover and bake for 15 minutes longer. Let stand for 5 minutes before serving.

Joy Kennedy-Swanson's Lobster Bisque with Roasted Corn and Potato Shreds

2 cups cooked lobster meat

2 to 4 tablespoons dry sherry or white wine

¼ cup butter

3 tablespoons flour

3 cups milk

1 teaspoon Worcestershire sauce

salt and pepper to taste

dash of hot-pepper sauce (i.e. Tabasco, Texas Pete)

1 cup roasted corn kernels, cooled (see directions below)

potato shreds, for garnish (see directions below)

Directions:

In a small bowl, combine lobster and sherry; set aside.

In a medium saucepan over low heat, melt butter. Blend in flour and cook, stirring constantly, until smooth and bubbly. Gradually add milk, stirring constantly. Continue cooking and stirring until mixture is thickened; stir in steak sauce and salt, pepper, and Tabasco to taste. Add lobster, corn, and sherry; cover and simmer for 5 to 10 minutes, stirring occasionally. If mixture becomes too thick, thin it out with extra milk, seafood stock, or water. Serve in individual bowls. Top with potato shreds. Makes 4 cups of lobster bisque.

To roast corn and potato shreds:

Cut corn off the cob (2 cobs for 1 cup of kernels.) Shred one russet potato lengthwise. Arrange corn and potato shreds on a well-greased sheet pan. Roast at 400 degrees for 10 minutes or until potato shreds are brown and crispy. Remove shreds and continue roasting corn for an additional 5 to 10 minutes until they just begin to turn brown. Remove and let cool before adding to bisque.

Christian Van Lorton's Sea Bass
with Beets and Fennel

1 bunch beets, peeled and quartered

2 fennel bulbs, chunked

7 tablespoons extra-virgin olive oil, divided, plus more
  for drizzling

salt and freshly ground pepper, to taste

6 cloves garlic, sliced

¾ cup dry white wine

½ cup fresh orange juice

6 pieces orange peel, each ½ inch

6 sea bass fillets, each approximately 7 ounces

Directions:

Preheat oven to 400 degrees. Toss beets and fennel with 1 tablespoon olive oil and salt and pepper to taste. Roast in oven for 20 minutes. In a large sauté pan over medium heat, warm 3 tablespoons oil. Add garlic; cook, stirring occasionally, until softened, about 5 minutes. Add wine, orange juice, and orange peel, heat to boiling, and boil 1 minute. Remove beets and fennel from oven and add them to the wine mixture; simmer 2 minutes. Remove from heat. Set aside.

Season fish with salt and pepper. Drizzle fish with 3 tablespoons of oil. Roast at 400 degrees until fish is opaque throughout, 15 to 25 minutes, depending on thickness. Remove from oven. Spoon the beet and fennel mixture onto a serving plate; place fish on top and drizzle with oil. Serves 6 to 8 people.

Kelsey Dison's Spicy Fajita Casserole

8 flour or corn tortillas, cut into thin strips

vegetable oil or cooking spray

1 tablespoon onion powder

1 tablespoon garlic powder

1 tablespoon ground cumin

1 teaspoon ground allspice

salt and ground black pepper

2 pounds boneless, skinless chicken breasts, boneless
 pork chops, or steak

4 tablespoons oil, divided

1 cup light beer

2 red bell peppers, seeded and thinly sliced

2 red onions, thinly sliced

3 to 4 cloves garlic, finely chopped or grated

zest and juice of 1 lime

¼ cup cilantro or flat leaf parsley, chopped

1 cup pepper jack cheese, shredded

sour cream, salsa, and/or guacamole, to garnish
 (optional)

Directions:

Preheat oven to 400 degrees.

On a baking sheet, toss tortilla strips with some oil or spray with cooking spray and bake in oven until golden brown, about 10 minutes. Turn halfway through the cooking time so they get brown on all sides.

In a small bowl, combine the onion powder, garlic powder,

cumin, allspice, salt, and pepper. Toss chicken with the spice mixture and set meat aside.

Place a large skillet over medium-high heat with 2 tablespoons oil. Add the meat to the pan and sear until golden brown and cooked through, 5 to 6 minutes. Add the beer to the pan and cook to reduce, 3 to 4 minutes.

While the meat is cooking, place a second large skillet over high heat with 2 more tablespoons oil. Add the peppers, onions, and garlic to the pan, and cook until brown around the edges and tender, 3 to 4 minutes. Add the zest and juice of 1 lime, chopped herbs, salt, and pepper to the pan, toss to combine and reserve.

When everything is ready, toss the meat, peppers, and onions, and toasted tortilla strips together in a casserole dish. Top with the cheese and melt under the broiler. Serve with sour cream, salsa, and/or guacamole.

Christian Van Lorton's Southern Fried Steak with Red Pepper Relish

1 large roasted red bell pepper, fresh or jarred

2 tablespoons cider vinegar

1 tablespoon maple syrup

1½ teaspoons, hot-pepper sauce, divided

1¾ teaspoons salt, divided

1 tablespoon vegetable oil

1 package (10 ounces) frozen corn kernels, thawed and drained

2 to 3 tablespoons green onions, chopped

4 (½ pound) beef cube steaks

2¼ cups all-purpose flour, divided

2 teaspoons baking powder

1 teaspoon baking soda

1 teaspoon black pepper

1½ cups buttermilk

1 egg

2 cloves garlic, minced

3 cups vegetable shortening, for deep frying

4 cups milk

kosher salt and ground black pepper, to taste

Directions:

Relish:
Peel, seed, and chop red pepper. In a large bowl, combine the vinegar, maple syrup, 1/2 teaspoon hot-pepper sauce, and 1 teaspoon salt. Gradually whisk in the oil. Add the chopped red pepper, thawed corn, and green onions. Toss to coat. Cover and refrigerate overnight, stirring occasionally. Let relish stand at room temperature before serving.

Steaks:
Pound the steaks to about 1/4-inch thickness. Place 2 cups flour in a shallow bowl. Stir together the baking powder, baking soda, pepper, and 3/4 teaspoon salt in a separate shallow bowl; stir in the buttermilk, egg, 1 teaspoon hot-pepper sauce, and garlic. Dredge each steak first in the flour, then in the batter, and again in the flour. Pat the flour onto the surface of each steak so they are completely coated with dry flour. Heat the shortening in a deep cast-iron skillet to 325 degrees. Fry the steaks until evenly golden brown, 3 to 5 minutes per side. Place fried steaks on a plate with paper towels to drain. Drain the fat from the skillet, reserving 1/4 cup of the liquid and as much of the solid remnants as possible. Return the skillet to medium-low heat with the reserved oil. Whisk the remaining flour into the oil. Scrape the bottom of the pan with a spatula to release solids into the gravy. Stir in the milk, raise the heat to medium, and bring the gravy to a simmer. Cook until thick, 6 to 7 minutes. Season with kosher salt and pepper. Spoon the gravy over the steaks to serve.

Nora Henderson's Blackened Mahimahi with Mango Butter

4 teaspoons salt

4 teaspoons paprika

3 teaspoons garlic powder

3 teaspoons finely ground pepper

2 teaspoons onion powder

1½ teaspoons cayenne pepper

1½ teaspoons dried thyme, crumbled

1½ teaspoons dried oregano, crumbled

4 mahimahi filets

1 cup all-purpose flour

2 tablespoons extra-virgin olive oil

2 tablespoons butter, plus ⅔ cup butter, melted, divided

2 ripe mangos

½ teaspoon cayenne pepper

½ teaspoon lemon juice

Directions:

Combine first 8 ingredients in a small bowl.

Slice filets to desired thickness, rinse, and dry with paper towels. Put one filet at a time on a dry plate, cover with the spice mixture, and gently rub it into filet. Have a cup of flour on another dry plate and roll filet until covered. Continue until whole fish is complete. Heat oil and butter in a large skillet on medium-high heat. Place 2 or 3 filets in pan and cook each side for 3 minutes or until dark brown/black.

Peel outside of mango and slice flesh away from the pit

and core. Chop fruit into ½-inch pieces. Put a small amount of butter in a small skillet and sauté mango until very soft. Put softened mango in a blender with butter, cayenne, and lemon juice. Blend until smooth. Serve on a warm platter with sauce on the side.

Acknowledgments

Preheat

Before I met fiction, I fell hard for poetry. I was blessed with amazing teachers: Michael Waters, who taught me everything I know about the importance of words and the tightness of good prose; Jim Harms, whose use and love of narrative showed me how to condense a lifetime in less than a page; and Mary Ann Samyn, who introduced me to different forms and structures—who essentially opened my mind to styles other than my own. I'm also indebted to the Mid Atlantic Arts Council and the Maryland State Arts Council, whose Individual Artist Award grants were blessings that allowed me to travel, think, write, and get here.

Combine

Some higher, *Glee*-loving, hair-metal power brought me my agent, Hannah Brown Gordon. She is my Cheerio. She is my CC Deville. I can't even begin to express my gratitude for her faith in me and my writing and for her encouragement and dedication to making this happen.

Champion is a noun and a verb—it applies in all ways when talking about my editor, Mary Kate Castellani. Her close reads and thoughtful edits took this book to places that made it far better than its former self. I'm indebted.

Serve

I'm incredibly fortunate to be surrounded by people who love me, even when I bury myself in an isolated writing world and don't come out for days. My parents, Ann and Dale Edgeington, are the epitome of supportive, and I'm extremely lucky to get to call them Mom and Dad. Throughout this process, Katie Wheeler has been my cheerleader, my sounding board, and my dearest friend. I also need to say a big THANK-YOU to Carly Keane, Lauren Martin, Ali Lazorchak, Ryan Edgeington, the MFA/English Department at West Virginia University, the English Department at Salisbury University, Ken Robidoux and the staff of Connotation Press, and the students and staff of Frederick High School. I'm also extremely grateful for the websites and associations that are so supportive of YA writers like me, especially SCBWI, YALitChat, and YA Highway. Also, a special thank-you to the Sands family, whose daughter, Nora, unwittingly lent me her name for this book.

Most of all, I owe everything to my boys, who gave me room to breathe and time to write, who spent so many evenings and weekends wifeless and mommyless so that I could dream my dreams. Matt, you've been there for everything the vows promise and then some. You've made me the luckiest girl in the world. And Max, you've taught me all the most important lessons about love. My writing, my world, my life, is better because of you.